ATTACK ON IWO JIMA

Bullets stitched the ground and brush, and there was an agonized cry as one of the marines was hit. Redhawk pressed his face against the rough scraping of rock and waited for a pause in the fire, then threw himself back down the slope, rolling like a ball until he reached the bottom.

"Move it!" the Navajo soldier shouted.

The six men on the recon patrol followed him as he zigzagged for cover. U.S. salvos began to fall again, the shells tearing up the ground in chunks and giving them a smoke-screen as they ran.

Grabbing a radio, the Indian code talker called in for more smokers to hide their retreat from the Japanese snipers. "Am taking heavy fire, repeat heavy fire. Have hawk drop eggs two hundred yards east. Repeat, two hundred yards east!"

Scrambling toward the underbrush, Redhawk and his squad dug in as the air attack started.

It would be a long night in the shadow of the enemy.

THE CODE TALKERS

CHUCK BIANCHI

PINNACLE BOOKS
WINDSOR PUBLISHING CORP.

PINNACLE BOOKS

are published by

Windsor Publishing Corp.
475 Park Avenue South
New York, NY 10016

Portion of actual Navajo Code appeared on pages 24-30 and 39-45 of Doris A. Paul's *NAVAJO CODE TALKERS* and are reprinted here with the kind permission of the author's publisher Dorrance Publishing Co., Inc., Pittsburgh, PA.

First printing: December, 1990

Printed in the United States of America

AUTHOR'S NOTE

Although this novel is a work of fiction, some of the events that occur in it are borrowed from actual experiences of several of the Navaho Code Talkers. Certain license has been taken in regard to actual training dates. I have tried to weave the most accurate accounts of truth and a minimal amount of fiction to recreate the historic battles of World War II as seen through the eyes of the Code Talkers. Some of the names of officers have been changed, of course, but the names of the operations, battles, and geographic locations have remained true to history.

Dedicated to the memory of my father, Charles Joseph Bianchi, Jr., U.S.N., who was wounded during the bombing of the Arizona *at Pearl Harbor, December 7, 1941.*

ACKNOWLEDGMENTS

First of all, I would like to thank the more than four hundred Navajo Code Talkers who served in WWII. They were brave and patriotic Americans who endured much to do their duty so well.

I also would like to thank my editor, Paul Dinas, for his patience. Special thanks to my wife, Virginia Brown-Bianchi, for her help and support. My sincere appreciation goes to Mr. Walter Zacharius, who believed in the project from its conception and lit the fires of inspiration.

Special acknowledgment goes to Mrs. Doris A. Paul for the painstaking research she did in the writing of her book entitled *The Navajo Code Talkers,* a laborious task that lent greatly to my imagination and saved valuable time in my efforts to research and write this novel.

An added thanks to Mr. Martin Link at the *Indian Trader Newspaper* and the Gallup, New Mexico Chamber of Commerce.

Last, but certainly not least, I would like to express my appreciation to Eugene Roanhorse Crawford, one of the original Code Talkers and the first to enlist, for his insight and assistance with this project.

My heartfelt thanks to all of you.

National Navaho Code Talkers Day

By the President of the United States of America

A Proclamation

Since the Revolutionary War, when General George Washington praised the Indians under his command, the United States has been privileged to have members of the Indian Nation serve in its armed forces.

From the bravery demonstrated at Valley Forge and the establishment of the U.S. Indian Scouts on August 1, 1866, to the present day, Native Americans have heeded the call to duty. Though often excluded from the annals of United States history, these people, nonetheless, have defended the only land they have ever known, asking for nothing more than opportunity in return.

The Navaho Nation, when called upon to serve the United States, contributed a precious commodity never before used in this way. In the midst of the fighting in the Pacific during World War II, a gallant group of men from the Navaho Nation utilized their language in coded form to help speed the Allied victory.

Equipped with the only foolproof, unbreakable code in the history of warfare, the code talkers confused the enemy with an earful of sounds never before heard by code experts. The dedication and unswerving devotion to duty shown by the men of the Navaho Nation in serving as radio code talkers in the Marine Corps during World War II should serve as a fine example for all Americans.

It is fitting that at this time we also express appreciation for the other American Indians who have served our Nation in times of war. Members of the Choctaw, Chippewa, Creek, Sioux, and other tribes used their tribal languages as effective battlefield codes against the Germans in World War I and the Japanese and Germans in World War II.

Beyond this unique role, American Indians serving in the United States military forces have established an outstanding record of bravery and heroism in battle. Many have given their lives in the performance of their duty. Their record should be recognized by all Americans.

By House Joint Resolution 444, the Congress has requested me to designate August 14,1982, as National Navaho Code Talkers Day.

NOW, THEREFORE, I, RONALD REAGAN, President of the United States of America, do hereby designate August 14, 1982, as National Navaho Code Talkers Day, a day dedicated to all members of the Navaho Nation and to all Native Americans who gave of their special talents and their lives so that others might live. I ask the American people to join me in this tribute, and call upon Federal, State and local officials to commemorate this day with appropriate activities.

IN WITNESS WHEREOF, I have hereunto set my hand this 28th, day of July in the year of our Lord nineteen hundred and eighty-two, and of the Independence of the United States of America the two hundred and seventh.

Ronald Reagan

"Were it not for the Navajos, the Marines would never have taken Iwo Jima. . . . The entire operation was directed by Navajo code."

Major Howard M. Conner
Communications Officer
Fifth Marine Division on Iwo Jima

Prologue

The sharp smell of sulphur burned the air. A bomb screamed through the sky before exploding, creating a huge crater in the raw ground and tossing men about like matchsticks. Thick clouds of smoke swirled in hot eddies, almost hiding a huge mountain that loomed just ahead. Trees had been flattened and were nothing but charred remnants. Yawning craters pocked the ground that had been chewed by bombs. Death surrounded the American soldier who lay belly-down with his hands over his head.

Twisting, gouging a hole in the ground with his body, Johnny tried to escape the inevitable. Shells screamed past him, exploding overhead to shower him with hot shards of metal, but he didn't feel any of it. He didn't feel anything but fear and anger as he lurched to his feet and ran in a zigzag line, his lungs bursting from the sharp burden of breathing sulphur and smoke.

As he ran, the same frightened, angry thought drummed over and over in his head: *It's not my war, it's not my war!* But it didn't really matter whose war it was, because he was there in the middle of it.

With his lungs near to bursting from the effort of running in the smoke-filled air, Johnny saw a man suddenly appear in front of him, a small man with slanted eyes, and a wide grin almost splitting his face in two. He held a rifle in front of him and was screaming in an incomprehensible language. A wicked bayonet was fixed to the end of the rifle, glittering in the light of exploding shells. When the small man lunged forward in a lightning-quick movement, thrusting upward with the bayonet, Johnny twisted out of the way, bringing up his own rifle and bayonet.

The blood of his Navajo ancestors surged hotly through his veins as the American soldier faced the enemy. His actions were instinctive. He sprang forward, eyes burning from the bite of smoke and death, screaming an old war cry as he slammed his bayonet into the enemy. It went in easily, but jarred his arm as it grated against bone and muscle and the enemy's natural resistance. Watching him, watching the small yellow man's eyes widen with shock, Johnny pulled it out with a jerk. He leaped back as the enemy sagged to the ground with a peculiar grunt, his grin fading and his eyes still wide and staring. Blood spurted from the wound and his open mouth, splashing all over Johnny's shirt.

It didn't matter. Nothing mattered but escape from the smoke and exploding bombs and constantly racketing gunfire. Men all around him screamed as they fell, and Johnny was afraid of the *chendi,* or evil spirits that would befall him because of his proximity to death. Every Navajo warrior knew that a dead body harbored its spirit and could cause grave harm to those foolish enough to linger nearby. All around him death stalked, and Johnny Redhawk was afraid.

Turning, Johnny ran. His arms and legs grew heavier and heavier as he stumbled over dead bodies and through rivers of blood. A crimson wave washed in front of his eyes, and he didn't know if it was blood or the haze of exhaustion as he ran. The smoke grew thicker, and he prayed aloud to the Great Spirit to take him away, to take him from this place of death and madness.

Then he felt himself flying, looking down over the carnage below as if he were on the wings of a great white eagle. He flew over a body of water stretched without end from horizon to horizon. There was the light sensation of weightlessness. A hot wind blew in his face—the breath of the gods—and he grew calmer. Then he was drifting, a feather on the wind, serenely floating without pain or worry.

It was the sharp jolt of landing that jerked him awake.

Sitting up, wiping away the sweat that drenched his face and body, Johnny Redhawk glanced around the dark, smoky interior of the hogan and felt a wave of relief. It had just been a dream, a hallucination. A strange peyote dream had invaded his mind, but now he was awake. He would not think of the dream again.

Part One

Chapter One
The Chase

Hot winds blew across the Arizona desert. Tumbleweeds and dust rode the air currents, and sand seeped into hogans and food, underneath clothes to scrape against the skin. The Navajo reservation squatted on the flat, open land like a giant, brooding bird of prey.

Several miles from the reservation, two horsemen rode across the broad horizon, tiny dark specks against the bright light that shimmered around them, giving them a surrealistic look from a distance. Humps of red rock undulated across the land like the waving spine of a serpent, occasionally broken by a sink, or small watering hole. The two men reined their mounts to an abrupt halt at one of the hidden seeps where water trickled over rock and formed a pool. The sharp echo of hoofbeats quickly faded away. Silence rode the wind, the silence of time and satisfaction.

Johnny Redhawk turned, a half-smile curling the corners of his mouth. A strip of cloth held long black hair out of his eyes, and his chest was bare and well-muscled. He wore moccasins and a dingy pair of jeans, and a beaded sheath held a long-bladed knife at his side. He looked predatory and pure Indian. "There will be good eating tonight," he said in a soft voice, and his cousin grinned.

Willie Johns had the same blood in his veins, but he'd chosen not to walk the same path as his cousin. He wore a chambray shirt, jeans, and boots, with a Stetson slanted over his face. The brim of his battered hat almost hid his black eyes as he nodded agreement to Redhawk's next comment.

"*Aiie,* the gods have a way of caring for Navajos and drunks," Redhawk said with a blurred grin.

"Then we have a double blessing, 'cause we're drunk half the time, Navajos all the time, and the rest of the time . . . well, it is true that some call us thieves and rustlers." Squinting against the light, Johns stood up in his stirrups, his saddle leather creaking as he leaned forward.

A sharp burst of laughter cracked into the hot, still air. "Thieves? Rustlers? Ha! We're doing what we have to do to feed ourselves. Just because these white men put down fences across the land does not mean that they own it. This is land for all men to use, men and animals. How stupid they are to think any man can own land." Redhawk's voice was thick with whiskey and contemptuous as he waved an expansive hand to indicate the land around them. "Can man own the stars? The wind? The water? Even this fat old cow tied to my saddle? I laugh at them!"

Turning in his saddle, Johns fumbled in his worn-out saddlebag for the bottle of whiskey he usually kept there. "Here . . . let's drink to the white man. And to the white man's war . . ."

Redhawk caught the tossed bottle in midair with an expert motion that smacked of practice. "Well," he said, "I don't think Connor would agree with us about the cow. He raised her from a calf. He thinks he owns her. But the cow . . . ah . . ." he said with a grin, "she gave herself to us for our hogans, so we would not starve."

Willie Johns shrugged. "We have no hogans, only

the sky for a roof and the stars for lamps. And I like it that way."

There was a moment of silence while the bottle was tilted up, then lowered. The memory of the peyote dream returned in a rush, and Redhawk shifted uneasily in his saddle. It had been real. Too real. He chose to ignore his cousin's remark about the white man's war, just as he'd chosen to ignore the war.

But Johns did not require acknowledgment. He looked at his cousin. "It's not just the white man's war," he said, as if reading Redhawk's thoughts. "It's our war, too. I heard on the radio about how they are fighting for the freedom of all Americans. We are the original Americans, aren't we?"

A soft lowing from the cow seemed to punctuate that sentiment, and the two young Navajos grinned, teeth white against the dark copper of their faces. Redhawk laughed.

"See, she agrees with you, even if I don't."

"Then she is a wise cow," Johns retorted. He swung down from his horse, glancing around the desolate landscape where nothing seemed to move for miles. "This is as good a place as any. No one ever comes here."

It wasn't long before the cow had been butchered and the ritual offering of thanks given for her sacrifice so that they might live. Redhawk spoke English well and he had attended the white man's school, but he was still a Navajo, steeped in Navajo tradition and customs.

A sacrifice was always offered to the spirit of an animal used for food. The heart was buried and words of gratitude were whispered, a token of appreciation to the creator for providing a means of survival.

Orange flames soon licked the edges of a fresh hindquarter section that was skewered on a fire-hardened stick placed across round, smooth stones. A warm wind blew from the south, making the fire dance. Hunkered down by the blaze, the two Navajo youths ate fresh meat, tearing off strips as they were cooked.

Hot grease ran over Redhawk's fingers and down his chin as he bit off a charred strip of meat, chewing slowly, and gazing into the fire. When he was almost full, when the worst of the hunger pains in his belly were quieted, he turned to his cousin.

"We are damn lucky to be sitting in the sun drinking good whiskey and eating good meat." He squinted into the distance, dragging his shirtsleeve across his mouth to wipe it. The dream still haunted him in spite of his resolve to forget it. He wondered if he put the dream into words it would lose its power over him and he would be able to dismiss it.

"Some of our red brothers are fighting on an island far away," he said abruptly, and Johns looked at him with surprise. "We have this, while they are risking their lives in the white man's war." Waving one arm to indicate the wide expanse of empty sky and land, Johnny said in a soft voice, "This is good. We are free and do what we feel like doing. Yes, this is good."

Willie Johns grunted in reply and hacked at another section of beef with his twelve-inch skinning knife. When he had devoured more meat and chased it with a healthy gulp of whiskey, he looked at his cousin.

"Dah, this is good. Right now. Tomorrow . . . ah . . . that may be another matter. Maybe our fighting brothers are the ones who are so lucky."

"How do you mean?"

Shrugging, Johns grinned through the hot grease smearing his mouth. "They have it easy. Three meals a day, new clothes, money for whiskey . . ."

"A roof hiding the sky, a white man standing over them telling them when to eat, when to get up, when to go to sleep, what to do every minute . . ." Redhawk spat on the ground. "No, we are still free men. They are sheep, following bigger sheep. We are men, free men."

Johns frowned. "But how long will we be free? I heard on the radio that if the Germans or the Japanese win this war, we will be conquered."

"What is that to us? The white man thinks he has conquered us, but has he? He already occupies lands that our fathers hunted on many years before he came here. But we are not conquered. Do you think others can manage what the white man could not?" Redhawk spat into the dust again. "I do not! I think we will always win the final battle, because we know how to be losers as well as winners. The white man, he thinks we are conquered because we go to his school and worship his god, because we follow his rules and smile and say yes, but inside—" he thumped his chest, "inside here we are the same. We are *Diné,* The People, belonging only to the wind and the sun and stars. We belong to a much greater plan than the white man's."

Johns remained silent. The wind blew across them, and the meat sizzled on the spit with a hissing sound.

Nothing else was said. Nothing needed to be said. The two youths were attuned to the other's thoughts and emotions without speaking. Dusk deepened into night and the fire grew dim, dying to only red and gray embers. They rolled into their blankets and fell asleep almost immediately. Few sleepless nights ever daunted them. They had long since learned the trick of the Navajo, how to fall asleep at once whenever possible. If need be, the two could stay awake for days, grabbing only moments of sleep to refresh them and keep them alert.

Even asleep, the slightest noise would wake them. It could be the high-pitched whisper of the wind over the scrubbed red rocks or the suggestion of noise as a snake slithered across the ground with a rasping sound.

But this time, in the cool clear hour just before dawn, it was the vibration beneath his head that woke Redhawk. He felt it, and his eyes snapped open. It was only the slightest tremor, but he recognized it. The sound followed in a few moments, the solid beat of hooves on the hard-packed ground that denoted a solitary rider.

Redhawk sat up, and Johns awoke. He looked at his cousin with a half-smile. "How does the Old One do it? He tracks us every time we take a cow."

Shaking his head, Redhawk curled his body into a half crouch. "If it is the Old One, then he will know what we are thinking." There was a brief pause as Redhawk considered for a moment, then he straightened in a smooth, lithe motion like the uncoiling of a rope. "Come. Let us go. You take the mesa canyon trail by the big rock. I will meet you at the wall."

Johns glanced at the neatly butchered remains of the cow. "And the meat for later—?"

"Must be left for now. Perhaps later we can come back for it."

Dust spiraled up behind them in a miniature whirlwind as the two youths caught and vaulted atop their ponies. Drumming their heels against the horses' ribs, they left the camp behind them. Their brief occupation was marked by the remains of the cow, glowering coals, and two indentations in the ground where they'd lain.

Less than ten minutes later, a lone horseman reined in his mount beside the charred ashes of the fire and the cow. Saddle leather creaked dryly as he leaned to one side and inspected the evidence. A faint smile touched thin lips, and he muttered, "*Aiie,* they ask for trouble, as always. I think this time, they have found it."

Lifting his gray head like a wary old elk, the tracker actually sniffed the air. After a moment, he turned his horse west, toward the mesa canyon trail. The tracks the two had left behind were easy to follow. They had not bothered to hide them, not really caring if they were caught. What did a few months in the stockade mean to them? Very little. Not when it was compared to being hungry. The old man sympathized, but he would do what he'd set out to do.

A faint light began to glow in the east, growing over the jagged edges of peaks that gnawed at the sky. The old tracker lifted his rifle from the saddle scabbard and laid it carelessly across his lap. He would show them that he meant business this time, that they must keep to the rules.

Hoofbeats pounded against the ground in the cadence of pursuit. As the morning sun rose hot and high, lather flecked the sides of the tracker's horse. He showed no evidence of heat or tiring, just a dogged determination.

Redhawk and Johns were well ahead, careless with youth and indifference. In this flat, dry land that held ancient secrets hostage, not much mattered. Life went on as it had for centuries, dawn dragging into dusk, life and death and endurance all melding one into the other. Nothing changed. Nothing remained the same.

Redhawk was the first at the high sandstone wall. It rose straight into the air for several hundred feet. Scrub oak fringed the foot of the bluff, and he hid himself and his paint mare behind a large clump of sage. He made no noise, just waited with a patience born of experience. Sweat trickled slowly and silently down his face as he stood with one hand over the mare's nose, a motionless statue without a single flicker of an eyelash.

There was a scraping sound as small rocks skittered over the edge of the bluff, bouncing down the wall and along the ground. Still Redhawk did not move. It was Johns, and he would be down soon. Redhawk waited, his black eyes flat, his muscles tensed for action. He heard more than one horse and wondered if Johns knew he was being closely followed.

Waiting until precisely the right moment, Redhawk exploded into action. He swung atop his mare and kicked her into a run, moving along the canyon floor to the left, where Johns would be. A shrill whistle pierced the air, and both horsemen flattened out across the ground at a dead run. The canyon narrowed abruptly, veering into a sharp vee at the opposite end, high rock walls rising hundreds of feet above them. Trees twisted by eons of wind and time thrust up from the ground at the apex, lining a thin trail.

"Annosozi," Redhawk threw over his shoulder, and Johns nodded. He understood the implied directions.

"The sacred dwellings should hide us well," he tossed back at his companion.

The *Annosozi,* the ancient Indian tribes who had once lived in those high white cliffs pocked with rooms, had left behind a legacy of mystery and myth. Montezuma's Castle held more than history, the Navajos believed. The centuries-old dwellings still housed the spirits of their former occupants in the rock walls. At least, Redhawk and Johns believed so, in spite of the white man's scoffs and derision. The ancient ones would not give away their hiding place, and few knew of all the tiny cubicles and hidden caves that riddled the cliffs near the old stone dwellings.

Rocks slid from beneath their horses' hooves as Willie Johns and Redhawk picked their way down the trail. They glanced back once, and saw a faint cloud of dust hanging in the air. Redhawk paused, his eyes squinting against the burn of sun as he stared into the distance. Then he gave a grunt. Johns nodded.

"I knew it was Yaphet, the BIA tracker. He will not give up easily," Johns observed. They reined their mounts up a narrow shelf of rock that passed for a trail.

"I know."

"He won't stop until we are caught."

"He'll have to if he can't find us," Redhawk returned sourly.

Johns nodded. "That is true, but he always finds us. Let us ride far, so that he will not want to give chase the next time."

More rock skittered from beneath horse hooves, and at one point the two Navajos had to dismount and lead the terrified animals with strips of cloth tied over their eyes. The slender ribbon of rocky trail clung to the mountainside in varying widths, and the nervous horses could well plunge over the side if not blindfolded.

"Mules are better," Johns muttered once, and Redhawk didn't bother to reply. Sweat shone on men and beasts alike.

When the trail widened, they remounted. Nothing could be heard behind them. Silence shrouded the area except for the constant keening of the wind through scrub and sculpted rocks.

"Perhaps he turned around."

When Redhawk looked at Johns, he shrugged. Neither of them really thought that would he true. Yaphet was not a man to quit. That was why the BIA used him. It was well-known that he would track a man for days, weeks, or months, until he got him.

"Perhaps," Redhawk finally said, but his voice held no conviction.

The trail slithered like a rattlesnake through the rock and scrub oak, doubling back on itself, then swooping as straight as an arrow for several yards before coiling back. The sun was directly overhead now, searing down, throwing distorted shadows along canyon walls.

"I hear the water," Redhawk, in the lead, said at last, and Johns allowed himself a smile of relief. *Annosozi.* At the base of the high white cliff dwellings flowed a constant spring that would refresh and rejuvenate men and horses.

The path narrowed abruptly, then widened again, and just ahead of them lay a rocky pass that led down the side to the spring. But when they rounded the final curve that led to the pass, a surprise awaited them. Shadowing the exit waited the old tracker, sitting motionless atop his horse, his Winchester .30-.30 glittering in the slanting sunlight. With the sun directly overhead, light glittered from the long barrel in blinding sharp starbursts, so that there was no mistaking what he held in his hands.

Redhawk did not move. The black eye of the rifle barrel was aimed at his chest. Only his eyes moved, opaque and empty as they shifted from the rifle to the old tracker's face.

The wind whistled down the narrow crevice, carrying his words to the old man.

"We are yours," Redhawk said flatly.

The old man chuckled. "There are worse things to be. I have much patience, but I am weary of following such stupid boys."

Stiffening, Redhawk did not respond. Beside him, Willie Johns was rigid from the insult.

"Perhaps you know the land better than we do," Johns began angrily, but the old man cut him off with a sharp jab of the Winchester in his direction.

"Do not insult an old man! I *am* the land, while you two are only like the buzzard, taking the leavings of others. Come with me."

Because there was little else they could do, the youths followed the old tracker from the path and into the grassy field beyond. They watered their horses and drank from the clear spring, keeping a wary eye on the old man, who seemed pleased enough to ignore them. He perched atop a flat rock with his Winchester held loosely across his knees.

His relaxed pose did not fool Redhawk or Johns for a moment. They knew that the Old One could bring that rifle up in the wink of an eye and that he would not miss if he chose not to do so.

"What do you want with us?" Johns finally asked, but the old tracker said nothing.

"Do not speak to him until he speaks first," Redhawk advised in a soft voice, his glance sliding slyly toward their captor. "He likes to play games."

Alert, the old man's head turned sharply toward them. "Play games? It is you two foolish boys who play games! You steal from the white man that which he claims as his, then run away like children. Are you not brave enough to say to him, 'I took this because I wanted it . . . Do what you will.' " He spat on the ground. "No! You steal and run away!"

Redhawk straightened slowly, his hands curling into fists at his sides. "And if I did what you say, went to the white man and said, 'My cousin is hungry and so am I, so we took your cow,' what do you think he would do? Do you think he would say, 'Why, you may have it, my red friend.'? No, he would not, and you know it."

"And that makes it right to steal what you know you will be punished for?"

Redhawk drew himself into a proud line. "We have always taken what we wanted. We are *Diné*. It is our way."

Yaphet gave a sad shake of his head. "No, it is not our way any longer. We must do what we must to keep food in our hogans, and stealing from the white man only angers him. It is not just ourselves that we must think of, but all of The People."

"So, you will take us to the stockade again," Willie Johns said.

"No. Not this time. This time you will be given a choice."

"A choice?" Redhawk stared at him warily. "A choice between what?"

The old tracker laughed aloud, throwing back his head and cackling with glee. "Between dishonorable death and an honorable death!"

"It doesn't sound like much of a choice," Johns muttered, but Redhawk stared at the old man. There was something else behind his words, and he was suddenly uneasy.

Chapter Two
The Recruitment

Window Rock arched between the two young Navajos and their future. It soared high in the sky, a stone rainbow that framed the three horsemen as they passed slowly beneath the natural bridge of rock. The town of Window Rock lay just beyond, a collection of wood, brick, and adobe buildings that did not seem at all welcoming to Redhawk and Willie Johns.

Redhawk sat his mare stiffly, staring straight ahead, his expression much more distant and composed than he felt.

A choice of deaths? Honorable or dishonorable? It sounded like peyote taking, not wisdom. No one in the BIA would hang them for stealing a cow. Prison, perhaps, or hard labor, but not death.

When Yaphet reined his mount in on the ridge overlooking the town, Redhawk and Johns waited to see what he would say. The Old One took his time. He shifted in his saddle, the leather creaking in protest, his old wrinkled face creasing even more than either of the youths had thought possible.

Redhawk stared straight ahead, schooling his features into complete disinterest. It did not fool Yaphet or Johns for one moment. The Old One grinned, a toothless grin that split his seamed face with mirth.

"Well," Yaphet said at last, "we are almost there, my foolish ones!"

Johns shrugged lightly, trying to be as careless and indifferent as Redhawk. His eyes flicked to the old man who was obviously enjoying himself too much. "It is not the first time we have been to Window Rock, Old One."

"No? Perhaps not. And perhaps I know that too well. The others, they tell me, 'Do not look for those two. They have eaten the wild grass.'—but I do anyway. I know you both as well as I know the coyote who runs and howls at the moon just as you do. . . ."

Stiffening, Johns snapped, "Do not be too sure, Old One! You know that we are hungry, yes, that our bellies scrape against our backbone at times. And you know where we ride, yes, but you must also know that we will not stay in the white man's jail forever."

"And what is forever to one of The People? Is it until the buffalo are all gone? They have been gone for years, my child. Is it until the coyote is gone? The coyote must hide for his life, my child." Yaphet shook his head. "Do not talk to me of forever. It is an unknown tongue."

Johns was silent for a moment, then he said, "It does not matter, Old One. We will go to the white man's jail for a while."

Yaphet shrugged. "There is another way. I told you of a choice. I did not speak falsely."

"What choice?" Redhawk asked.

"There is a judge in Window Rock who claims to be sick of the sight of your faces every other full moon. He has said if you come back to his court, you will go away for a long time." There was a lengthy silence, then Yaphet said softly, "I may not tell him of this last cow."

"You spoke of death, Old One," Redhawk said. His eyes were flat, but a betraying muscle twitched in his jaw.

"Death is not to be feared," Yaphet said.

"We live with death. We do not fear it. Only cowards and small children fear death."

Yaphet nodded approvingly at the youth's bravado. "It is true. That is what I told the men who came to the reservation asking."

Cautiously, Johns asked, "What men were these?"

"Marine recruiters."

Redhawk spoke sharply. "Do not talk to us of the army!"

Yaphet leaned forward, fixing Redhawk with a narrowed gaze as he spoke slowly. "This is not the army, not like you think. This is not the men your grandfathers speak of, the cavalrymen who rode herd on The People like they were nothing more than cattle. No, these men were from the Marine Corps, trained soldiers like The People were once trained."

Still unconvinced, Redhawk asked in an abrupt tone, "What do they want?"

Yaphet's horse shifted beneath him, hooves scrabbling on rock. The old man tugged at the battered hat shading his eyes. "I have been told they want the help of The People. They came especially to Arizona to recruit Navajo youths for a program set up to aid the war efforts." This last was said in a singsong voice, as if by rote, and the old man shook his head. "Young men are needed who can speak fluent English and read and write. They need The People to help fight the enemy."

"They *are* the enemy!" Redhawk's lips curled with contempt, but Johns said nothing. Silence rode the wind as they sat their mounts.

Recalling his peyote dream, the smell of sulphur was suddenly as real to Redhawk as the hot wind that blew over him. "What do they want of us?" he demanded so harshly and loudly that Johns jerked and stared at him.

Yaphet didn't answer for a moment, then he said,

"You are young men in need of discipline and direction, not like the young men of old. Young men these days do not have what their fathers had, the strength and discipline of The People. Bah, but I will not speak of that now. Now it is enough to know that the white man's army needs The People. We are all part of America and must fight. Do you understand what I mean?" The old man raised his voice a little with the question.

Johns looked at him. "Yes, I understand too well what you mean. I remember that my older brother joined the Marine Corps less than a year ago, and we have not heard from him since then. What is the difference between the white man's army and his jail?"

Shrugging, Yaphet said, "The choice is yours. Jail or the Marines."

There didn't seem to be much of a choice for the two young men. Redhawk had the thought that to sit in a small cell and not smell the hot wind or see the sky would be worse than death, and now he understood what the Old One had meant when he said death with honor or dishonor. He knew that imprisonment would just be another form of death, a lingering death.

Nudging his mare into a trot, Johnny Redhawk led the way down the rocky slope. After a pause, he could hear Johns's mount picking its way down the slope behind him.

As the three riders approached the outskirts of the town huddled forlornly on the Arizona desert, they saw the gleaming metal trailer. Parked close to it was a dull green jeep marked with official insignia. The sign on the side of the trailer read *U.S.M.C. Mobile Recruiting Station.*

Yaphet escorted Redhawk and Johns inside the narrow trailer. Two uniformed men glanced up as they entered, their faces reflecting surprise at the sight of two recruits being ushered in by an armed guard. One of them shook his head, then looked back down at his paper-littered desk.

Glancing around the small area, Redhawk nodded to several of the young men lining the walls. Two of them were not even fifteen years of age, and were burdened with leather day packs, hunting rifles, and saddle blankets. One of the older youths had ceremonial war paint smeared across his high cheekbones and the bridge of his nose.

Several hours dragged by as Johns and Redhawk completed endless written forms and took oral and written tests to assure the two recruiters of their proficiency in the English language. During that time, the two fifteen-year-old boys were quickly dismissed, and the two taciturn men with experience seamed into their faces were brusquely turned down. They left, humiliated because of their deficiency, and Redhawk had only a small flicker of gratitude that he would not be so humiliated by a lack of knowledge.

One of the recruiters shoved a piece of paper toward Redhawk and looked up at him curiously. "How is it you can read and write English so well?"

When Redhawk remained silent, Yaphet replied for him. "His parents died in the tuberculosis epidemic many years ago. So did Johns's parents. They were sent to the Catholic Mission School here in Window Rock. Of course, the priests taught them well, and they are skilled in English."

What Yaphet didn't tell the curious recruiter was that the boys had rebelled after their graduation from the school. They had chosen to live a free existence in the desert and rocks rather than to be ruled by a priest or one of the black-robed nuns. But Yaphet also knew what the two young men did not—that without a return to some sort of self-discipline, they would end up in prison or as hopeless alcoholics, the way so many of the young men had gone. And he understood these two young men, sympathizing with them even though he would never tell them so.

Shifting the Winchester he still held into his other hand, Yaphet watched both young men lift their right hands and take the oath.

Their voices blended with the hot wind outside, the winds of time blowing down the dusty streets of Window Rock and forming rocks and trees and lives. Johnny Redhawk and Willie Johns were in the Marines.

"Report here at 0900 hours Friday morning," the marine recruiter told them, not bothering to glance up as he began the endless routine of paperwork. He didn't see the brief flicker of confusion on Redhawk's face.

"What does that mean?" he asked Yaphet when they were outside the small metal trailer. "0900 hours . . . it does not make sense to me."

"Nine o'clock." Yaphet shrugged. "It is the marines' way of telling time."

There it was again—time. A marking of minutes, hours, days, months, years by the irritating clicking of a watch, a man-made instrument ticking away a man's life.

Get up at five o'clock, dress and be in the eating hall at six, rang through his memory. Nuns in voluminous black robes like crows flicked through his memory, their faces stern, always admonishing, sometimes comforting. But always there had been a time for everything, a time to eat, to pray, to sleep, even a time to think. The inner clock that woke a man, made him rise, sent him out to hunt, had been ignored. Individuality had been ignored. Everything was done in groups. He'd hated it then; he would hate it now.

For centuries, Navajos had depended on an unenforced clock to govern their lives, such as the rising of the sun or the turning of the leaves. Now the white men had come and wanted them to forget all that, to forget the seasons that had once been their "clocks."

Shaking his head, Redhawk reflected that everything was changing. It would never be the same.

"What did he mean by *a wall?*" Johns asked Yaphet. "I heard him tell the others that if they were not there at the right time, they would be *a wall.*"

"AWOL. Absent without leave. It means you must be here on time or you will be in big trouble with the Marines." When there was no reply, he emphasized, "And if you get in trouble with the marines, you will go to jail."

Ignoring that, Redhawk said, "Friday is two days away. Are we free until then?"

Yaphet hesitated. The officials would not understand it if they found out that he had allowed the two young men to go free until Friday, but he also knew that once they left Arizona, they might never come back again.

"Yes," he said. "You are free until then." He saw from Redhawk's faint smile that he understood the situation, and Yaphet nodded slowly.

"We will be here, Old One," Redhawk said in a quiet, grave voice.

"I know you will."

Chapter Three
The Purification

"What do you have?" Willie Johns stared down as Redhawk's fingers uncurled to reveal two small buttonlike buds in his palm.

"Dreams."

Johns was already shaking his head. He recalled the last dreams. "No. Not for me. It is against tribal law."

"Since when did you ever care about the law?"

"Since the mission teachers told us it is bad medicine and you can die if you eat it." Johns glanced reluctantly from the small bluish-green knobs and thin silk-hairs growing on the outside of the seed to Redhawk's determined face. He knew what Redhawk had in mind. He wanted the dream again, the dream of the great white bird and the faraway mountain of sulphur.

Johns was right. Redhawk both dreaded and longed for the dream, wanted to explore it again, was afraid of it, yet knew that somehow it was more than just a dream. Was it a prophecy, perhaps? Did it mean that he would die in battle? Or did the white eagle signify his rise above death? He had to find out, had to know more. Perhaps a shaman could interpret the dream for him.

It was late that afternoon when they rode their

horses to a high butte near the edge of the reservation. They had not bothered with provisions other than the skins of water they carried.

While Johns hobbled the horses, Redhawk built a ring of stones two feet in diameter and a foot high. Then he laced together a framework of long, slender branches. When it formed a domelike shell, he covered it with blankets, then stooped to enter the small wickiup. Squatting in the closed interior, he built a fire inside the ring of stones, fueling it with twigs and branches until the rocks were hot to the touch and glowing with red embers.

Both young men stripped naked, then sat cross-legged in the close hot air of the tent. Redhawk began pouring water over the rocks. Steam curled swiftly upward, filling the tent in a matter of seconds. Sweat poured from the two young men in rivulets, dripping over their taut-muscled frames to the thirsty ground.

Redhawk removed the small peyote buttons from a leather pouch. He began to intone an ancient chant. Closing his eyes, the old words came to him without conscious thought as he rocked back and forth. Johns watched silently.

He didn't approve of using the peyote unless there was a ceremony. It wasn't the way he'd been taught, and it wasn't to be used lightly. But in spite of his disapproval, he understood what his cousin wanted.

"Here," Redhawk said after a moment, and held out one of the buttons. "Chew it slowly. Do not swallow it. Suck the juice."

The bitter taste of the peyote made Johns shudder, but he did as Redhawk instructed. He did not like the dreams, did not want to summon them.

For several minutes Redhawk sat motionless except for the slow, steady movement of his jaws grinding the bitter button. Johns felt a churning in his belly, and his face altered from a flushed red to a sickly green hue. Half stumbling, he pushed aside the tent flap and staggered outside. Redhawk could hear him gagging.

It was part of the ritual, and after a few moments Redhawk joined him. Sweat poured down his face as he retched, and he sucked in a deep breath before muttering, "It will pass."

When it did pass, they returned to the sweat lodge. Nothing was said. The only sounds were the crackling of the fire and the hiss of rising steam. They sat opposite one another, their eyes closed, their bodies drooling sweat and their muscles tense.

Johns was the first to see his vision, and he gave an involuntary moan. Blood was all around him, running like spring rivers through a treeless valley, and men lay prone in the postures of death, their faces contorted. When he would have run away, he found himself surrounded by men shorter than any Navajo, small men with rifles and knives. He was hemmed in and could not escape as black walls closed in on him. He reached out blindly but found no one.

Unable to breathe, Redhawk crawled slowly to the flap and shoved it aside, then made his way to the edge of the butte. Far below him stretched rocks and scrub. He waited. Finally, he saw it, a great white eagle soaring in the distance. Circling and circling, it drew nearer to him. The colors of the sun were brighter, hotter, more intense as the light cast eerie shadows against the distant mountains.

A loud, keening cry pierced the air, echoing from peak to peak. Redhawk waited expectantly. The eagle flew nearer, and it was much larger than he'd thought it would be, larger than he remembered it. He wasn't surprised when the eagle landed in a graceful motion and looked at him, close enough for Johnny to reach out and stroke the white feathers. Its hooked beak opened slightly, and he saw the pulsing movement of its tongue as it seemed to say, "Come with me."

There was the whooshing sound of great flapping

wings, and the eagle lifted effortlessly and soared into the air. A feeling of euphoria enveloped Johnny, and he leaped from the edge of the butte in pursuit.

Redhawk soared high above the land, riding air currents over towering snowcapped peaks, dipping low over green valleys that stretched like velvet ribbons below him. He cried out in delight and surprise. Was it the vision or was it real? He could not distinguish between reality and dream; only the rush of euphoria was tangible.

Then the land faded away and they were skimming over blue waters as far as the eye could see, stretching to infinity. When small green islands flung across the water like a handful of jewels appeared, the eagle circled to land.

A cone-shaped mountain thrust upward from the sea and the eagle landed lightly, its talons scraping treetops before it came to rest on a sloping hill. Redhawk landed beside it, and there was the brief sensation of well-being. It was peaceful. Clear skies shimmered overhead, and a gentle wind brought the scent of flowers as it touched his face. Trees were sparse. A gray beach curved at the base of the sloping hill and waves crashed against it, making a loud roaring sound that filled his ears.

Turning slowly, Johnny looked at the eagle. Sunlight filled the air, a blinding white as bright as the eagle's feathers. He closed his eyes against it, and when he opened them again, the eagle had begun to change colors. Its beak opened soundlessly, and there was the constant roaring of the ocean waves in his ears as Johnny watched the white feathers slowly change to a smoky pink, then a light red, and finally deepening to an iridescent purple.

One hand lifted to touch the eagle, but he drew it back quickly as the huge creature began to blur. He didn't understand at first, then saw it begin to melt like a wax figure in the fire. Frozen in place, Redhawk watched helplessly as the eagle dissolved into a huge crimson puddle that flowed rapidly down the hillside.

A feeling of horror gripped him, and he knew then that it was blood, that the swiftly running streams were blood and there was nothing he could do. He tried to stop it, to stem the tide that bubbled over his feet and rose to his knees, but he couldn't. The blood flowed down into the valleys below, then rose in a cloud of smoke that stung his eyes and made his stomach rebel.

Falling to his knees, Johnny shut his eyes tightly and prayed for the dream to stop. He could feel blood beading on his body, pouring over him in a drowning surge. His heart was beating so loudly it sounded like the drums of war, and his stomach knotted.

A wave of nausea enveloped him and he vomited. Weak from retching, he waited for it to stop but it didn't. It wasn't until a blast of water crashed against him that it subsided, and he was suddenly limp with relief.

Redhawk looked up finally, dazed and shaking, and saw Johns pouring water from their water skins over him. He was saying something, but it took a moment for the words to penetrate his fogged brain.

"Wake up, cousin," Johns was saying with a worried frown. "Wake up."

"I'm all right," Redhawk said, shaking water from his hair like a dog would do. The movement made his head spin again, and he sucked in a deep breath. "I'm all right. It was just a dream."

Chapter Four
The Beginning

Fumes from the bus crept in through the opened windows as it sped through the deserts of Arizona toward the train that would take them to California. It was hot, and even the sight of the small towns that sprang up like cactus in the middle of the flat land could not erase the feeling of uneasiness that pricked at Redhawk. It was more than the dream, though its vivid memory still clouded his thoughts. Regret and uncertainty mingled with the vague feeling of disquiet, and he could tell from the taut expression on Johns's face that his cousin felt some of the same.

The bus was almost full, and there was an air of expectation. Some of the other Navajos laughed and joked and generally treated the ride as a lark. Others felt as alien as a man traveling to outer space. Fighting would be easy, for after all, the Indian had grown up with a weapon in his hand. But leaving the security of the reservation was vaguely frightening, especially to the younger men. The familiar things in life were gone. Hot winds and fast ponies, the high red rocks that offered shelter and privacy and an air of timelessness, were replaced by a gray band of asphalt and the steady roar of an engine. Their world had been encapsulated into this bus filled with fear, excitement, and dread.

Redhawk smiled faintly at his cousin when Johns peered out the open window of the bus and said, "I never thought I would see such things."

"Do you like this better than the free air we are used to breathing?" Redhawk asked. "Sometimes I think you like the white man's ways too much."

"Maybe I just don't see the advantage in resistance," Johns said after a moment. "What has it gained the Navajo?"

"Dignity."

"And how filling is dignity to our bellies? Does it keep the rain from our heads or the snow from covering us?" Johns shook his head. "It only makes it harder. And a man can keep his dignity if he knows how to make peace."

"A man can't serve two masters. Can a man be Navajo and white, too? Look at you . . . Willie Johns. What kind of name is that for a Navajo? Where is the name your grandfathers took pride in?" Redhawk shook his head. "Sometimes I think we have given up too much."

After a moment of silence, in which only the roar of the engine could be heard, Johns said, "Maybe we just know how to survive."

Redhawk looked at him, and some of the tension and anger faded from his harsh expression. "*Aiiee,* we know how to survive."

The need for survival was not lessened by their arrival at Camp Elliott below San Diego, California. A huge hulk of a man greeted them as the troop bus from the train station rolled to a stop and the new recruits piled out onto a hot stretch of pavement. Standing with his legs planted like trees on the concrete and his arms folded across a chest that looked as wide as the front of the bus, the marine bellowed, "Fall in!"

Immediate confusion followed that booming voice

as the recruits reacted. Some just fell to the pavement in a sort of lotus crouch, following his order to the letter. Others froze in place, waiting for an explanation, and some of the raw recruits formed a ragged line, hoping for the best.

Redhawk quickly sized up the beefy marine as a man to be avoided. He was huge, with a face of stone and vinegar, and his voice reverberated like rolls of thunder as he gave the order again to "Fall in!"

Three assistants quickly stepped forward to shove the men into a straight line, snapping at them to put their arms at their sides and face straight ahead. Redhawk allowed himself to be shoved with the others, but he hated the rough way he was handled and the faint sneers on the faces of the men who told him to listen to the drill sergeant.

"Fall in!" the DI roared again. His face reddened and his lips drew back from his teeth in a grimace as he glared at the new boots now in a ragged line. It had grown quiet, and no one spoke as the DI stomped toward them. He stopped, his hands clasped behind him, his legs spread as he balanced on feet that seemed too big to belong to a human. Redhawk could feel the man beside him quiver slightly, and he felt a pang of sympathy.

Drill Sergeant Marshall bellowed and roared, belittled and sneered at the raw men, pacing up and down an invisible line in front of them, pausing occasionally to thrust his stony visage in a man's face and spew out a stream of abuse. Each man recoiled, fear written in his features and his heart pounding with dread as DI Marshall outlined the coming days.

"Lissen up, shitbirds," he snarled. "My job is to turn you buncha losers into fightin' men—*real* fightin' men, not just Saturday night brawlers. I'm not here just to teach you how to fight for your country . . . I'm here to teach you how to fight for your lives! And I'm gonna do it, even if it kills most of you.

Got that? And my assistant, Corporal Andrews here on my left, will help me find out who's the weakest, who's the dumbest, and we're gonna change all that. You're gonna learn to run until you can't run anymore and to stay awake even when your eyeballs hurt. I am in charge of meting out pain"—he paused to smile, a curling of his lips that was more a smirk than a look of amusement—"and I mete it out without prejucide," he continued in the same snarling roar.

Marshall paused before Redhawk, raking him with a narrow glare. "I hate all of you equally," he said, and to Redhawk it seemed as if he were speaking especially to him. "I don't hate any one of you more than the other, and I think each and every one of you is equally stupid. But you will change," the DI bellowed, finally moving along the line to another recruit. "You will become men! You will become . . . *marines!*"

Pivoting on his heel, Marshall stalked back toward Redhawk. He sized him up slowly, watching for a reaction. There was none. Redhawk continued to stare straight ahead, his black eyes opaque, giving nothing away. Inscrutability was his refuge, his retreat, a trait learned hundreds of years before by his ancestors. It usually worked, but not this time.

Marshall reached up to snatch off Redhawk's bright red headband, and he flung it to the ground with a gesture of contempt. "You don't have a past. You don't have a future. You only have me. You no longer have families! You no longer have anyone in your life who is more important than I am! I am your daddy. I am your god. You have to ask me before you can even shit! Do I make myself clear? What? I can't hear you!"

Led by Andrews, the men shouted, "Sir! Yessir!"

Ramrod straight, with sweat streaming down their faces and soaking their clothes, the recruits learned to preface every remark with "sir" and to end every reply with "sir." Failure to do so met with dire penalties. Marshall interrogated them like prisoners of war, pounding out rule after rule while the hot California sun beat down and the heat shimmered up from the concrete. One of the men—not a Navajo—slipped to the ground in a dead faint, and the DI ignored him. There were to be no allowances for human weaknesses, no allowances for human preferences. They were not to think, not to feel, not to react. They were merely to be machines, well-oiled machines in marine issue. They were to act as a body of men, not individually.

Redhawk hated it. He hated Marshall and Andrews and the acres of concrete surrounded by fences and guard houses. He hated the government issue uniforms that sagged on his body like hand-me-downs. And he hated being made to sit erectly in a barber chair while an enlisted man took an electric razor and shaved his head.

"Looka here, Geronimo," the barber said with a laugh, and handed Redhawk a hand mirror. "Don't you look cute?"

Disdaining the mirror—he could see Johns's bald head and knew what he looked like—Redhawk tugged the cape from around his neck and stood up from the chair. He felt naked suddenly, exposed, and didn't want anyone to know it. Only Willie must have sensed some of what he felt, for he had the same kind of half-embarrassed expression on his face.

Standing there awkwardly, in the issue clothes that sagged, his head shaved, Redhawk began to doubt the wisdom of having chosen the marines over prison.

"Move it, shitbird!" came the bellowed order, and Redhawk moved to the line of men already shaven.

He'd been issued a small carrying case an enlisted man had referred to as a ditty bag, holding a razor and shaving soap, toothpaste, soap, and other toilet articles. He carried it under his arm as he was marched with the others across the bare grounds to a line of barracks. His new boots pinched his feet, and he'd had to surrender all his personal possessions when he'd been issued government gear. His hunting knife was gone, as well as the sheath he'd carried it in. The red headband he'd worn had disappeared, and the comfortable moccasins that he'd made from the skin of a venerable old cow several years before had been tossed into a huge bin like yesterday's newspaper. Redhawk reflected on the injustice of the marines as he was halted in front of a Quonset hut, which was indistinguishable from a dozen or more other such huts.

"This is your new home, shitbirds," Andrews was saying in a voice thick with a nasal twang. His smirk was a poor replica of Marshall's, but it was evident he was striving to rival it. Clasping his hands behind him, Andrews paced in front of the men.

Though accustomed to the white man's way of sprinkling his conversation with curses that were usually incomprehensible to the Navajo, Redhawk found himself amazed at the versatility of the English language in lending itself to such colorful phrases. Andrews used liberal amounts of curses and epithets, but still couldn't quite match the DI's earlier abusive words.

"I think we should be given a course in profanity," Johns muttered to Redhawk when they were at last allowed inside the barracks. "The English the nuns taught us didn't include any of these words, and our language has none."

A faint grin flickered on Redhawk's face, and he gave a short nod. "I don't think this kind of English is taught."

He slung his gear on the bare mattress of an upper bunk and leaned against it. Metal footlockers stood at the end of each set of steel beds. The recruits were instructed to make their racks and stow their gear, then wait for inspection.

Andrews strolled down the aisle of racks lining the walls and paused beside Johns's. He took the sheets and swiftly made the rack, showing them how to tuck the corners and blanket so tightly a coin would bounce when tossed to the surface. Then he stripped it and handed Johns his linens.

"Now, you do it, shitbirds."

The men made their racks exactly the way Andrews showed them, then stepped back for him to inspect.

"What?" Andrews bellowed in a fair imitation of the DI. "That's not the fuckin' way I showed you!" He stopped beside a bed and stripped off the sheets and blanket, tossing them onto the floor. "Do it again. All of you! And do it right!"

They made and remade their racks six times before Andrews was satisfied. By now it was late afternoon, and they were to line up for chow. Redhawk found that he was to march in formation to the mess hall for his meal, grab a tray, hurry down the line while men in dirty aprons flung food on a divided tin plate, then gobble his food as quickly as possible before being ordered outside again. In the days that followed, he was grateful for that first leisurely day in boot camp.

Occasionally, there wasn't time for meals. Sometimes, due to a rack not being made well or a wrinkled uniform, the recruits missed chow. Then they had to wait for the next mealtime, while the DI bawled them out not to be crybabies, that it wasn't their mama in there cooking pabulum for them. Those were among the kindest things he said, and Redhawk found himself becoming inured to most of what was said to him.

The days passed in an endless blur of shouted orders, repeated over and over, marches in the blistering heat, and drills that haunted the few hours of sleep he got. He found himself in lines for everything, from food to getting the required inoculations. Everything in the Marine Corps seemed to be assembly line.

Redhawk learned not to call his weapon "a gun."

Marshall pounced on Redhawk like a cougar on a rabbit when the Navajo made the mistake of referring to the M-1 Garand rifle he'd been issued as a gun.

"A gun?" Marshall's voice rose to a shrill squeak that held Redhawk momentarily spellbound. "Did I hear you call this a *gun,* shitbird?"

Realizing he'd made a mistake, Redhawk hesitated. He could feel all eyes on him, and a cold knot formed in his belly as he slowly nodded. "Sir, yessir."

Marshall stuck his face right up in Redhawk's, so that their noses were almost touching and Redhawk could smell his breath. "Well, this isn't a gun, shitbird! *This*"—he snatched Redhawk's rifle away—"is a rifle, a weapon, or a piece, but never, *never* is it a gun! Do you have that, shitbird?"

Wincing at the spittle that flew from the DI's mouth, Redhawk said, "Sir, yessir!"

"Yes what?"

"Sir, this is a rifle, or a piece, but never a gun, sir."

"That's right, shitbird!" Marshall shoved the rifle back at Redhawk. "Let me show you a little exercise to help you remember the difference between a rifle and a gun. . . ."

For two hours, Redhawk marched in a straight line outside his barracks, holding his M-1 in one hand and his crotch in the other, chanting over and over until he was hoarse, "This is my rifle"—hold up the M-1—"and this is my gun"—grab his crotch. "This is for work"—up went the M-1 again—"and this is for fun"—another grab at his crotch. It was humiliating, but he knew he would never refer to his rifle as a gun again.

Along with his dislike for Marshall, Redhawk felt a growing respect. Whenever the recruits marched, Marshall marched. Whenever they drilled in the hot sun, Marshall drilled in the hot sun. And he was constantly challenging them to greater efforts, using his scorn as a whip and his rare nod as a reward.

"Any man tired of walking," Marshall was fond of saying on long, exhausting hikes, "can start running!"

For the Navajos, the running was play, however. They'd run longer distances when children, and their endurance was as admirable to their white counterparts as it was irritating.

"Shee—it," one marine grumbled when he lay across his rack soaked with sweat and exhausted, "you guys look like you just got back from a fuckin' Sunday afternoon stroll!"

"Didn't we?" Johns asked, and the marine groaned.

Most of the Navajos were assigned to the same barracks. There were other Navajos in the marines, but this group was special. Their training was different, Redhawk noticed, and their daily classes included subjects the other marine recruits didn't have. He wondered what Yaphet had not told them, and it made him uneasy. Why were they special? Why hadn't they been told why they were receiving specialized training?

Johns shrugged wearily when Redhawk broached the subject one night after taps had played and they were lying in their racks. "I don't know. I do know they'll tell us when they're ready for us to know."

"But what could it be?" Redhawk persisted. The memory of his peyote dream still haunted him, still lingered in the recesses of his mind to make him wonder if he were to be part of a suicide mission. It wasn't dying that bothered him; it was the thought that he wasn't being given a choice in deciding his own death. At least his ancestors had known how they were to die, had known how it would be. All he knew was that he was to fight in some foreign land, with weapons that were foreign to him. "Don't you wonder about it?" he leaned from his bottom rack to ask Johns, but his cousin was already asleep and didn't answer. Redhawk lay there a long time staring up at the dark ceiling and thinking about the days ahead.

It wasn't all grueling work without letup, however. Occasionally, there would be flashes of humor.

As usual, the San Diego weather was uncompromisingly hot. The recruits had been marching in drill formation for hours, preparing for an inspection, when Andrews came up with the brilliant idea of having the Navajos count out the cadence in their own language. Hot, tired, and longing for a diversion, Redhawk exchanged glances with Johns. No one offered the information that to count aloud in Navajo would mean the platoon taking three or four steps to a number.

"Johns!" Andrews bellowed, "Start the counting!"

By the time Johns reached three, the Navajos had begun adding words of their own, counting aloud and calling Andrews inventive names. Confused and mad, Andrews just stood on the parade ground with a red face as the Navajos began doubling over with laughter. He gave the order to line up again, and once more the Navajos chanted nonsense in their native tongue. It wasn't until the entire platoon was in complete chaos that Andrews admitted defeat.

"Go back to English," he growled to the hoots of laughter from a watching platoon.

"Say, what were you guys saying?" a recruit by the name of Whitworth asked Redhawk later. "I couldn't understand a damned thing you were saying!"

Redhawk shrugged. "We were just doing what Corporal Andrews told us to do." Pushing up from his rack, Redhawk walked away without looking back, leaving Whitworth alone with Johns.

"What's with him?" Whitworth turned to ask Willie, and the Navajo smiled.

"We don't know many white men. Since coming here, my cousin says we know too many."

"Yeah?" Whitworth shrugged and offered Johns a cigarette. "I don't know any Indians, neither. You guys are the first." He gestured toward the other Navajos scattered throughout the barracks. "Are you all related?"

Shaking his head, Johns said, "No. I never met any of the others until we got onto the train together."

"Funny, ain't it?"

"What?"

"How war can make friends as well as enemies."

Johns smiled. "Yes, that's a good joke."

"No, no, Chief, that ain't what I meant. Funny as in peculiar, or odd, not *ha ha.*"

"Oh."

Whitworth, a tall, lanky man with a shock of sand-colored hair and light eyes, grinned at Johns. "You guys are pretty damned good, you know."

"What do you mean by that?"

Whitworth puffed at his cigarette. "I mean, during field exercises, you guys don't look like it bothers you at all to march in the sun without water for hours and hours. Hell, half of our platoon fell out from heat exhaustion the other day, and we look over and see you guys just marching along like it's a spring day in Boise!"

"If you mean we're used to the sun, you're right," Johns said. "There are no 'spring days in Boise' where we come from."

Whitworth grinned, and Johns awkwardly puffed at the cigarette he'd given him. "Scuttlebutt has it you guys are earmarked for something big," Whitworth said as he blew a smoke ring toward the ceiling.

"Scuttlebutt?"

"Gossip, you know . . . talk. Anything to it?"

Johns shrugged. "I don't know. No one has told us anything yet."

"Still, I bet it's something big the brass has cooked up for you guys," Whitworth said. "And I'll bet old Vogel had a big hand in it, too."

Major General Clayton Vogel was the Commanding General of Camp Elliott, and he did, indeed, have a hand in what was going on. But it wasn't until a civilian visited the camp that the new recruits began to have an inkling of why they had been recruited.

Chapter Five
Specialized Training

Morning hit with all the force of a hammer—or more to the point, with all the force of the DI's swagger stick hitting on the ends of the boots' metal bunks. It jerked them from sleep to awareness like an exploding grenade.

"Grab your cocks and put on your socks, you buncha mama's boys!" Marshall bellowed in his endearing voice. "You got five minutes to shit, shower, and shave! Except for you Indian boys who can't grow any hair like a man . . . a marine! You guys shave anyway, just in case you grow into marines one day. Then, ladies, after a short five-mile trot around the compound, you can all grab a little chow. Get a mo—o—ove on!"

The stick banged against a metal bunk again, the noise reverberating through the barracks as Redhawk rolled from his rack and to the floor. He scrambled for his clothes and ditty bag, then made a mad rush for the head. If he didn't get there first, he could count on not getting to use any of the facilities. Some of the men had been sent to the infirmary because it had been too long since they'd had the opportunity to use the head.

Five minutes later found the platoon forming a

straight line in front of the barracks, with Sergeant Marshall stalking in front of them like an avenging grizzly. The customary scowl creased his face, and if anything, he was even louder than ever. The fact that the platoon was shaping up well did not seem to impress him.

"Lissen up, shitbirds!" he bellowed. "You've got five miles to run before chow! I don't want any stragglers, and I don't want any shortcuts!" His face contorted into what passed for a smile as he added, "You've got some new instructors coming and I want you to impress them with your shit-for-brains mentality! Now mo—o—ove it!"

Redhawk reflected that it was easy enough for Marshall to conduct a five-mile run when he followed them in a jeep, watching them like a hawk, bellowing at any man who slowed down the slightest bit. But Marshall didn't realize that the Navajos were used to running, that they didn't have that many vehicles on the reservation, and that many of them didn't even have a horse. Sometimes, at night, Redhawk had gone out onto the desert and just run, for no reason other than that he felt like it. No, running wasn't hard for the Navajos at all.

By the time the five-mile run was over and they were lined up in front of the chow hall, the sun was hanging in the eastern sky. Two flapjacks and a scoop of powdered eggs later, the recruits were back in front of the mess hall and ready for their new instructions.

Marshall strutted up and down the graveled walk, his swagger stick under his arm, his voice shaking the boards of the buildings.

"Men, this will be a little test of what you've learned these past weeks. And I want you to know that I expect you to win. A contest has been devised, a game between us and Second Company. You *will win!* There will be no quarter for failure."

Marshall briefly outlined the details of the contest,

a battle between First Company—Red—and Second Company—White—Redhawk grinned.

"Men, here's the plan: First Platoon will be the reconnaissance platoon for this operation. Second Platoon will be backup, and Third Platoon will be the artillery unit," Marshall was saying. "I will give out a map, but the lines are not exactly set. You can tend to that in the field. Your job is to take the 'white' army. This is your final test in the field, and I'll know just how much attention you shitbirds have paid by the time it is over. Fail . . . and you'll have me up your asses every minute of every day until I think you know more than how to hold your cocks. Do you read me?"

A resounding chorus of "Sir, yessir!" rumbled the rooftops until the DI seemed slightly satisfied.

"All right, ladies, now lissen up! These seven men here," Marshall said, shoving a beefy arm in the direction of uniformed men wearing black helmets and arm bands, "are the referees. It is their judgment that will determine the outcome and performance of this battle. When a referee states that you have been killed, you must surrender your arm band, and report back to base camp. There will be no live ammo issued. And you radio men will call in coordinates that will be monitored and judged. If you are in the quadrants that have been shelled, these umps will take your arm bands. If you get close enough to the enemy without detection, notify the nearest ump and he will make the call. Understood?"

"Sir, yessir!"

That day was spent in preparation, and early the next morning the Red team fell in at 0400 hours. They were loaded into half-tons and driven out to the woods and fields where the games were to take place. Very little was said as they rode along dirt roads rutted from heavy trucks and field equipment. The half-tons rocked up steep slopes, and Redhawk realized that they were headed into the ridged foothills of the surrounding mountains. Second-growth evergreens stubbed the knolls and ridges.

When the half-ton rolled to a stop and the men piled out, Redhawk sucked in a deep breath of freedom. No fences. No guardhouses. Nothing but miles and miles of empty land—empty but for the intrusion of the Red Company. The remainder of the day was spent in setting up a camp for base operations, and somewhere in those mountains, the White Company was doing the same. For the next two days they were to play cat and mouse, hunting and hiding.

Redhawk grinned to himself. At last . . . a game he knew how to play.

Redhawk and Johns were chosen to be scouts. He relished the opportunity to range freely without constant supervision, and the platoon trusted his ability to do the job. This was his element, his instincts told him, and he could get closer to the "enemy" than any other man.

Redhawk chose Johns to be his partner, and they were issued walkie-talkies. They were to find the enemy without being detected, then report their position back to the command post at base camp. Then the squads would be given their instructions, with a platoon flanking left, a platoon flanking right, and another to go up the middle. One platoon was to be sent around to the back in an effort to try and catch them in a vise, surrounding them and forcing surrender. It was a simple plan.

Or it was when the lieutenant used his topographical maps and outlined his strategy. Employing it would be a bit more difficult.

Just before noon, Redhawk and Johns slipped from camp armed with their walkie-talkies and red arm bands. They moved quickly at first, not speaking, just walking as they had walked through the New Mexico and Arizona hills.

"Reconnaissance," Johns said after they'd walked a

mile or two. "It's just a fancy way of saying hide and seek."

The air was crisp, with a cool wind blowing through the boughs of the evergreens, the sharp scent spicing the wind and making Redhawk think of home. He hadn't realized how much he missed the freedom of ranging through mountains and even the hot dry rocks until now. There was always something to do, someone standing over him telling him how to do it—or how not to do it.

But, oddly enough, instead of the earlier resentment he'd felt, he accepted it now. There was no hatred, no prejudice, just the determination that every man there—red, black, or white—would be a marine. Teamwork was stressed, the instinctive reaction as a body instead of an individual, and Redhawk supposed that was necessary during battle. Perhaps that was the secret to the white man's ability to annihilate their enemies, to have forced the Indian into defeat—teamwork.

"What are your plans?" Johns asked in the quiet around them. "You're thinking too hard."

Redhawk grinned. "Something just occurred to me, cousin. The white man stresses teamwork, right?"

"Right."

"Then I think we should work as a team to search out the enemy."

Johns frowned. "I don't know what you mean."

As they walked down a slope and through a gully, a helicopter buzzed on the horizon, and they quickly dove under cover of some brush. They waited as it passed, flying low and obviously scanning the area. No air power was to be used during the games, but Redhawk and Johns instinctively hid from even the referees. They crouched in the bushes and waited until the copter was a distant buzz.

Johns listened intently when Redhawk proposed a plan. "Do you think it will work?" he asked when

Redhawk finished speaking, and Johnny shrugged.

"I don't see why it wouldn't."

"It's worth a try."

"Old Stone-Face would swallow his swagger stick," Redhawk returned in a dry tone.

Several hours later found them in a shallow depression in the ground, lying and waiting for the light to grow dim. They had not attempted to communicate with their home base, knowing the White team would pick up on their transmission. They lay there with all the patience of their race, chewing silently on strips of dried beef from their packs. They traveled light, with only canteens of water and scant food, but that was the way Navajos had traveled for centuries. Water was found in barrel cactus on the Arizona desert, and food was provided by plants and animals the white man would usually overlook. The piñon tree provided small cones that could be dissected and the nuts eaten. Even the cactus could be eaten if one knew how to pluck the fruit, and yucca plants offered a fruit that was sweet and juicy early in the summer. No, they wouldn't starve even if they had not brought tins of food in their packs.

Dusk finally blanketed the land, lying in soft shrouds that blended the trees and bushes into one long outline. Redhawk smiled at his cousin.

"I think it is time."

A thin moon gave little light overhead, and in the unfamiliar territory the rustlings of night creatures was overrun by another sound. Their sharp ears picked up the noise of men in the distance, and Redhawk stopped, knelt, and put an ear to the ground. He looked up at Johns with a wide white grin.

"I hear them. They are only a few miles ahead. Maybe on that far ridge."

Pulling out the topographical map he'd been given, Redhawk picked his memory for the details of the orientation class he'd taken. He struggled to pinpoint the quadrants of the map so his teammates could easily read it. It wouldn't do him any good to know where their camp was if the members of his team couldn't find the enemy or he couldn't give them the proper coordinates over the radio.

Johns shinnied up a tall, slender pine and perched in one of the forks like a giant raven. He gave a wave of his hand when he was situated, and Redhawk moved silently ahead.

He'd discarded his pack and canteen because of the slight clinking noise they made when he walked, and he had rubbed dirt on his face so that it would not reflect the moonlight. It was an old trick, one used by his ancestors in the form of war paint. All he carried was his M-1.

Crawling on his belly, Redhawk edged closer to the origin of the sounds, until his keen night vision located a small boulder with two smaller humps jutting up from behind it. The two smaller humps were marine helmets, and his mouth stretched in a faint smile. He paused, crouched motionless and silent, waiting. Then he saw the brief, bright spurt of a match flare and laughed softly to himself.

This must be the forward guard post for the base camp. And they were obviously careless or confident, or they would not have lit a cigarette. He could smell the smoke on the wind.

Tilting back his head, Redhawk cupped one hand around his mouth and gave a lilting birdcall that he knew Johns would recognize. They'd used the sign since they were small boys playing at war in the desert. An answering call drifted back, and he knew Johns had understood.

Still crouched low, Redhawk moved quietly through the underbrush, circling the guard outpost. It took nearly half an hour before he was behind them, crouched in the dark bushes and waiting for the right moment.

He could hear the two men talking quietly, laughing occasionally, and still smoking cigarettes. Quietly bringing up his M-1. Redhawk straightened slowly, rising up out of the cover of the bushes. The muzzle pointed steadily at the two guards still deep in conversation, and he smiled as he stepped out of the bushes and into the small clearing.

The two marines jerked around, cigarettes dropping as they fumbled for their weapons, but Redhawk gestured with his rifle and they paused. The two men exchanged stunned glances, then looked back at Redhawk.

"How," Redhawk couldn't resist saying, and both marines burst into laughter.

"Shit! You scared the hell out of us, Chief, but I reckon you got us," one of them said, shaking his head.

His companion let the radio he was holding slide between his knees, the unused mike dangling uselessly. "I never heard you coming," he said in amazement.

Redhawk wasn't surprised. "Give me your arm bands, now. And the radio," he added.

Peeling off their arm bands, they tossed them at Redhawk, then reached for the radio and weapons. The first man said, "Here you go, Chief. I still don't understand how you snuck up on us so quiet-like. I didn't hear a damned thing."

"Just lucky, White-man," Redhawk returned, deftly catching the M-1 the marine tossed at him. He caught the other one, then laid them down beside the radio that was nudged toward him.

While the two captured marines shook their heads in disgust, Redhawk used his walkie-talkie to radio Johns. He spoke instinctively in Navajo so it would not be received and understood by the White team. The radio crackled with static as he waited for a reply, impatiently thumbing the button. Finally, it came.

"I hear you," Johns said, speaking in English. "What are your coordinates?"

Redhawk thumbed his button again, and the mixture of English and Navajo words flowed into the mike. "I have captured two of the enemy. I am in quadrant 1101. Repeat, quadrant 1101. Do you receive?"

"Affirmative," came the reply broken by static. There was a pause, then Redhawk heard Johns hesitant voice. "Do we keep to plan?"

"Affirmative," Redhawk replied without hesitation. He switched off the radio and smiled down into the mystified faces of the two listening marines. "Don't you agree with me?"

Grinning, the taller marine shook his head. "Hell, I ain't got no idea what you said, Chief, and you know it!"

"I thought you didn't, but I was just checking," Redhawk said. He sat on the edge of a rock and fished in his shirt pocket for one of the strips of dried meat. Biting off a hunk, he chewed it and waited.

Willie Johns arrived in a reasonably short time. He glanced at the two prisoners and grinned. "Not bad, not bad for a day's work."

"Oh, we're not even close yet," Redhawk said. He'd been thinking while waiting and decided to discard their original plan. Why let all the company have the glory when the platoon of Navajos could do it? "Lissen up," he said to Willie, then proceeded to outline his plan in Navajo.

"Sounds good to me," Johns said.

They radioed back to the base camp and gave their position, then asked for reinforcements. "Send First Platoon out," Redhawk instructed.

After turning the captured marines over to an umpire, the two Navajos set off down the hill, slipping quietly through the scrub and brush while a thin moon shone down. A fresh breeze sprang up, and

Johns lifted his head to sniff the air like a wary elk.

"I can smell their camp," he whispered to Redhawk. "I can detect the fumes of gas and exhaust."

"We'll take out the other guards," Redhawk decided, and Johns nodded agreement. They crouched in the thick brush, while moonlight washed the gully and their adrenaline pumped high.

This, Redhawk thought, was more like the games he liked to play. This was the art of warfare instead of the reality of it, but it proved that not everything had to be learned from the white man's book. There were a few tricks the Navajo could teach, too.

In the next two hours, the Navajos used all their native skills to slip quietly around the perimeters of the camp and take out the White team's guards. It was easy for them, almost laughably easy. Flushed with victory and with their adrenaline pumping, Redhawk and Johns paused to wait for the rest of their platoon with a fistful of arm bands in hand.

Their daring plan didn't seem quite so impossible now. Almost every one of the guard posts had been captured, and all without alerting the main company. Time was the most important element now, for if the rest of the Red platoon took too long to get there, the element of surprise would be eliminated when the guards were changed. Redhawk radioed a message in Navajo and, received the answer immediately: First Platoon was almost at the rendezvous spot.

Returning to the quadrant radioed to the base camp, they met up with the rest of their platoon. Holding up a fistful of the white arm bands, Redhawk grinned at them.

"It will be a slaughter," he promised, and the platoon grinned back.

Swiftly marshaling their forces, the platoon moved out in accordance with Redhawk's plan. The White command post was situated in a canyon below a tree-studded knoll, not easily seen and not easily accessible. So how to get in?

It was Redhawk who voiced his idea to use the white arm bands they had captured from the enemy.

"Why not put them to use instead of just carrying them around?" he asked, and the platoon exchanged glances.

One of the men, Bell Wood, spoke up. "But aren't we supposed to just call in our coordinates and let the umps know the situation?"

"That's what we're *supposed* to do, yes. But when have we ever followed the rules?" Redhawk looked from man to man and said, "Wouldn't the DI be surprised if we managed to capture the entire command post?"

"It'll never work," another man disagreed with a doubtful shake of his head.

"It might," Bell Wood argued, and his face split into a wide grin. "I think it *will* work!"

In a matter of minutes, the white arm bands had been passed around and replaced the red arm bands. A ripple of excitement went through the platoon crouched in the shadows and bushes, and muted laughter added an air of high spirits that made the plan seem more like a prank than serious training.

The platoon of Navajos split up, taking two more guards and forcing them to exchange their white arm bands for red. One force fanned out to wait for the signal, while the other marched boldly into the White camp, their "prisoners" pushed ahead of them at riflepoint.

"Don't speak," Redhawk warned the prisoners. "Pretend I have real bullets in my rifle. Who is your CO, and which tent is his?"

"You told us not to talk," one of the captured men said in a sour voice, and Redhawk jabbed him in the back with his M-1.

"I also said to pretend I have real bullets."

The other prisoner laughed, enjoying the charade

in spite of his defeat, and pointed the way to the CO's tent. "His name is Morgan."

Captain Morgan and an umpire were in the canvas tent erected at the base of the canyon. A guard was posted outside the area, and he barred the way.

"Reporting two Red team prisoners," Redhawk said, and hoped the guard did not shine his flashlight over him. The dim light of the moon provided enough shadow to keep his Indian features from being recognized. He was in luck. The guard played his light briefly over the telltale arm bands, then motioned them through.

Captain Morgan looked up with a pleased smile as Redhawk strolled in, shoving two of the "enemy" ahead of him. "Well! I see that you men have been busy tonight," he said.

"Sir, yessir," Redhawk replied, keeping his chin down as he maneuvered the prisoners to one side. He could hear Johns right behind him and could feel the tension in his cousin. "Reporting the capture of fourteen arm bands, sir," he said to the captain, and saw his face sag in astonishment.

"Fourteen? Damn, but that's excellent! Excellent! I am absolutely amazed at your aptitude! What's your name, Marine?"

Pushing back the brim of his helmet, Redhawk lifted his face to look at the captain. He saw recognition register in his eyes along with shock, and he grinned.

"Recruit Redhawk, sir." Bringing up his rifle in a swift motion, he fired harmlessly into the air. "That was a signal. Your post is surrounded, and you, Captain Morgan, are my prisoner, along with your men."

Morgan had half leaped to his feet and stood frozen as he heard the unmistakable sounds of men shouting and shots being fired. "I don't believe it!"

The umpire seated at the table began to laugh. "I think you'd better," he said. "Looks like the Red team outdid you, Captain."

Morgan sagged back into his chair, shaking his head. "Never in all my years in the marines has this happened! I fucking don't believe it! What . . . how did you men do it?" His voice was faintly pleading, still slightly skeptical as he looked up at the Indian recruits.

Redhawk's face was solemn as he asked, "Sir, does the name *Custer* ring a bell, sir?"

Chapter Six
Training Introduction

Redhawk shifted uneasily from foot to foot, and Johns looked at him curiously. "Is something the matter?" he asked, but Redhawk didn't reply for a moment.

Then, shaking his head, he said, "I don't know what this *special training* is about. Does it mean that we are to be a special force?"

Shrugging, Johns looked dawn at the paper he held. "It doesn't say anything like that. I don't know. Maybe we are to get special training because we did so well at the games they had us play. Even Sergeant Marshall was pleased. I have never seen him laugh before."

"He probably never has," Redhawk said with a flicker of amusement. "The white man has a strange sense of humor. I don't often understand their jokes."

"And they never understand ours."

"Which is all right. I'm not sure I want the white man to understand us, do you?"

Johns shook his head slowly. "No, I guess not. But it would be better if we could understand how his mind works, I think."

A voice from behind them said, "We already know how! It goes *click, click* like a money counter."

Turning, the two cousins smiled at Bell Wood, the Navajo youth from Fort Defiance. He had ridden on the train with them, but things had been so strange and frightening that they had not taken the opportunity to become acquainted with one another. Now they were more relaxed and more confident, and had begun talking freely among themselves.

Gesturing toward the long clapboard building where they were to gather for "special training," Bell said, "You are to attend a class here, too?"

Redhawk nodded. "Yes. But I don't know what it is about yet, do you?"

Taking a step closer, Bell said, "I was told that it has to do with the fact that we are all Indians. And more than that . . . all Navajos. Have you noticed that there are no other tribes in our outfit?"

Redhawk thought about it a moment. "Yes, I see what you are saying. We have been singled out for some reason. What do you think it is?"

Bell Wood grinned. "It must be because we are cleaner and can march all day without water!"

Willie Johns laughed gleefully and began to do an imitation of some of the white marines they'd seen. He let his tongue loll out of the side of his mouth and crossed his eyes, then dragged himself heaving and panting across the paved street until Redhawk and Wood were weak with laughter at his impersonation.

"I am on a one-mile hike!" Johns said, and dropped to the ground to pretend to crawl. Redhawk and Wood doubled over with amusement.

When they straightened, they saw Marshall standing with his feet planted a yard apart and his huge fists on his hips. He wasn't smiling.

"Ten-SHUN!" he bellowed, and Redhawk and Wood snapped to a stiff posture while Johns scrambled up and brushed dust from the legs of his uniform. "What in the hell do you men think you're doing?" Marshall snarled when they had stood stiff and motionless for a full minute and a half. "Do you think you're funny?"

"Sir, no sir!" the three chorused. They knew what was expected of them.

"Then what were you doing?"

At the bellowed question, Redhawk replied quickly, "Sir, a new exercise, sir."

"A new exercise?"

"Sir, yessir," Wood said immediately, picking up on Redhawk's cue.

Redhawk stared straight ahead. He knew better than to tell the truth. No white man ever saw the humor in what they did. Most would be insulted if they realized how the Navajo mimicked them.

Marshall was glaring at the three Navajos, not quite believing them but not sure what to think. He reacted with the normal response of a marine DI.

"Five laps around the compound! Double-time! If you've got time to do exercises, I want to see them! Move it, move it, Mo—o—ove it!"

As they ran, Johns looked at Redhawk and Wood and grinned. "This is better than special training, I think."

"It is less dangerous than joking the white man," Redhawk shot back. The rest of the run was completed in silence.

One of the most difficult things for the Navajo recruits to become accustomed to was the white man's fondness for repeat phrases and personal names. It seemed ridiculous to Redhawk that a question like: "Can you hear me? Do you hear me?" should be asked over and over. Or, personal names were used all the time. Even with his cousin, he used his name sparingly. To borrow it too often would be an invasion of Johns's privacy.

But in spite of all his reservations, Redhawk was slowly beginning to feel more comfortable. He realized he might not understand a great deal of the Anglo way of thinking, but he could respect their right to their own views. And maybe one day, the white man would feel the same, he reflected with a wry twist of his mouth. But perhaps that was too much to hope for.

That opinion was only slightly revised by the new communication school's instructor, Philip Johnston. A pleasant-faced man with thick glasses, Johnston addressed the class composed entirely of Navajos in their own language. It was both startling and gratifying at the same time.

"Now that you have successfully completed boot camp, your skills are required for a new program," Johnston said after introducing himself. "Not only will I be your teacher for this course, but you will teach me and each other." He gave them a faint smile. "This will not be easy. In fact, it will be one of the most difficult tasks you have been assigned." He perched on the edge of a heavy oak desk and took off his glasses, letting the silence extend to just the right length as he polished the lenses. Then, as the men began to stir, he replaced his glasses on the bridge of his nose and said loud enough to startle them, "Only *you* can participate in this program, a program designed to outwit the enemy at every turn! No other marine is qualified to take this training . . . only the Navajo."

A dropped pin would have sounded like a barrage of enemy fire in that silent room as the bronzed faces stared intently at Johnston, who smiled again.

"And now, men, you have a forty-eight-hour leave. Your return time is 0600 hours Monday morning. Dismissed."

Redhawk, Johns, and Wood exchanged glances full of questions and relief. Finally, Redhawk shrugged. "Well? We still don't know any more than we did when we went into the room."

"Who cares?" Johns shot back with a jubilant smile. "I smell whiskey!"

"We only have forty-eight hours," Wood pointed out. "I don't think we can drink enough before we have to be back."

"We can try."

Redhawk shook his head. "Johnston spoke very good Navajo. Where do you think he learned it?"

"Trading post," Johns said promptly. "That's where most white men learn to speak our tongue. Those who bother to, anyway. Most white men say we must learn to speak English, but they never bother with learning even one word of our language, as if it might make them Indian."

"But most can only speak phrases or words, not with the right sentences," Wood said. "He is right in thinking it is odd."

"And Johnston said only the Navajo could take this training." Redhawk stood stock-still with his brow furrowed in thought, then finally shrugged. "We will know more than we want to very soon, I think."

A chugging noise cut through the hot air and dust, and the three Navajos glanced up to see a bus lumber to a halt.

"Hey, come on!" another Navajo called to them, waving them forward. "We have a ride into town!"

Dust boiled up behind them as they sprinted toward the bus with more energy than they had shown in their entire six-week training.

An hour later found many—maybe most—of the Navajos in a smoky bar in San Diego. Laughing and proud in their spic-and-span uniforms and sharp creases, the men crowded close to the bar and ordered drinks with exotic names, such as Tom Collins, Whiskey Sour, Martini, and Vodka Gimlet. Some stuck to what they knew—plain whiskey in a glass, no ice, no water.

"Look at this!" Johns said with a trace of admiration in his voice. He was rolling a bottle around in one hand, staring at the label and occasionally sniffing the open top. "It's much darker than that we drink, cousin! But it does not have the same fire."

Bell Wood laughed. "It does not have the same fire because it is much better than that rotgut I'm sure you are used to drinking!" He pointed to the shelves of differently labeled bottles. "See? Scotch, vodka, gin, brandy—they all have a kick, but they are not as rough on a man's stomach. Unless a man drinks so much he walks on air."

"My cousin always thinks he can walk on air after he drinks whiskey," Redhawk remarked with a grin. "And I swear that I have seen him do so!"

"No, it is *you* who has flown with the eagle, not me," Johns said, and then regretted the reminder. "I spoke too hastily, cousin."

Redhawk's grin had immediately faded as he remembered the peyote dream, and he stared at Willie Johns in the smoky light. For a brief instant it had all flashed through his mind again, the blood and death and clouds of smoke and sulphur. Tilting back his head, Redhawk gulped down the last of his drink, then splashed more in the small glass.

"They should give a man a bigger glass," he said. "This is too small."

Johns nodded agreement. "*Aiee.* We are more used to this bottle than a glass." He grabbed the bottle and drank from it, then dragged his sleeve across his mouth.

"Hey!" the bartender said. "Drink from a glass like a white man, Injun!"

Redhawk stiffened at the implied insult, but Wood's warning hand on his arm kept him from saying anything. He'd had just enough whiskey to make him bold, make him forget all the lessons he'd learned in his childhood. Redhawk took up his glass between his thumb and index finger, and with his little finger held at an exaggerated angle, he pursed his lips like a woman and sipped. He said nothing, but kept his flat black eyes on the bartender as he drank with a surplus of dainty motions.

He was defying all his hard-learned lessons about "never joking about the white man," but he didn't care. Whiskey and anger had made him reckless.

The bartender eyed the young Navajo. He saw the anger in his eyes, and he saw something else, too. There was a dangerous quality to the steady gaze, the broad shoulders, and the set of his jaw, and he decided not to pursue an argument.

Shrugging carelessly, the bartender said, "Suit yourself," then stalked away, his jaw set and ugly.

"Why did you do that?" Johns demanded. "Now he has seen what you think of him. You know that is dangerous! You know better, and it was you who reminded me of it just yesterday afternoon!"

Redhawk shrugged. "I don't care."

"Let's go somewhere else," Wood suggested. They left the bar in much lower spirits than they had entered it.

Once out on the sidewalk in the fresh air, the three men stood silently for a moment. Redhawk was seething with anger and resentment, and Johns knew it. It was a familiar emotion to all Navajos.

"No matter where we go, we will always be *Injuns,*" Redhawk said after a moment. "We can wear the white man's clothes and his uniforms, and we can fight for the same land, but when it is all over, we will still be *Injuns.*"

Bell Wood looked up at the white clouds scudding in the sky, then sucked in a deep breath. "It doesn't matter. No one ever promised any man an easy path in life."

"He's right," Johns said. "We still have our pride and our dignity, and the white man has not been able to take that away from us. . . ."

Redhawk turned on him with a furious glare. "How can you say that? How can you say that we still have our pride and dignity, when you have seen the old ones lying in the gutters of every town, sleeping whiskey dreams and forgetting themselves? Do they look dignified lying in the dust and dirt? Do they look dignified when they shuffle down the street begging for money for more whiskey?" He spat on the ground. "I will not drink it again. I am one of The People, and I will not sell myself for a bottle of empty promises again."

Wood and Johns stared after him as Redhawk turned and stalked away, his hands in his pockets and his shoulders hunched. They followed slowly, and none of them spoke about it again. Instead, they went to a movie called *The Flying Tigers,* starring John Wayne, a man they were more accustomed to seeing fighting Indians on the wide screen than Japanese soldiers.

Redhawk felt a cold chill run down his spine. The small men in the movie were very much like the small men in his dream.

Chapter Seven
Specialized Training

Instructor Johnston paced the floor of the classroom with firm, steady steps. "Gentlemen, this is our problem: Our enemies are adept at deciphering every code we have been able to devise. We have used American slang, profanity, and any vocabulary that has seemed feasible, and they are still able to intercept and decode our messages. It is vital that we devise a new code, one that will not be decipherable. It must be quick and easy, in order to be transmitted in the midst of a heated battle. There will not be much time to send or take messages under some circumstances, yet vital orders must be radio transmitted." Johnston paused to glance at the men. A faint smile curved his mouth as he saw the gleam of comprehension in some eyes.

"I see that there are a few of you who already know what it is the Marine Corps wants from you. This is it: a new code must be devised using the Navajo language. It will be sent by Navajos to Navajos, working in teams, and it will use words familiar to all of you. Yet, for safety's sake, we must still code the Navajo language."

Pausing in front of his desk, Johnston leaned back and folded his arms across his chest, affecting a casual pose. "Of course, fluent English and Navajo are prerequisites to this course, and it has taken a great deal of weeding out to come to this group. You men are all intelligent, able-bodied marines who have passed basic training and shown an aptitude for communication skills. It took me a long time to gain approval for this and it has undergone quite a few changes since its inception, but now we are here and we will show them that it will work.

"Employing only the most frequently used words in military lexicon, we shall supplement our code with the Navajo alphabet to spell out proper names or places, and any other words not included in the syllabus. These must—and I stress the word *must*—be memorized, for there will be no time in battle to look up unfamiliar words. Any error could be fatal. It will not be easy, but if we all work together, I think we can devise a workable code that will baffle the enemy."

Johnston paced the floor in front of the chalkboard, and eyed the silent men. Redhawk met his gaze steadily, and there was the glitter of excitement in his eyes as he realized he would not be just another marine, another Indian whose worth was not recognized and would soon be forgotten. He could make a difference, he and his brothers. This was not just another dirty job given to the Indian because he was easily replaceable and would not be missed. No, they were *needed,* and that gave him a sense of pride.

He listened with renewed interest as Johnston turned to the chalkboard hanging on the wall and began to sketch out a series of ideas using Navajo words. And Redhawk wasn't the only man there who was fascinated with Johnston's proposal. After a few moments, everyone sat forward in his seat. Chalked words began to appear on the board, quickly drawn, and his interest was piqued by the use of the written word in a familiar tongue.

"*A*," Johnston was saying, "can be interpreted by the word *ant* in English, but the Navajo translation for *ant* is *wol-la-chee. B* will stand for *bear,* and in Navajo that is—"

He was interrupted by a chorus of voices saying, "*shush!*"

Johnston looked up with a pleased smile. "Correct. And *C* for *cat* would be—"

"*Moasi.*"

At the end of the alphabet, from *wol-la-chee* to *Besh-do-gliz* the Navajo equivalent of *zinc,* the Navajos went over the code. They began to smile at one another, obviously thinking it was too easy. Then Johnston threw them a curve.

"I suppose you think this is simple. Maybe it is, but if it's too simple, it's too dangerous. So how do we arrange the alphabet to disguise it even further, just in case there are some of the enemy who know Navajo? I'm not certain if you men are aware of the fact that for the past twenty years, German students have made a practice of coming to America and studying various Indian dialects."

There was a brief silence before he added, "Only the Navajo tribe has been eliminated from that number, for whatever reason. The Navajo dialect is not intelligible to other tribes, even though it bears some resemblance to Apache. Nor is it intelligible to other races, with the possible exception of a few Americans. For this reason, it is virtually undecipherable by the enemy, in my opinion. But we *must* be certain! We must transpose our words in some instances, then memorize those changes."

After a moment, one of the men asked, in a doubtful tone, "Does that mean that you wish us to call things by different names?"

"Correct. We all have to agree on the words. As

one Navajo word can have four different inflections, thus four different meanings, it is my opinion that we should use just the words that are not so subtly shaded. For instance, we could use *chicken hawk* for "dive-bomber," or in Navajo, *gini*. "Transport" would be *eagle,* or *atsah.* Do you understand what I am trying to do?"

Words for letters of the alphabet were taken from nature, using the names of animals in most cases, but agreed-upon terms in others. Names were given to organizations as well as to communication terms, military officers, airplanes, ships, seasons, and months. A general vocabulary was also devised, with coded terms to represent commonly used words or actions. "Bombs" were referred to as *eggs,* or *a-ye-shi:* "Fortification" was given the Navajo name of *An-no-sozi,* or *cliff dwelling,* a term suggested by Redhawk and Johns. "Invade" would be *moved into,* or *a-tah-gi-nah.* Even geographical locations were given code names. *Slant-eyed,* or *Beh-na-ali-tsoisi,* was the term for "Japan." "Africa" was *Blackies,* or *Zhin-ni.* When it came to "Italy," the men could not think of a code name until one man suggested they call it *Stutter,* or *Doh-ha-chi-yali-tchi,* because he knew an Italian who stuttered. Laughing, they all agreed. And so it went, a different term for names, dates, and places, totaling over four hundred and eleven different terms in the vocabulary.

Day after day the words were repeated by rote. Then tests were given, with the instructor saying the word or phrase in Navajo, and the men translating it into English printed on sheets of paper.

"Ni-ma-si," the instructor would say, the Navajo word for "potatoes," and the recruits printed *grenades* in English. *"Ha-a-cidi"* he would say, Navajo for "inspector", and the correct response was *reconnaissance.* The instructor repeated words

and phrases slowly at first, then more quickly as the recruits learned them. A "military unit" was sent as *da-az-jah,* translating into the Navajo term for *bunched.*

They progressed from rote and dictation to using code words by commanding operational orders. The recruits were issued a manual entitled "Sample Operations Orders," and they used it as a basis. The instructor, usually pacing in front of the class and speaking quickly, would rap out orders in code, and the class was expected to print the English translations on test sheets. Orders such as "machine gun fire on right flank" and "continue to advance" were given out until the class had no hesitation in translation.

It was an eight-week course, a rigorous exercise in testing mental and physical capabilities. The final two weeks of the course were to be spent concentrating on field experience.

It wasn't easy for the Navajos, who still had to complete their basic training in radio and communication skills as well as study the code. Nights were long and were spent poring over their notes, repeating the words over and over until they became as natural as breathing, as natural as their native tongue. Sleep became a thing of the past.

Philip Johnston became an unofficial mother hen, watching over the students and his pet project, worrying about the outcome and level of success it would achieve. He frequently queried the instructors, and Redhawk overheard him one day.

"Are you certain Private Wood is ready yet? He seems to be confused at times."

The instructor—another Navajo—shook his head. "Some of the men are naturally slower than the others. Private Wood has a very good basic understanding of what is required, but he prefers to go more slowly rather than speed through his lessons like Private Redhawk."

"And this Redhawk . . . does he know his code?"

The instructor smiled slightly. "Like he knows the back of his hand."

"Let's put that to a test tomorrow out in the field," Johnston shot back. "I think they're ready now."

"I know they're ready," was the instructor's reply.

Redhawk stepped quickly away from the door where he'd been listening. He felt slightly embarrassed that he had not let his presence be known, because it was very ill-mannered to eavesdrop, but he was also glad he had. He would study doubly hard that night and would be ready for the next day.

Willie Johns, Wood, and Redhawk studied together. The code words flew back and forth between them as they quizzed one another. If a mistake was made, no time was wasted in recriminations, only the correct answer repeated over and over until it was deeply embedded in all their minds.

The field training was grueling. They were divided up into teams and sent out.

"I will send ten messages," one instructor said to Redhawk and Willie Johns, "and after the final message, you are to act according to my instructions. Do I make myself clear?"

"Sir, yessir," was the prompt answer, which seemed to please the instructor. Several other men repeated their orders twice before understanding, and a few still seemed confused. Bell Wood was one of those who was kept behind.

Trudging up a hill, loaded down with radio equipment, Redhawk did not allow himself even a glance back at Johns. Willie was to send the messages, while Redhawk would receive and act upon instructions. A flutter of excitement in the pit of his stomach was not lessened by the hasty breakfast he'd eaten that morning, and Redhawk had the wry thought that Johns had been right about marines eating three good meals a day. It was too much. Hunger kept a man on edge, made him sharper, while a full stomach made him lazy and too relaxed.

When he reached the top of the hill, Redhawk radioed his position back, then waited on the messages. They came quickly, in rapid Navajo, and he wrote them down as quickly as they came through the mike. He didn't stop to think about it but reacted instinctively. Each message began and ended with time and date, but the instructions differed.

On the tenth message, he packed up his radio equipment and crossed to another position indicated by the message. Marshall and the instructor allowed themselves a brief exchange of congratulatory glances before ordering Redhawk back to base camp.

The following days were spent in simulated situations. Plane to ground, messages from moving tanks and half-tracks, and even ship to shore messages were simulated. The code talkers excelled at every turn, surprising the brass and gratifying their instructors, especially Philip Johnston.

Johnston beamed as he walked around a simulated field position, listening to messages being decoded as they came in, as if they had been sent and received in English. Some of the brass were frankly skeptical, but after viewing the results for themselves—sending runners back and forth between the key positions—they had to admit they didn't know how in the hell it was being done so quickly. And so accurately.

The area was crisscrossed with wires running from position to position, resembling the inside of a radio, Redhawk thought as he sat back and watched for a while. He grinned when he heard one of the top brass say, "It must be rigged. *No* one can send and decode a message that fast!"

Chewing on a fat cigar, he glared at the mild-mannered Johnston, who didn't back down an inch. "Sir, why don't you send a message yourself, just to prove that it can be done. I think you will be surprised at the results."

Colonel Crawford continued to chew on his cigar, his hand behind his back as he dictated a message. He watched with eagle-sharp eyes as the man spoke into the mike in a series of grunts that sounded incomprehensible to anyone who didn't know the Navajo tongue. "Well?" he demanded when the message had been sent. "Send a runner to retrieve a written copy of what I just said! And I'm going to be watching closely."

Johnston didn't turn a hair, and Redhawk watched with interest as a man ran down the hill to the position on the far slope. He was handed the paper and immediately turned and ran back, while Colonel Crawford kept his eyes on him.

Crawford took the paper out of the man's hand and scanned it swiftly, then looked up at Johnston. The fat cigar drooped from one corner of his mouth as he shook his head.

"Well, I'll be goddammed! I didn't think it possible. Can he do it again?"

"As many times as you want, sir," Johnston shot back confidently. It was tried again with the same results. The colonel left completely convinced of the reliability of the code, but still skeptical that it would be as effective under extreme battle conditions.

"Perhaps the colonel thinks we are men who are afraid of death," Redhawk observed softly, and Johnston turned to look at him.

He smiled. "Perhaps he just doesn't know the Navajo as well as I do."

Redhawk smiled back. "No, he does not."

"You are called Johnny Redhawk, aren't you?" Johnston asked after a moment of companionable silence, and Redhawk nodded.

"Yes."

"You came here from Window Rock?"

Again Redhawk nodded, slowly rising to his feet. "I did."

"What do you think? Do you think that the code will work under battle conditions?"

Faintly flattered that the man who had conceived the idea of a Navajo code would seriously ask his opinion, Redhawk thought for a moment before he replied. He did not want to insult Johnston by giving him a trite answer, an answer a white man would expect, but he did not want to say other than what he believed.

"If it is given a chance to succeed, I think it will work under any conditions," he finally replied.

Johnston read between the lines, and his smile gave him away. "I see. You think that there will be difficulty among some of the white officers in accepting the code?"

Redhawk just looked at him. "The white man has always had difficulty accepting the Indian. Why would he change hundreds of years of prejudice just because there is a war?"

It was as blunt as he dared get, and his gaze was faintly challenging as he met Johnston's steady glare. Philip Johnston didn't bat an eye.

"I agree. It will have to be proven to them that it works, and I'm counting on you and men like you to do that for me. It's vital that we have an unbreakable code, and I think this is it. No, I *know* that this is it. I believe in it, and I want you to believe in it, too."

"I believe in it, but there are those who will not. It is not the Navajo who has to be convinced, but some of the white men who have no vision." Redhawk's voice was flat, and his eyes shifted politely away from Johnston's face. He did not want to challenge him with his eyes or stance, but only wanted to make his point.

Johnston understood. "I have been to Window Rock before. My father was a missionary, which is how I learned to speak your tongue. We lived not far from the Navajo reservation, and as a child, I played with other children my age. I learned a great deal about the *Diné,* and have always held a high affection for The People. I was also a translator for my father and even went to the White House when I was only nine years old. My father appealed to President Roosevelt for fair and humane treatment of the Hopis and Navajos."

Redhawk was still listening politely, his attention trained on Johnston, who stood amidst the hum of activity generated by radios and men, and took the time to talk. It was flattering to be singled out, and some of his natural reticence faded as Johnston talked about himself and what had given him the idea to use the code.

"I served in World War I, came back to California, and enrolled in the university. I have a degree in Civil Engineering, but I have never forgotten my days as a child. After Pearl Harbor, I happened across a newspaper article about an armored division in Louisiana attempting a secret form of communication in their practice maneuvers. They were using some of their Indian personnel. It gave me the idea to use the Navajo tongue because of its complexities in language. I immediately visited Lieutenant Colonel James E. Jones, who was Area Signal Officer here at Camp Elliott, and I asked him what he thought of a device that would absolutely ensure him of total secrecy for battlefield messages. Of course, Jones was frankly skeptical and told me it couldn't be done. But he didn't know what I had in mind!"

Redhawk laughed. "Neither did the Navajo when we first came here. We thought that special training meant we would be sent in first to battle."

"In a way, you are. But not in the capacity you think." Johnston stared over the frenetic activity of radios and men still sending and receiving messages, and he let a satisfied smile slant briefly across his face. "It has far exceeded my expectations. I knew the Navajo capable of effectively completing the tasks but was not at all certain of my ability to convince the top military brass."

"You haven't succeeded yet," Redhawk pointed out, and Johnston gave him a rueful smile.

"Don't I know it! But I will. The key to the success of this plan is that we don't need to use written messages that could easily fall into enemy hands. I had to convince Colonel Jones that the main difference between using the Navajo language and any other language was that we would devise a *code* of Navajo words, equivalents for military terms. He wasn't at all sure it would be practical, but now he's one of my biggest supporters. He's seen how effective you men are."

"That will be proven once we leave here, I think," Redhawk said.

Johnston's expression sobered. "Yes, I believe it will."

Chapter Eight
Guadalcanal, 1942

The huge bow of the transport ship cut through the gray waves, leaving behind a wake large enough to engulf any craft not at least as large as a football field. Gigantic engines churned heavily, a constant hum beneath the feet of men who had never been as far away from home as the ship was long. It was unsettling. It was dangerous. It was exciting.

Sailors had rigged huge booms to the heaviest of the landing lighters so that they could be launched swiftly. C-rations had been issued from several stations during the day, including tins of concentrated coffee, biscuits, the inevitable tinned meat and beans, vegetable stew, and some D-ration chocolate bars. There was enough for up to three days, adequate time for field kitchens to be erected on the island after landing.

Fortunately for the landing force, the sky was overcast, cutting visibility by a great deal. Still, the waiting was tense, as all the men aboard expected at any moment for the Japanese to spot them.

It was the night before D day. The squawk boxes cracked with the order, "All troops below deck."

Much more silently than usual, the men filed below. No one bothered to insult the squawk box for its anonymous order as was customary; there were no playful shoves or nudges, no laughter. Tense with apprehension, the men all went about the checking of packs for the last time before landing. Clean socks and underwear, cigarettes, shaving gear, rations, a Bible, maybe letters from home or a photo of a pinup girl. Along with the unavoidable odor of several hundred men in the same compact area was the scent of fear. It was almost tangible, riding the small spaces like a great-winged bird.

Redhawk could smell it. He felt it all around him, and it made him tense. Retrieving a small tin of shoe polish from his ditty bag, he sat cross-legged on the floor and began to smear thin streaks across his high cheekbones and over the bridge of his nose. No one said anything, just watched warily. It was so quiet they could almost hear the fish swimming in the Solomon Sea.

Ignoring them, Redhawk began to chant softly, an old song remembered from his early childhood. His grandfather had sung it the night before he died. After a moment, he heard Willie Johns join in, then one after another, the other Navajos on board smeared paint over their faces and sang death chants.

Uncoiling his body, Redhawk stood up, and the songs abruptly ended. He had somehow unleashed the desire in his red brothers to revert to the old ways, and now they looked to him for guidance. Silently, he stripped to just a towel wound around his lean waist.

"What are you doing, Chief?" one of the marines asked curiously.

"Praying that the strength of the enemy will be sapped, allowing us an easy landing," Redhawk replied after only a brief hesitation. The curious marine had not seemed to be hostile, only interested.

"To God?"

Shrugging, Redhawk said, "To *yei,* the Navajo gods, or if you prefer to say just God, yes." He knew better than to suggest that there might be another god besides the white man's.

Anglo marines watched curiously, most showing respect for the Navajo ceremony. As Johns and another Navajo by the name of Little Wolf Smith solemnly beat a steady tattoo on metal footlockers, Redhawk completed the circle dance in a shuffling movement, his bare feet slapping against the metal decks of the ship with a peculiar sound. He was joined by a Navajo from Fort Defiance, William Brown. Soon, there were four other men chanting prayers in Navajo as they danced. Their guttural voices echoed eerily off the steel bulkheads of the ship.

Redhawk barely felt trickles of sweat down his body or heeded the glistening sheen that made his skin glow under the dim lights of the ship. He closed his eyes against the curious stares of the white men, transporting himself back in time and place, almost feeling the hot whip of the Arizona wind across his body and the bite of sand under his bare feet. Echoes of yesterday sounded in his mind, until he could hear his father's voice.

Seek the light, my son, and the gods will always protect you.

His father had not intended that he remain an observer but had wanted him to always put himself forward, to enter into and participate in life, as he had done. Willie Johns was more passive, more willing to compromise, but he, Redhawk, would not allow himself to be ignored, as his father had wished.

To end the ceremony, it seemed fitting to sing the "Marine Hymn," as they had done at Camp Elliott. Redhawk sang it in Navajo, and his companions joined in. The Anglo marines recognized the song and looked at each other in amazement as the Navajos repeated the familiar verse in unfamiliar words.

"Nin hokeh bi-kheh a-na-ih-la
Ta-al-tso-oo na-he-seel-kai
Nih-bi-kah-gi do tah kah-gi
Ta-al-tso-go en-da-de-pah
Tsi-di-da-an-ne ne-tay-yah
Ay be nihe hozeen
Washingdon be Akalh Bi-kosi-la
Ji-lengo ba-hozhon."

The words faded into silence, and the stunned Anglo marines didn't utter a sound. Grinning, Redhawk began singing the same verse in English.

"We have conquered our enemies
All over the world.
On land and on sea,
Everywhere we fight.
True and loyal to our duty.
We are known by that.
United States Marines,
To be one is a great thing."

Several of the marines began to laugh, and as the verse ended, one of them said, "I knew it sounded familiar, Chief! But it sure does sound different in Indian than it does in English."

"We could say the same thing to you," Little Wolf Smith said.

A wiry marine stepped forward to say, in a slow, belligerent drawl, "Well, I'm from Texas, and I say the only good Injun is a dead Injun!"

"Knock it off, Simms!" one man exclaimed, but the Texan shook him off.

It grew quiet again, and Redhawk's black eyes

narrowed as he faced the Texan. Simms was taller, and there was an ugly expression on his face. His manner was challenging, his pale eyes hostile. Shaking off Johns's hand on his arm, Redhawk said, "Some white men are quick to speak and slow to think. Perhaps you are one of those."

"And maybe you'd like to join your dead ancestors!" the Texan shot back. His fist slammed into Redhawk's jaw, knocking him back against the bunk, which was still up in its chains against the bulkhead.

Redhawk bounced back, lashing out with quick punches that sent Simms slamming into the bulkhead. Ignoring the shouts of encouragement as well as the ones from those who wanted to stop him, he followed the sagging Texan with three more quick blows, feeling a grim satisfaction as his fists thwacked into bone and muscle.

"Company coming! Secure the butts!" someone shouted and there was a flurry of movement and rattle of bunks being dropped into position. Redhawk allowed Willie Johns to pull him away from the bleeding Texan, and slowly the mist of fury began to subside.

Thrusting his clothes at him, Johns scrambled to put on his own, snapping at his cousin in their native tongue, "Are you crazy? Fighting a white man like that?"

Redhawk wiped a hand across his face, smearing streaks of shoe polish over his palm. He didn't offer a defense. It had always been he who had said one must never fight the white man on his own terms, and now he had. There were other paths of resistance that worked much better, but he had allowed Simms to provoke him.

By the time an officer appeared in their quarters, the lights were out and all the men were in their bunks, fully clothed and apparently sleeping. Not many of them slept that night, however.

It was still dark when marines laden with packs and rifles lined the starboard rails. A gigantic black land mass thrust sharply ahead, jagged peaks gnawing at the sky and just dark enough to contrast with the lighter horizon. There was no enemy fire yet, no jovial banter among the marines, only the slap of water against the ship's sides and the quiet rustle of men shifting position. They were all silent, waiting and watching.

The wind flattened the legs of their uniforms against them and tugged briskly at their heavy packs. Redhawk looked forward, straining his eyes, and finally saw a dark blur on the horizon. They rounded the hump of Cape Esperance and cruised into Sealark Channel, the stretch of water separating Guadalcanal from Tulagi.

Redhawk stood at the rail beside Johns, leaning on the metal and looking down at the brownish froth boiling up as the ship sliced through the Sealark Channel. He'd never been this high up before, this far above land or water.

Except for the peyote dream, when the eagle flew so high and far above everything . . .

No light silvered the waters or revealed the presence of the fleet to the enemy. Hunching his shoulders against the blast of wind and spit of spray, Redhawk turned to Johns. "They say we'll land in an hour."

Johns nodded, lifting his voice to be heard over the roar of wind and mighty ship engines. "Yes. I heard that, too."

The U.S. fleet had been split just before reaching Savo, with ships heading northerly toward Tulagi and ships steaming down toward Guadalcanal. The ship drew closer, and he could barely make out the paler gray stretch of sand and clumps of green trees dissected by a river. Behind rose a steadily climbing knoll. Redhawk remained silent, watching the coastline become clearer in the growing light of dawn.

General Quarters sounded over the squawk box, drowning out the sound of wind and sea, and Redhawk flashed Johns a quick glance. Not an enemy shot had been fired yet. And now it was time.

Redhawk peered over the rail toward the island that lay like a sleeping dragon. Then an explosion assaulted his ears and sent him reeling.

The huge guns aboard the ship boomed, rocking the craft in the sea, and Redhawk grabbed at something to hold on. It seemed as if all the gun turrets had opened fire at once. Salvos of eight-inch shells arced through the air toward the island. Black, acrid clouds of smoke mushroomed in the air, drifting on the wind, seeping above and below decks to fill lungs and noses. It wasn't thick, just strong enough to make the world reek of sulphur.

Time exploded into activity as a blinding burst of yellow-green light erupted from a cruiser on the starboard bow. Slender crimson lines of shells arced gracefully through the smoldering sky, plummeting to earth on the island shore in a strangely beautiful explosion. That was immediately followed by a rhythmic cannonading punctuating the lightening sky.

"Shit!" a marine said in an awed voice, and Redhawk silently echoed his sentiment. Shit, indeed.

Two more cruisers began firing as salvos sped toward their destination on Guadalcanal, an overpowering rumble of chained explosions that rocked the ship and assaulted the ears. As tracer bullets stitched the shoreline, the sound of airplane motors could be heard above the din. The U.S. planes were strafing.

Several minutes later, still leaning on the starboard rail and watching the spectacular light show, Redhawk heard someone say, "Fuckin' A! We hit a Jap ship!"

A gigantic sheet of orange and yellow flame lit up the surface of the water ahead of them, slowly inching out into a long, thin line, growing steadily into a triangular inferno. The U.S. naval guns increased tempo, slamming out salvos in a steady rhythm, the wind whipped up by the shells swooping back across the decks of the ships. Dive-bombers flew gracefully low over the island, and in the growing light of dawn, Redhawk could see a variety of colors as the bombs landed. Crazily, he was reminded of the song the nuns at his school had them sing every morning after the pledge of allegiance to the flag, one particular line standing out in his memory. ". . . the bombs bursting in air . . ." He had never been able to visualize it until now.

The incandescent lines of the tracers from the planes chewed into the ground, then bounced back, forming a thin, shallow V, adding to the thick, black clouds of oily smoke billowing up from the Japanese ship burning in the bay.

"Prepare to move out!" came the shouted order, and Redhawk and Johns exchanged glances. This was it.

They had been drilled so many times their movements were automatic. Flak jackets, helmets, life preservers, and man positions. As radio men, Redhawk and Johns were not given key battle positions, but were assigned to the communications area. The radio room was frenetic with activity and the buzzing crackle of radios as they wedged their way into the small area. They found themselves beside an Australian officer.

His leathered face was creased in a frown as the report crackled over the radio, ". . . scouting plane shot down by our cruiser . . . no other enemy activity reported . . ."

"Is that one of the Ferdinands on the radio, sir?" a man asked the Australian wing commander, and his granite expression eased slightly.

"Aye."

Nervously dancing from one foot to another, Willie Johns eyed the Australian for a long moment. "Ferdinand?" he asked. "What company is that?"

The Australian turned to eye the short, stocky Navajo. He must have decided to be affable. "It's a nickname, laddie. He's an Aussie, like me, but one of our coastwatchers. Surely you've heard of the Australian coastwatchers?" When Johns shook his head, the officer gave a sighing shrug. "That's th' trouble with fame. It's all too fleeting at times."

"They're already stationed in the Solomons?"

"Aye, laddie, since 1919 they've been stationed there! The Royal Australian Navy put them there back then, and along the coasts of Australia as well. There are a great many islands in the Solomons, and our brave volunteers have been reporting planes, ships, and any unusual activity for a long time. Even the coconut farmers and the missionaries have been taught to use a special code and transmit it on a monitored radio. If it's of value for security reasons, they report it. Our Ferdinands have been seeing Japanese activity since 1939."

"Why the name Ferdinand?" one of the radio men asked curiously.

The Aussie officer grinned. " 'Cause like that daft bull in the old story, our coastwatchers are ordered to prefer smelling the flowers to fighting."

The radio man grinned back. "And you, sir? Do you prefer flowers to fighting?"

"Ah, give me a weapon over a radio, laddie, and I'll die a happy man!"

"Shit, ain't it kinda embarrassing to be a Ferdinand?" the radio man asked, and the Aussie shook his big head.

"Not at all, laddie! Not at all! If it wasn't for our Ferdinands, word would not have come as quickly about the Japs taking Tulagi back in May. The Brits lost their administrative capital in the Solomons as well as one of the best ship anchorages in the entire chain of islands. And it was a Ferdinand who reported in June that the Japs had a work party that crossed from Tulagi to Guadacanal to build an airfield on Lunga Point." He grinned. "That's why we get to join the party now!"

It was frighteningly clear that the Japanese intended to use the base on Lunga Point in the middle of the island's north point as a pivotal air base to launch strikes against other islands in the Allied hands—the New Hebrides, New Caledonia, the Fijis, and Samoa. If those fell, Japanese bombers and battleships launching from Tulagi would be in an excellent position to hit at the main shipping routes from the United States to Australia. It was vital that Guadalcanal and Tulagi be retaken as quickly as possible—before the Japanese could complete the building of their airfield.

No transmission from shore reached the ship rocking on white-capped waves, and the order was finally given to go ashore just east of the Tenaru River and the airstrip the Japanese were building.

"Land the landing force!" came the order, and Redhawk and Willie Johns found themselves swept along in the tide of confusion and gathering momentum as the marines prepared to disembark. Men flung open hatches and threw out heavy booms to lower cargoes of equipment and supplies. Higgins boats were swung aloft from davits, and nets were slung over the ship's sides for the marines to scramble down with swift, crablike motions. Landing was more painful than they had considered it might be. As the marines lowered themselves over the gunwales, they stepped on the fingers of the men below them in the nets and had their fingers stepped on by those above. Rifle barrels clattered loudly against metal helmets, and the unfortunate men laden with heavy machine guns or mortar parts groaned beneath the pain of carrying them. Redhawk panted slightly as the weight of his radio equipment dug into his back, and he could see from Willie Johns's expression that his cousin was feeling the same burden. The small boats bobbing on the swells below them seemed to defy their efforts to board, and they had to jump three or four feet to land in the erratically moving craft. Deep-laden boats chugged to the assembly areas, forming circles before finally spreading out in a wide line and speeding toward shore with hulls down.

Redhawk felt the sea-spray hit his face, and he felt the churning of his blood. Adrenaline pumped high excitement through his veins, and his throat was tight as he waited for return fire from shore. None came. There was no opposition from the enemy as the first wave of marines stormed ashore, feeling relieved and faintly ridiculous at the same time when no one opposed their landing. When his boat bumped into the shallows, Redhawk sludged through the water with the rest, feeling his feet sink deep into the muddy sand on the ocean floor. It was hard moving through the water, and he was glad when they finally stumbled onto the sandy beach that stretched in a smoky curve. Fires still burned here and there from the ship's salvos, and he could feel the hot wind carry a dusting of black ashes.

"Move it Move it! Mo—o—ve it!" came the order, and they jogged faster across the wet sand.

"Ever feel like you've gone to a party and there ain't nobody else there yet?" a marine asked no one in particular as they ran in a heavy rattle of equipment and rasping breath.

Redhawk grinned. "Disappointed?"

The marine grinned back. "Like hell! I was hopin' for a whole buncha Nips!"

"Be careful what you wish for, doggie," another voice cut in. "You may get it."

Ninety miles long and thirty-five wide, Guadalcanal seemed large enough to hide the enemy for a while. The only mobile targets the marines found ashore were wild pigs that squealed through the thick underbrush where orchids grew wild. Coconuts dotted the ground at intervals, and several marines stopped to hack them open with their machetes. Guard posts were established and the supplies aboard ship began being unloaded.

Redhawk found himself assigned to a group unloading the stacks of boxes and steel drums. His radio equipment lay to one side as he worked in the sand and sun, and he actually began to feel good. His tension had eased, and he could listen to the marines' banter with a smile, though some of it seemed obscure.

"They're callin' this *Operation Shoestring* instead of *Watchtower,* I hear," a tall, lanky marine said around the cigarette that dangled from one corner of his mouth. "And we ain't fightin' for MacArthur no more, but Nimitz."

"I thought we were fighting for America," Redhawk said as he heaved a heavy cardboard box, which was still damp from rain, atop a growing stock. "Does it matter if we fight for one man or the other?"

"To some of us, it does." The tall, red-haired marine paused to eye the shorter man warily. "You look more like a Jap than an American. What's your lash-up?"

"We're waiting to be assigned to a division and regiment, as needed."

A suspicious stare, then, "Where are you from?"

"Arizona."

"Sure you don't mean Tokyo?"

Shrugging, Redhawk let the remark pass. He was used to it by now. Several had made the comment that the Navajos resembled the enemy more than they did the Allies, but it still rankled. Another man stepped quickly into the breach.

"They put Nimitz in charge of Guadalcanal because he wanted to attack Rabaul with the First Marine Division and two of Nimitz's carriers, the way I heard it. The old man didn't like the idea of MacArthur getting hold of his precious carriers on a risky maneuver. So, the Joint Chiefs of Staff just moved the line of demarcation between MacArthur's and Nimitz's commands, that's all."

"Still sounds like a bad deal to me," the first marine grumbled, but his attention had passed from Redhawk to the peculiarities of the Joint Chiefs of Staff in Washington.

Redhawk offered no more comments as the marines tossed scuttlebutt back and forth. He felt left out and didn't know if he was grateful for the second man's intervention. Why should he be? He had a right to his opinion, just like any other American. Did the white man think only he could have the right views?

Catching Willie Johns's glance at him, Redhawk allowed his anger to ease. Anger was a useless emotion when it came to the prejudicial remarks he encountered, and he should remember that. He would also remember the red-haired marine who disputed his right to have an opinion.

The first wave of marines had been on the beach for only two hours when the emergency "Bells" radio frequency sounded. Monitored by every combat ship in the fleet, the coded message *FROM STO: 24 TORPEDO BOMBERS HEADED YOURS* alerted the Americans.

One of the coastwatchers on the Japanese-held island of Bougainville, three hundred fifty miles away on the air route between Guadalcanal and Rabaul, had sighted the enemy planes. He was only slightly in error: There were twenty-seven Japanese planes burning the air toward newly occupied Guadalcanal. It gave the marines one hour to get ready.

The unloading operations ceased immediately. Ships rocking in the sound raised anchor and got under way: the antiaircraft gunners slapped on their helmets and scanned the skies. Two carriers, the *Enterprise* and the *Saratoga,* that were cruising with the carrier *Wasp* just south of Guadalcanal, sent aloft entire squadrons of the squat Grumman Wildcat fighters. They clawed through the air in metallic streaks, rising to take positions over the fleet.

Two-engine Mitsubishi "Bettys" hummed toward the island to drive back the American invasion forces. Fortunately for the Americans, the planes had been originally sent out on a bombing raid at Milne Bay on New Guinea's southeast coast. After receiving urgent orders to head for Guadalcanal, they had not stopped to exchange their load of bombs for the more effective torpedoes that would have inflicted heavy damage on the American ships. High-level bombing would not do much damage to sleek vessels that were ready and maneuvering at high speed.

On Guadalcanal, the men heard the orders to cease the unloading of supplies with dismay. Already cut in half by a torrential winter rain in New Zealand, the supplies left had been cut from a ninety-day ration to sixty. Thirty days of ammunition, food, and fuel was still in the bellies of the transports as they steamed away from Guadalcanal. What was already unloaded was only enough for thirty days. Less than half of the ammunition had been unloaded, and only eighteen spools of barbed wire were stacked on the beach. Thousands of sandbags necessary to build bunkers were still aboard the ships, as well as essential tools. Shovels, axes, saws, radar sets, 155mm howitzers, and coastal defense guns were snug and secure at sea instead of at Guadalcanal. All of the heavy equipment vital to the completion of the unfinished airstrip was still in the holds, except for one lone bulldozer.

"We go on short ration, men," the marines were told, and short ration it was. . . .

It was hours before Redhawk attempted to give his orders to a commanding officer, but none seemed to know anything about the men sent to relay messages in code.

"Go find the general," he was told by a beleaguered colonel.

"Where is he?"

"Behind the lines somewhere. . . ."

Redhawk led his squad of eight Navajos from post to post, until they found the general.

"Sir, here are our orders." He gave the general seated behind a table the pages of orders, but the officer didn't bother to glance at them.

"What the hell are you talking about, Marine?"

"We were sent to assist operations by code talking," he replied, but the general just gazed at him blankly, as if wondering why he was wasting his time with nonsense.

"I've got more on my mind than codes right now! Hell, we're sitting here like ripe pigeons, and you want to talk to me about *codes?* Dismissed!"

Redhawk backed away, snapping a salute before he pivoted on his heel and stalked out of the tent.

"Well?" Johns asked, and Redhawk shrugged.

"Let's go back to the colonel on the beach. Maybe he can tell us where to go."

As chief of staff, the colonel listened to the orders again, shaking his head and grumbling about passing the buck. "Okay . . . lissen up. You two men"—he pointed to two of them—"go to the Third. You two go to the Second, and you two men"—he pointed to Redhawk and Johns—"report to the Fifth Division."

"Permission to transmit code, sir?" Redhawk asked, but the colonel gave an irritated shake of his head.

"No time to fool with that crap now! Just go to your regiments and follow orders."

"Maybe we're not so special after all," Johns observed as they trudged toward the Fifth Division, and Redhawk nodded.

"I think you're right. Learning all that code seems to have been a waste of time as far as Colonel Crawford is concerned. He obviously doesn't have the same tolerance as the Colonel Crawford at boot camp, in spite of the same name." He lapsed into silence for a moment, then said, "We'll have to prove it works."

"Since when did you get so gung ho, Marine?"

Redhawk grinned and gave his cousin a nudge. "You're beginning to sound like the rest of the dogfaces!"

Both Navajos laughed softly at the subtle jest.

The Fifth Division, Second Regiment was assigned to search out the coconut plantations to the west. Laden with radio equipment as well as weapons, Redhawk and Johns marched with their regiment through thick underbrush and coconut groves. In case of enemy attack, they were to keep in communication with the base. But the first skirmish happened so quickly there was little chance to radio before it was over.

After several hours of marching through sand and fording shallow creeks, the men arrived at the perimeter of the uncompleted airfield. A burst of fire greeted them from the trees overhead. Dropping to one knee, the point men fired back, and three Japanese soldiers fell to the ground like ripe fruit.

Redhawk's throat was tight, and the hand gripping his rifle was damp with sweat. No other shots rang out, and in a moment the sergeant in charge signaled for them to move forward. As they moved cautiously through the trees, a few more Japanese were sighted in full retreat. Marine fire gave them added speed in their flight, but they escaped without harm.

"Dammit," Sergeant Jones said, but didn't seem particularly bothered. "There's probably a lot more where those came from." He turned to Redhawk. "Okay, Chief. Show us your stuff. Radio base and tell them we have achieved our objective."

Dropping to their knees, Redhawk and Johns tried to set up the heavy TBS unit and found it almost impossible. In the end, they were forced to hook the bulky generator to the sturdy security of a coconut tree instead of the shifting sand that would not support it properly. Johns straddled it, steadily churning the crank to provide juice while Redhawk transmitted the message.

While the Navajos radioed position, the rest of the company moved forward to secure the airfield and installations that the Japanese had been constructing. A twenty-six-hundred-foot airstrip was nearly completed, and Jones broke into a satisfied grin. "Chief! Add the intelligence that we have also captured over a hundred Nip trucks and nine road rollers to finish this lovely little runway!"

Redhawk relayed the information to base, then pitched in to help inventory the captured prizes. Revetments, repair sheds, and blast pens were already finished, making it obvious that the Japanese would have brought in their first planes in only a few days. Wharves and machine shops had been slightly damaged by the American bombardment but could be quickly used. In their retreat, the Japanese had abandoned huge quantites of gas, oil, kerosene, cement, and a variety of machinery, even surgical tools. And to the marines beleaguered with *Operation Shoestring,* the finding of hundreds of cases of canned meat, fish, and fruit was a welcome surprise. There were tons of rice as well, and a loud cheer greeted the discovery of a machine for making ice. In the humid climate of Guadalcanal, it would be greatly appreciated.

One quick-witted marine painted a sign on the shed housing the ice machine, and Redhawk grinned in appreciation of the white man's humor.

"TOJO ICE FACTORY," it read, and in smaller letters beneath, "Under New Management."

"Not bad for a day's work," Colonel Crawford greeted his men that evening. "Now, if we can just hold on to it."

Those words were more prophetic than he thought.

It was after four in the afternoon before the Navajos were given the opportunity to prove themselves. Frankly skeptical, the colonel finally yielded to repeated pressure from Redhawk.

"All right, dammit, show me what you can do! But make it quick. It's been a long day, and I'd like to catch a little shut-eye before I have to start this shit all over again tomorrow."

Not allowing himself to feel any resentment at the colonel's attitude, Redhawk set up his equipment. He called the Second on his radio and gave them a message, then sat back to wait. Response was immediate and surprising.

As the wires crackled with code, alarmed personnel sent runners to report to the colonel that the Japanese had taken over the radio waves.

"Sir, Captain Morton sent me to tell you that the

enemy is on our frequency, and nobody can tell what in the devil they're saying!" a breathless runner reported.

Colonel Crawford rocked back on his heels, staring at the man with annoyance. "Tell Captain Morton that it's our men on the radio! Do you understand? . . . *Our* men are talking on the radio!"

The runner hesitated. "But, sir, I heard them, and it sure don't sound like none of our men, even in code."

Exasperated, Colonel Crawford raked a hand through his sparse hair so that it stood on end, then bellowed, "Well, tell Morton that it *is* our men!"

As the runner backtracked and Redhawk and Johns exchanged wary glances, the colonel wheeled to glare at them. "What was that gibberish you were talking?"

"Code, sir."

"It doesn't sound like any code I've ever heard before!"

"That's the general idea, I believe, sir," was Redhawk's dry response.

That seemed to halt the colonel, and he muttered after a moment, "You guys are going to be causing trouble, I have a feeling." He paused, then added, "This is liable to cause a stir, you know, if they think the Japs have gotten on our frequency."

"Yessir."

Another pause, then, reluctantly, "Tell you what. . . . I'll keep you guys if you do one thing: You beat my code and you can stay."

"Sounds fair to me," Redhawk shot back.

The colonel gave a doubtful grunt. "Go to it."

A man was summoned to send a code the usual way, with a white cylinder that clicked out a message. The same message was sent out to several units, and the answer was clicked back on the white man's cylinder, as well as returned by Navajo voice. The colonel paced behind, then leaned forward to ask Redhawk, "How long will it take you to decode, Marine?"

Redhawk looked up at him with a carefully blank face. "I have already decoded one message, sir, and as soon as I have received, I will have decoded the others."

The colonel's eyes narrowed, and he asked the other man abruptly, "How long to decode, Marine?"

Startled, the man replied, "Sir, it will take me an hour or two to figure out the message. . . ."

Colonel Crawford swung his head back to stare at the silent Navajos. Redhawk held out a paper with his decoded messages printed neatly. Crawford snatched it up and scanned the paper, then broke into a reluctant smile.

"Well, I'll be damned!"

Leaning back in his chair, Redhawk allowed himself a surge of triumph. "Ready to give up your cylinder and give us a chance to transmit code, Colonel?"

Shaking his head, Crawford muttered, "Hell, you guys are a *walking* code!" He was still shaking his head when he walked away, and Redhawk and Johns slapped one another on the back with congratulatory grins.

"How did you guys do that?" the other radioman asked. "It sure beats the hell out of this way!"

Grinning, Redhawk said, "We learned it as babies!"

Baffled, the radioman shook his head. "Well, I have to admit that it works."

"We intended for it to work," Redhawk replied. "That is why we were trained."

The feeling of triumph lasted for hours, and Johns and Redhawk began to feel vindicated.

"I was beginning to think we would have to go back in disgrace," Johns said as they pitched their blankets on the sand for the night. "Johnston would have been very sad to see us return."

"No sadder than I would have been."

Johns unhooked his equipment belt and slung it to the ground, then gave his cousin a curious look. "Have you changed your mind about the 'white man's war,' then?"

"Maybe."

It was as close as he would come to admitting aloud that he felt very involved now, much more so than when he had first been forced into joining the Marines. Perhaps the Old One had somehow known he would feel that way. Or perhaps he had just hoped he would. Johns did not pursue the subject.

Chapter Nine
"Tojo Time"

That first night, huddled in thin blankets on the sand, Redhawk listened to unfamiliar night noises. Johns was lying beside him, rolled in his blanket and sleeping as soundly as if they were on the Arizona desert. Redhawk gave him an irritated nudge.

"Wake up."

"Wha–?"

"Did you hear that?"

Johns rolled over, peering into the thick darkness that smelled of fetid jungle. Shrill screeches pierced the air.

"The birds?"

"No. It sounds as if someone is chewing rocks."

Johns listened carefully, then heard a rasping, crunching sound. The noise was interrupted by a burst of fire from nearby, and he grinned. "Maybe they will stop now."

Another burst of rifle fire sounded in the dark, and they could see the quick stab of orange flame. Someone in the distance shouted, "Knock it off! It's just land crabs digging in the sand!"

"They must be pretty big crabs," Redhawk muttered, but felt better. He was as edgy as the others, who started at every unfamiliar sound. Rifle fire had punctuated the night since the sun had set, and nervous marines reacted to every noise.

"It must be the 'know-your-enemy' lectures they gave us in class that has everyone on edge," Johns whispered. "Do you remember? The Japanese always attack at night."

"Just like the Indians," Redhawk shot back, and Johns laughed softly.

"*Aiee,* just like the Indians."

The night dragged on in a cacophony of tropical noises and marine fire. Boys unaccustomed to the rigors of war made nervous enemies of even their allies.

Before midnight it began to rain, a little at first, just enough to sink quickly into the sand, then it began to pour. Torrents of rain washed over the men lying on ponchos and blankets, making them thoroughly miserable. Redhawk just pulled his blanket up over his head, detaching himself from the misery of the night. Jagged flashes of lightning lit up the night sky, providing a spectacular light show for those too miserable to sleep. Heavy rumbles of thunder formed a continuous chain that sounded almost like the booming of ships' guns.

Redhawk did his best to ignore it, curling into a ball and catching moments of sleep. Two hours passed, and a deep, rattling thunder jerked him awake. It wasn't thunder; the rain had stopped. Sitting up, fully awake now, he saw bright flares spurt into the air, then drift seaward. Huge, booming explosions rent the night, and blinding flashes arced in the direction of Savo Island. Instinctively, he grabbed his rifle, and saw that others had done the same. The marines watched with a sense of helplessness and fear as a naval battle was waged.

"It looks like the whole fuckin' Japanese and American navies are out there!" someone muttered, and no one argued with him.

It continued for an hour, occasionally puncuated by massive explosions and billowing clouds of orange smoke and flames. Then it seemed to move away, and some of their tension eased slightly. Flares lit the night and the D-2's phone continuously rang, announcing alarms throughout the fight. A flare plummeted landward off Tulagi, and another one soared down over Beach Red. One hit closer over Lunga Point, and in the midst of it all, a plane droned overhead. Redhawk and Johns hit the communications shack, waiting for an opportunity to help, but they were largely ignored.

"Not now!" a sergeant snapped when Redhawk offered his services. "This is no time to be experimenting with new codes!"

Redhawk and Johns shrugged. "It will take time," Johns observed, and Redhawk knew what he meant. It would take a while for the marines to learn how useful the Navajos could be in tense situations, but he intended to prove it to them.

A sergeant from the Eleventh Marines called in to report that Japs had landed on Beach Red, and Colonel del Valle quickly dispatched a patrol to investigate.

"Do you want us to go along to relay messages in code?" Johns asked, and the colonel shot him an irritated scowl.

"No time for that! Just get back to your outfit!"

Another shrug lifted their shoulders, and the two Navajos went back to their rain-soaked gear still stretched on the beach.

"We tried," Johns said by way of comfort, and Redhawk nodded.

"You men!" Jones said before they could lie down again. "Go with this patrol to the beach. Japs are reported to have landed on the beach north of here. Hold a line at the CP."

Redhawk and Johns found themselves in a patrol

marching under the coconut palms, their feet sinking into the wet sand as they headed for the beach. In the water just off the beach, the patrol could make out the slinky movements of small craft in the water and they opened fire. A rattle of return fire made them all hit the ground.

Spitting sand from his mouth, Redhawk squinted down the barrel of his rifle and fired again and again, not even taking the time to fully aim. At this distance, it would be pure luck to hit anything anyway, he figured. He could hear the chaos in the water and suddenly realized that he was listening to American voices throwing curses with their bullets.

"Lieutenant!" he shouted, "I think it's our own men!"

A cease-fire was called, and the lieutenant, sprawled in the wet sand a few feet away, heard the familiar marine curses curling the air. He turned to Redhawk and grinned.

"I think you're right, Private. That ought to teach 'em to identify themselves before they sail up the beach in the middle of a full-scale naval battle!"

"What in the hell were you doing?" a red-faced marine bellowed as he sloshed from the Higgins boat ashore. The veins on his neck were corded, and his face was mottled with rage. "You could have killed us!"

"What in the hell were you doing out on a pleasure jaunt in the middle of a battle?" the lieutenant countered.

"Pleasure jaunt, hell! We were moving supplies up the beach to Kukum!"

"Bad timing, Sergeant," the lieutenant returned coolly. "Now, if you boys are through playing around, we're going back to our cozy little beds."

Leaving the infuriated sergeant standing in the shallow water and cursing, the patrol went back to the command post and reported that no enemy had been encountered, then returned to their soggy blankets.

It was to be a night of mistakes for the Americans.

The next morning, the story made the rounds of how the night before a jeep without its lights on had approached a marine position on the beach. Most of the passwords being used by the marines had been chosen because of the common knowledge that the Japanese had difficulty pronouncing the letter *L,* and would not be able to say words such as *lollipop* or *lollygag.* As the jeep rumbled down the beach, the sentry challenged it.

"Halt!" the sentry shouted, but there was no reply. Now alarmed as the jeep continued rolling, the sentry shouted again, "Halt, damn you, and give the password!" No reply, and the jeep kept coming. The sentry fired, and when the bullet smacked off the vehicle's side, the jeep immediately braked and a voice cried out in a fervent Tennessee drawl, "Hallelujah, brother, hallelujah!"

Even the Navajos could understand the white man's humor in that situation and they laughed with the others.

It was several days before the marines would find out just what had happened the night of the eighth.

Shortly before eleven that night, General Vandegrift, the commander of the marines on Guadalcanal, had left the island and gone by small craft to the flagship *McCawley* still in the sound. After conferring with Rear Admiral Richmond Kelly Turner, commander of the amphibious force, and Rear Admiral Victor A.C. Crutchley, the Englishman in charge of the escort force of American and Australian destroyers and cruisers who were to protect the invasion armada from enemy attack by sea, he took back disturbing news: Turner reported that a Japanese naval force had been sighted en route from Rabaul. To make matters even more grim, Vice Admiral Frank Jack Fletcher, commander of Task Force 61, intended to remove his three carriers from the area. That precipitated Turner's removal of transports he then felt would be vulnerable because of the air cover the carriers would no longer provide. Fourteen hundred marines were still aboard those transports, and more than half of General Vandegrift's needed supplies still lay in the ships' holds.

Vandegrift had returned to shore within an hour, determined to keep his troops unloading throughout the night. Maybe the marines on Guadalcanal could make it on limited supplies in the few days it would take for the carriers to refuel and return. Higgins boats were dispatched to haul supplies up and down the beach.

Unfortunately, bad news came in on the radio in the early hours of the morning. Johns took the message, his pencil scratching furiously as the coded words took shape. His face was grayish as he hurried the report to Crawford.

"Dammit to hell!" the colonel swore when he received the message. He crumpled the paper in one hand and smacked his fist into his palm. "Expect some losses? What in the hell is going on out there?"

The truth was not told for several days.

Crutchley had six cruisers and six destroyers patrolling off Savo Island, the tiny dot of land that lay at the western entrance of the sound. Crutchley's flagship, the cruiser *Australia,* was twenty-five miles away at the conference with Vandegrift and Turner when small floatplanes buzzed overhead at the exact time the American conference began. It was eleven at night, and the ship's officers aboard Crutchley's cruisers mistakenly thought the planes friendly because their running lights were on and no communication had advised them of an alert. The consequences were disastrous.

This was the Japanese naval force Turner had mentioned. It was much larger than he'd been informed—and much closer. Seven cruisers and a destroyer steamed into the channel between Savo and Guadalcanal. No American ship gave the alarm until the *Patterson,* an American destroyer within two miles of the southern section of Crutchley's force, spotted the enemy. By then it was too late.

Torpedoes from the Japanese cruiser zipped through the ocean waters to slam into American ships. Within seconds, the brilliant light from flares dropped by his scout planes lit up the sea, and Japanese guns commenced firing. Some of the American ships were hit while their general alarm was still sounding. It took only forty minutes for the battle of Savo Island to end—with two Allied cruisers sunk and another two so badly damaged they were unsalvageable. A number of American floatplanes were lost as well, and one of the destroyers was heavily damaged.

Japanese Vice Admiral Gunichi Mikawa emerged virtually unscathed, except for the destruction of a chart room aboard the *Chokai,* which had taken a direct hit from the *Quincy.* The Japanese rejoiced over the Americans' faulty communication system. Instead of pressing his advantage over the now unprotected transports, Mikawa made great haste on his voyage home, leaving behind over a thousand dead Australian and American sailors. Burned and exhausted Allied men bobbed in the shark-infested waters, waiting for rescue.

In the predawn hours, so many ships were sunk in the Sealark Channel that it received a new name.

"Hey Geronimo," a weary marine lieutenant said to Redhawk when the grim news was reported, "what's your code name for ship?"

"Battleship, carrier, minesweeper, or destroyer?"

he countered. "There are different names, such as *besh-lo,* or *iron fish* for submarines."

"Iron fish," the lieutenant repeated slowly. "That's pretty appropriate. . . . There are so many ships on the bottom of the channel they should call it Iron-bottom Sound."

Somehow, the name became popular as the days dragged on and the enemy attacks increased. Tulagi was finally secured after a stiff initial resistance by Japanese forces dug into the hills honeycombed with caves. Enemy interest swerved to a fresh object.

And on Guadalcanal, the marines endured. With the carriers that protected them gone, they were left wide open to enemy fire. Japanese planes buzzed in to annoy and bomb the next day at noon, an hour that soon became known as "Tojo Time." To make matters worse, Japanese cruisers or destroyers appeared on the horizon just out of reach of their guns, shelling the hapless marines along the exposed four-mile stretch of Lunga Point.

"Shit," Sergeant Jones grumbled as the endless firing wore on his nerves. "Won't those bastards ever stop?"

Johns huddled in a foxhole, his radio clutched to his chest. The small arms fire didn't bother him, but the constant rattle of the huge guns made his insides quiver with anxiety. He glanced toward Redhawk, who let nothing show on his face.

Only the white knuckles that held his radio equipment gave Redhawk away, that and the fine white lines bracketing his mouth. He stared out from under the metal brim of his helmet, past the white sandy beach and froth of curling waves washing ashore, toward the endless stretch of blue sky and horizon. He tried to detach his mind from reality, from the steady pounding of the guns and the rattle of dirt and metal fragments that showered over them.

Someone behind him muttered a wish for confiscated beer, and Redhawk silently did the same. The marines had discovered a warehouse filled with sake and Japanese beer, and they had quickly emptied it, hiding the booty from the officers. It would certainly have come in handy during the shelling. Anything would have helped.

Nature itself seemed to be on the side of the enemy. Cogon grass higher than a man's head boasted sharp edges capable of slicing through unwary hands. Furry red spiders as large as a man's fist huddled in shadowy spaces, waiting for the chance to bite. Giant lizards, some of them as long as a man's leg, scuttled from beneath rocks, more frightening to encounter than dangerous. Leeches covered tree limbs, falling onto men and latching on tenaciously, sucking blood furiously. White ants swarmed in expansive armies, their bite as painful as fire, and scorpions lurked under almost every rock, waiting to sting, their touch inflaming and festering human flesh. Rats and bats as big as domestic cats thickened the underbrush, and the rivers were riddled with crocodiles. The fetid smell of the jungle pervaded a man's nostrils until he could smell nothing else, and the humidity sank heavily, rotting human flesh and everything else. It was a wet, stinking heat of rain forests and traps designed by the fiendishly clever Japanese.

There were small compensations.

The unfinished airfield had to be completed for Allied use. With only one bulldozer unloaded before the transport ships had pulled out, it would have been almost impossible without the equipment left behind by the Japanese. Using Japanese dynamite, the engineers began to laboriously extend the runway, clearing obstructing trees from the north end. Then, with the aid of three earth tampers operated by Japanese air compressors, they packed new fill that was excavated by marine-powered Japanese picks and shovels. Japanese trucks fueled by Japanese gasoline carried American marines to the site. The marines used latrines built from Japanese lumber and covered with Japanese screens. When the Japanese sirens shrilled the approach of enemy planes, marines took cover in holes dug and roofed by the industrious Japanese. There was certainly a grim satisfaction in knowing that.

For the Navajos, the monotony of the raids was broken by their radio communications.

". . . 1400 hours, chicken hawks dropping eggs on *tah-bahn* . . . 1400 hours."

"The only way I can tell when you guys get finished with a message," Jones said ruefully, "is when you say *nos-bas*. That's the Navajo word for *zero*, isn't it?"

Redhawk allowed himself a smile. "Yes."

"I thought so. Since every transmission begins and ends with the day and time, that's how I can tell!" He ducked quickly as another enemy shell lobbed toward them. When the inevitable shower of fragments had finished, he looked up again. "I figured that out all by myself!"

"Very good, Sergeant," Redhawk said in such an obviously patronizing voice that the officer laughed.

"Why does that tone sound familiar, Chief?" he asked with a grin.

Redhawk froze. Had he made the mistake of "joking the white man" again? But Jones didn't notice his sudden silence, and the moment passed without further comment. For some reason, Redhawk could not get comfortable in his own skin, not around the Anglo marines. He almost envied Willie Johns his freedom of speech and manner, but then recalled his father's frequent admonitions. No, it wouldn't do to grow too close to men so vastly different in culture and thought. Only battle brought them together, anyway, and once the war was over, it would revert to how it had always been. He should know that well enough. There would never be a time when the white man and the Indian could accept one another on equal terms.

Part Two

Chapter Ten
The Blooding

"What'cha think of this guy, Chief?" a grinning marine asked as he gave a shove to the man in front of him.

Redhawk turned to look and saw a short, slender man in torn, bloodied khakis. His features were Asiatic, his eyes slanted and glittering with hatred. Redhawk looked at the marine, a man from the Fourth Battalion named Hanks.

"What am I supposed to think?" he asked carefully.

"Don't'cha think he looks kinda like one of you guys?" Hanks persisted. "I mean, he's short, and except for the eyes, he looks a lot like one of you guys. Don't'cha think so?"

Shrugging, Redhawk glanced at the captured Japanese again. He had to admit that to a white man, there would be a great deal of resemblance between the two races, but he could not see it as well. There were too many differences that he could see: the yellowish cast to the Japanese captive's skin, the dark eyes that slanted downward at the outer corners, and the almost fragile appearance of his body in spite of a layer of fat and muscle. No, to Redhawk there wasn't a great deal of similarity, but he could understand why the Anglo marines would think so.

"I see why some of you think we look alike," he replied when it became apparent that the marine wanted agreement.

Still grinning, Hanks moved past with his prisoner and the comment, "You Indians better wear white so we'll know you in the dark!"

"That may not be a bad idea," Johns said, looking up from his can of C-rations. "In the bush yesterday, one of our guys jumped me from behind, thinking I was the enemy."

"Everyone is jumpy these days, with the daily sniping and raids, and the enemy hammering away at us with barrages of fire every time we move."

"Yes, but I don't think I look *that* much like one of the enemy," Johns said, shaking his head. "I thought he might shoot me, he was so nervous."

"But he didn't."

"No, he just talked at me, asking a dozen questions without waiting for me to answer." Johns grinned slyly. "A barrage of questions must be a new weapon the white man has invented."

Redhawk gave him an oblique glance and said softly, "No, it's still the same old weapon they have always used!"

They laughed together, quietly, so no one would ask what they found amusing. Maybe not all the Anglo marines were effusive conversationalists, but they sure seemed like it compared to the less talkative Navajos. The difference was apparent when there was free time, and the white men would joke and talk without letup, while the Navajos would just sit quietly.

"I think," Redhawk said after a moment, "that the white man uses talk as a means of releasing his tension. I've noticed that they say much without meaning it, like using our names over and over, as if we don't know who we are."

"But they do that to other white men, too," Johns pointed out. "I don't think they mean to single us out."

"Maybe you're right," Redhawk agreed after a moment. "Maybe you're right." He dug into his pack, then came up with the bitter yellow tablets that would hopefully ward off disease. Atabrine, Halzedone, and salt tablets were a staple of the marine diet, and still men came down with dysentery and malaria. Just as many marines were dying of disease as bullets, another form of death inflicted on the invaders.

"Chief!" Sergeant Jones bellowed from a short distance away. "You and your buddy go help the others move the new command post."

Division headquarters was moving to a new command post that was intended to be permanent. A Colonel Thomas and one of his assistants had chosen the site. Situated on a grassy knoll overlooking the airfield from the south, the site was to be in a thicket of scrubby trees on the landward side of a low outcropping of coral.

"Why there, I wonder?" a weary marine asked, and was answered with a waggish, "Because it's got a great view for the new officers club!"

The marines' personal opinions aside, the location provided an excellent command post. On the morning of the tenth, General Vandegrift collected his regimental and battalion commanders on the site and advised them that they must move the mountains of supplies from the beach to more secure dumps within the perimeter, then set up defenses on the beaches west and east of Lunga Point and as far inland as possible. And of course, the runway must be completed to allow American air traffic access as soon as possible.

"Scuttlebutt has it that the Japanese have formidable strength massing near Rabaul," Jones told his men. "If they throw any of it our way, Japs could come across the beaches and retake the airstrip. We can't allow the Nips to do that to us, can we?"

Beach defenses were organized. The Eleventh Marines placed batteries of 75mm and 105mm artillery south of the airstrip so they could be fired on any segment of the line that came under danger. Machine gun nests were placed along the water's edge, backed up by 75mm half-tracks. When the marines ran out of barbed wire, they substituted wire from plantation fences, stringing it across the areas most likely to be approached by the enemy.

There wasn't the manpower to throw up a continuous line of defense across the southern edge of the perimeter, the side where thick jungle grew, providing ample cover for the Japanese. For the time being, specialized units were to bivouac the areas south of the airfield at night, becoming the nighttime defenders.

Defense of the beach was organized from the mouth of the gently winding Tenaru River in the east, along the sluggish outlets of the Lunga River, to a point just west of Kukum, where the marines found a primitive base of operations the Japanese had built for small craft. The marines returned fire on the Japanese riflemen and machine gunners they encountered. Crouching among the pineapple plants and behind coconut trees, they suffered only a few casualties, but it was enough for them to decide to return to Kukum.

The defense line ran close to a mile inland from the Tenaru in the east, up to the first ridge inland from the coastal strip in the west. The long southern edge curved south of the airfield. It encompassed an area of about ten or eleven square miles. Redhawk was in the group sent to secure the airfield. He soon discovered that "securing it" meant cleaning up after the enemy had abandoned it, rather than taking it by force.

"Have you noticed?" Redhawk asked Johns and Smith when they were seated with Sergeant Jones in the shade of a coconut grove during the noon break.

"Noticed what?" Smith swatted at a huge insect buzzing close to his head. "That we've become ditch diggers instead of code talkers?"

Sergeant Jones looked up from his C-rations. "Hey, you guys know our radio equipment is still sitting on the supply ships—except for the equipment we've been using, that is, and it won't reach much farther than the perimeters we've established here."

Redhawk looked at him in surprise. "No, no one told us. Is that the reason we've not been used as code talkers?"

"That's it, Chief!" Jones turned his attention back to his skimpy meal. "Is that what you were noticing?" he asked around a mouthful of food.

"No, but that is worth noticing. What I have noticed is that there are only a few men manning the outposts, with long, empty stretches between. The line runs about five miles along the beach."

"What's your point?" Sergeant Jones asked around the last mouthful of pressed ham he had dug from his tin can. He looked at Redhawk with curiosity. Something about the young Navajo interested him; perhaps it was his innate stoicism, or the way he did whatever he was told to do without offering the usual complaints. Most of the white marines did what they were told but kept up a stream of constant abuse, directed toward the higher-ups and whatever fates had led them to Guadalcanal. The Navajos were equally efficient but much more accepting of whatever orders they were given. Redhawk and Johns were almost unfailingly polite, and given their appearance—the slightly dangerous glitter in their dark eyes at times and the confident way they carried themselves—he deemed it courteous to listen to whatever comments they might make.

"My point," Redhawk said, "is that we are very vulnerable in a lot of areas."

"Nothing we can do about that, Chief," Jones said with a shrug. "Comes with the territory."

After a moment of silence, broken only by the sound of the earth movers cleaning up the airstrip, Redhawk said, "I saw a Japanese today. He is the first I have seen."

"The prisoner Hanks brought in? He's been a fountain of information," Jones told them. "Seems like there's lots of Japs like him hiding out in the woods. According to this one, they want to give themselves up. They're starving, and all they want is a good meal, if we're dumb enough to believe him." Jones frowned. "Thomas is organizing a patrol to bring them in."

Redhawk stared at the sergeant. "I thought the Japanese did not ever surrender."

"Normally, they don't. This guy claims he was forced to work for the Japanese, that he's a civilian." Jones emptied his C-rations and tossed the tin can to a pile of rubbish. He looked at Redhawk and Johns and shook his head. "Thomas needs men for this patrol, and he's pulling some out of a few outfits. Mine is one of them. I volunteered you two for the mission. You're more likely to come back than any of the others I've got."

Redhawk said nothing, just stared at the sergeant. He could feel Johns tense with excitement, but he wasn't sure he cared much for the idea.

"I heard scuttlebutt about the patrol," Redhawk said after a moment. "It's headed by a man with no experience in leading a patrol. The mission is ill-defined, and there's probably a hot-box of enemy sitting there and waiting. Is this right?"

Jones shrugged. His voice was irritated. "You heard right, Chief. If you don't want to go, tell me."

"No. I want to go. I just wanted to know the situation first."

Shaking his head, Jones stood up. "I don't always agree with the higher-ups, and this is one of those times. You're a good man, Private."

A smile briefly flashed. "I need a good fight."

Jones snorted rudely. "What you need is a good blooding to get it out of your system. Suit yourself, Chief. But it ain't gonna be no picnic, I can tell you that. Even if those Nips are sitting out there begging us to bring them in, I wouldn't want to be on that patrol."

"What do you mean 'good blooding'?" Redhawk asked.

"First kill, like when you're a boy deer hunting and someone smears the blood of the deer or elk or whatever you're hunting on you to give you a taste of what it means to kill."

Redhawk lifted an eyebrow. "And the white man says the Navajo is barbaric?"

This won a reluctant smile from Jones. He shrugged again. "Point taken! Get your gear. You and Johns move out at 1400 hours."

Willie Johns didn't hesitate. He was getting to his feet even as Redhawk glanced at him, and he was grinning with excitement.

"It will be like the old days, when we rode into the canyons hunting bear," Johns said. "Do you still feel like hunting the bear?"

A slight smile flashed as Redhawk looked at his cousin and mimicked a New Jersey twang, "Fuckin' A right!"

Sergeant Jones gave a loud burst of startled laughter, slapping his thigh and saying, "Attaboy,

Chief! You're getting the hang of it, all right. *Fuckin' a doodle de do!"*

When his initial surprise wore off, Willie Johns shook his head and grinned. "Looks like the marines have taught you more than they meant to."

Thirty-eight men went on the patrol led by a lieutenant colonel named Gerard. Gerard had the prisoner in tow, as well as a corpsman. They were to take the Higgins boats and travel the coastline to the mouth of the Matanikau River west of the Lunga. Marine patrols had reported seeing a white flag flapping near a village called Matanikau, just beyond the river mouth.

Redhawk and Johns were among the first to show up at the jetty at Kukum. The patrol was largely drawn from the division D-2 section and Fifth Marines. They waited in the hot broiling sun for the Higgins boats to return from a patrol. Unaffected by the heat, Redhawk and Johns squatted in the sand and talked quietly in Navajo, while their Anglo counterparts sweated and swore. Finally, one of them walked over to the two men.

"Hey, Injun, do you remember me?" a soft voice drawled, and Redhawk looked up with narrowed eyes.

"Yes, I remember you. You are Simms."

"Yeah, Geronimo, that's right." The Texan swaggered a bit as he stepped closer, and when Redhawk rose slowly to his feet, he paused. Sweat-damp strands of red hair stuck out from beneath his helmet, and his uniform had wet patches on the back and under the arms. The Navajos looked as cool and composed as if they were basking in the soft sun of springtime. Simms looked Redhawk up and down, his expression openly contemptuous. "How can I be sure you Injuns are fighting on the right side?"

"You can't."

Taken aback, Simms didn't know what to say for a moment. He had obviously expected Redhawk to defend himself with claims of American loyalty, but the smaller man just looked at the Texan with an impassive stare that was unnerving.

"Hey, cut it out, Simms," a youngish corporal said in an uneasy tone. "He ain't done nothin' to you!"

"Shut up, Mullen!" Simms snapped back, and the sergeant walked up.

Sizing up the situation, Sergeant McIntyre from the D-2 obviously decided to make light of it. "Hey, Simms, don't turn your back! You might find an arrow in it!"

The rest of the patrol found the situation amusing, too, but none of them were hostile. Surprisingly to Johns and Redhawk, they had encountered very little prejudice since being in the Marines. Most of the enlisted men and officers regarded them as capable fighting men, maybe more reticent but just as brave and willing as the others. Only a few men like Simms had confronted them or the other Navajos.

"Secure the butts, Marine!" McIntyre barked when Simms bristled angrily and took another step toward Redhawk. The Texan's hands were knotted into fists, and his mouth was set in an ugly line. Redhawk did not back down, nor did he allow himself to react. He wasn't afraid, but he had no intention of allowing Simms to provoke him into something that would only end badly. "Shove off, Private!" McIntyre bellowed again, rising from his seat on a loaded pack to glare at Simms. The sergeant meant business, and the Texan had no choice but to obey him.

Simms's face was as red as his hair as he pivoted on his heel and stalked away. Redhawk just turned back to his conversation with Johns as if never interrupted. He had a feeling that the Texan would not forget that night on the ship, nor would he forget the laughter of his comrades now.

By the time the three Higgins boats showed up at the jetty, it was dark. Lieutenant Colonel Gerard and Sergeant McIntyre debated the wisdom of cancelling the expedition, with McIntyre for it and Gerard against it.

"No, Sergeant," Gerard finally said. "We move out. Our destination is only three miles north, and we have already been delayed long enough. We must liberate those men who wish to surrender."

McIntyre, a beefy man with a shock of white hair, shook his head, his square jaw set. "Yessir, Colonel, but I have to advise you of my doubts. It's after dark, we aren't certain of our informer, and we aren't certain of the enemy's position. I was informed that those bastards are dug in well and meaner than hell. We could be walking into a trap."

"War is risky business," was Gerard's snappy reply, and the marines clambered into the landing crafts to chug the three miles to Matanikau.

Redhawk sat in the prow of the second boat, his ears filled with the noise of the rasping engine. If it was so loud, couldn't the enemy hear it, too? he wondered, but it wasn't his place to point that out to the lieutenant colonel, who had made it clear to Sergeant McIntyre that the mission would go on as planned.

The boats bumped ashore as planned, just beyond the river. They formed a defensive line near the beach, men fanning out to forge inland. The old familiar feeling of being watched trickled down Redhawk's spine, and he moved cautiously through the wet grasses. Johns was to his left. Stiff-necked and proud, Gerard was striding ahead as tall and as unconcerned as if marching on a parade ground. He had tied a length of rope around the prisoner's neck and told him to lead. McIntyre and three other marines swung out to the right, several feet apart, moving carefully. It was dark, and as his eyes became accustomed to the night shadows, Redhawk saw a flicker of movement just ahead of them.

"Sergeant!" he hissed quickly, and McIntyre stopped dead in his tracks, instinctively crouching down.

"What is it?"

"I don't know, but it's just ahead about two hundred yards."

"Dead ahead?"

"Southeasterly."

Sergeant McIntyre nodded, motioning with his hand for his men to get down. They crouched in the tall grasses, listening to the night sounds, the occasional grumble of a crocodile, and the piercing screeches of the tropical birds. Other than that, it was as silent as death. Even the birds sounded distant, as if they had moved to the north, away from where Redhawk had seen a flicker of movement.

No moonlight lit the sky, and clouds scudded overhead in silent scrutiny as the men waited with cramping muscles and swift-hammering hearts. Nerves were stretched to the breaking point, and up ahead, Redhawk could see Gerard rise from his crouch.

"Better get down, Colonel," McIntyre advised, and Gerard turned toward him.

"You're too goddamn jumpy, Sergeant! Have you forgotten that these men want to surrender?"

Still crouched in the sharp-edged grasses, McIntyre shot back, "I'm not taking the word of a Jap on that!"

"A *civilian* Jap!" Gerard snarled. "This is a direct order, Sergeant: Get your men up from the ground and move forward!"

Redhawk and Johns, alert for any alien sound,

heard it at the same time: the familiar click of a rifle being hammered back. There was no time to shout a warning, and the blast picked up Lieutenant Colonel Gerard and flung him several feet. He lay still, never having uttered a sound, the shallow water of the wetlands rippling about his body. The Japanese prisoner met the same fate just as silently. The force of the bullets threw him back across Gerard.

McIntyre rapped out orders: "Spread out! Get a buddy and stick to him like glue, but not in bunches. Back to the boats."

If it was a lone sniper, they had a chance. If the area was full of enemy, it was a long shot any of them would make it out alive. Quick, rapid bursts of machine-gun fire rapidly removed any doubt that it was a single sniper, and soon the jungle was alive with intense fire. The marines returned fire, but it was evident they were outmanned and outmaneuvered. The situation was growing more hopeless by the minute, and they had only been there for no more than ten minutes.

Lying beside Johns, Redhawk snaked forward on his belly, ignoring the foul water that lapped at his nose, ears, and mouth. He ignored the insects and the leeches that sucked greedily at any bare portion of his flesh. His concentration was focused on survival, not on comfort. What did it matter? The Navajo had never found life very comfortable, anyway.

Shots rang out, always followed by a cry of pain and the sound of a marine hitting the beach or the marshy ground that sucked at clawing hands and feet. Redhawk saw McIntyre get it, the bullet spinning him around and pitching him face forward onto a mucky clump of wet grass. Redhawk didn't pause, didn't allow himself to feel anything. Now wasn't the time for it.

Breathing came hard, with short, rasping breaths being sucked in and usually bringing a gulp of foul-tasting water with it. It didn't matter. It was enough air to keep him going, to keep him alive. He could hear the Japanese behind him, their voices lifted in triumph and hate, the rifle shots ringing out.

"Fuck you, GI! Fuck Babe Ruth!" came the shrill calls in the night. The Japanese sounded triumphant, as if they knew they had the marines where they wanted them. Their jeering calls were interrupted by blasts of machine-gun fire that hewed down saplings and mowed the high grass.

No marine dared move for a while, each one crouching in the high grass and holding his breath, knowing that to allow a rustle of movement would be to invite a bullet. Time dragged agonizingly by, and Redhawk tried to count the men left. He could only detect the darker shadows of fifteen men. Fifteen out of thirty-eight!

Finally, when one of the men could take it no more, he leaped, screaming, into the air, firing his rifle wildly at everything that moved. The Japanese responded with a withering barrage of bullets that actually kept his body upright and spinning like a child's top. When the firing stopped, the marine's body pitched forward like a log and lay still. No other sounds followed until another Japanese voice called out in the quiet, "Death to marines!"

Gesturing, Redhawk tried to signal to all those who could see him in the dark. They had to move out. The enemy knew their position, and they were like sitting ducks.

More snaking through the swampy murk, his mind detaching itself from the reality as he moved along, hearing Johns not far behind him. The Anglo marines were not as familiar with this type of movement and inevitably gave away their positions by the waving of grasses or the slapping of water.

Rifle shots punctuated the night, orange bursts of flame like tiny fingers of death stabbing the blackness that shrouded them, and another marine would die.

The Japanese were jubilant. Echoes of bayonets thudding into marine bodies made Redhawk's teeth clench, but he kept going. Anguished cries from the wounded marines being bayoneted on the beach filled the air, and he fought the urge to turn and fight. He could feel Willie Johns at his side and just behind. It gave him a dogged determination to get through the swampy area. Were they now the only survivors?

Grass cut his face and blood dripped into his eyes. Perspiration stung the cuts, and Redhawk had the detached thought that Navajos did sweat, after all.

It was at about that time that he heard a familiar voice choke out, "Gawd, I'm hit! Oh Jesus Gawd, help me. I can't move! Corpsman! Marine!"

He froze. Friend or foe? The Japanese were known to imitate wounded GI's, then kill the man who stopped to help.

The voice came again, agonized, familiar, and Redhawk ducked as a bullet whizzed close overhead. "For the love of Gawd, help me! McIntyre! Somebody!"

Then he saw the bulky shape just to his left in the darkness, thrashing like a whale in the marshy shallows.

Pouncing on the wounded man, Redhawk smothered his hysterical words with his palm, snapping in his ear, "Shut up! You'll give away your position, and I don't intend for them to find me because of you!"

Simms stared up at him with pale eyes. When he saw Redhawk's slitted eyes boring into him, he shuddered and lay still.

"Can you move?" Redhawk bent close to whisper against Simms's ear. The Texan shook his head and tried to motion with one hand. Slowly removing his palm, Redhawk cautioned him to silence.

"We'll carry you." Johns snaked forward, half on his belly and half on hands and knees, and glanced up at his cousin.

"It looks bad," he said in Navajo. "His leg is half gone."

Redhawk shrugged. Better to be alive than left to the mercy of the enemy. Battle wounds were honorable; surrender was not.

"We can drag him, then." Turning to the wide-eyed Simms, who had begun to shake, his eyes glazing over, he said abruptly, "Make no sound, or we will leave you to the enemy."

Simms put out a tongue to wet his lips. He seemed to have lost all control of his arms, and they flung out wildly. When Redhawk and Johns laced their arms together under him to lift him from the ground, Simms let out a hoarse cry.

"Its my leg. My leg is shot off. Oh Gawd!"

That was all he had a chance to say before Redhawk's fist swung out to hit him square in the temple. Simms lapsed into silence, his head falling back. Almost running, crouched over with the bulky, cumbersome Texan cradled between them, the two Navajos stumbled along the shoreline. It was just as well that Simms was unconscious. Razor-edged chunks of coral sliced their shoes and flesh as they splashed through the beach shallows toward the boats, but they never slowed.

Relief shone in their eyes when they saw the dark shapes of the boats bobbing in the water where they'd left them. Dragging Simms, Redhawk and Johns heaved themselves into the welcoming bottom of the nearest craft.

Only one Higgins boat churned through the water

back to the beach. Redhawk could barely see for the blood and sweat in his eyes, and Johns was dazed with exhaustion and a bullet crease along one arm.

"Is it bad?" Redhawk asked, but Johns shook his head.

"No. Only a scratch. Not as bad as a clump of cactus."

They both smiled. Cactus was the code name for Guadalcanal.

"It ought to make Sergeant Jones happy to know that we got our 'good blooding,' cousin," Redhawk said as the boat neared the jetty they'd left just a few hours earlier.

Willie Johns did not bother to reply.

Chapter Eleven

Japanese or Marine?

Driving themselves to the last of their strength, the two marines managed to bump the boat onto a stretch of beach they hoped was American-held.

"Think we can make it?" Johns muttered to Redhawk, and received an affirmative nod.

"Dah, we can do anything we have to do."

Johns smiled and wiped a hand over his face, leaving behind smears of mud and swamp. In the darkness, he certainly didn't resemble the clean, shiny marine who had started out, but Redhawk figured he didn't look much like one either. Blood smeared over him from Simms, and he had the thought that the Texan wouldn't last much longer if they didn't get him some medical attention real fast.

"How's the tourniquet on his leg holding out?"

Bending close, Johns gave it a cursory glance and shook his head. "Not that well."

"The bleeding would slow if we'd had some spiderwebs to smear over the wound. Or some bark from an oak gall."

Johns grinned. "Couldn't you see the faces of the corpsmen if we suggested that?"

"White doctors could learn a lot from a shaman," Redhawk shot back. He heaved his body over the side of the boat and into the shallows, grimacing as sharp edges of coral sliced into his boots. His trouser legs were already slashed to ribbons by the coral along their flight from the mouth of the river to the boat, and he'd lost his helmet somewhere back in the swamp.

Splashing forward, he dragged the boat the last little bit up the beach, until it was secure enough to lift out Simms. Willie Johns helped him, and they pulled the wounded marine onto the sand and crouched down beside him.

A sudden flare of bright light made them look up, and before they could react, they were surrounded by hard-faced men with M-1 rifles and Thompson submachine-guns bristling in their hands.

"All right, you slant-eyed bastard!" a marine growled, jabbing the muzzle of his M-1 at Redhawk, "Get your fuckin' hands off of our man!"

Warily lifting his hands chest-high, Redhawk said, "Private Redhawk from the Fifth Marines reporting back from patrol, sir."

"Yeah, and I'm Groucho Marx!" one of the marines spat as he chewed on the end of a fat cigar.

Redhawk stared at him uncomprehendingly. Was he supposed to know this Marx? "Reporting back to base . . ."

That was as far as he got before the marine lashed out with a booted foot to catch him square in the chest, sending him sprawling back on the wet sand.

"Think we don't know how you Jap bastards speak English as good as we do?" came the sharp question. "Think again, Nip!"

"Kill him, Sarge," one of the men said. "Shoot both of them! Looks like they were about to do in one of our men here."

Another marine bent over Simms's mangled body. "Bullet wounds to the leg, sir. Looks pretty bad."

Johns spoke up. "We were part of the Gerard patrol

sent out to take prisoners up around the mouth of the Matanikau River. If you'll just talk to—"

Swinging the butt of his rifle up, the sergeant caught Johns just under the chin, smashing back his head and laying open a wide gash. Redhawk sprang to his feet.

"Kill the sonuvabitches!" a furious marine shouted. "It must have been an ambush!"

A rifle cocked, and Redhawk's chin lifted. He stood quietly waiting for the bullet that would send him into the next world.

It didn't come. A higher power in the form of a captain strode quickly forward. He eyed Redhawk's quiet stance, the stocky frame and calm demeanor, and put up a hand.

"Halt! Take these men prisoner, and we'll interrogate them at the CP."

Redhawk felt no relief, nothing. He didn't allow himself to feel anything, not even anger at the mistake. It was easy enough to mistake a Navajo for one of the enemy in the dark, and he tried to remember that as he was roughly marched to the CP.

Sergeant Jones happened to be in the tent, and he looked up in surprise as Redhawk and Johns were shoved into the area by a burly marine.

"Caught these Japs tryin' to pass themselves off as marines, Sergeant," the man said. Sergeant Jones just looked at him.

"Is that right?"

"Yessir. They had one of our men down on the beach. Tried to claim they're with Gerard's patrol."

"And you were smart enough to see through their little masquerade, Private?"

The private smiled. "Yessir!"

"You dumb-fuck, these *are* marines! Can't you see how much bigger they are than Japs? Have you ever seen a Jap with muscles like that?" Jones jerked a thumb toward Redhawk, then stalked forward to examine Johns's bleeding chin. "Get me a medic. Now! And get the general. I have a feeling something's gone wrong."

The private fled, mumbling something that sounded like "How in the hell was I to know they weren't Japs?" as he disappeared out the tent flap. They could hear his boots pounding over the ground outside.

"It was like you said, sir," Redhawk told the sergeant. "An ambush."

Shaking his head in disgust, Jones muttered, "Looks like you got your blooding, Chief. Heads are going to roll for this."

He was wrong. No heads rolled. The top brass were too embarrassed by the ineptitude and failure of the mission to want to admit they had done nothing to stop it. It was widely agreed that the mission should have been postponed until daylight, but no one took the blame for it. The real blame lay with Lieutenant Colonel Gerard, and he had paid for his mistake with his life.

Two things came out of the night's disaster. One was the realization that the Japanese would not expect or give any quarter. Their brutal bayoneting of wounded marines was ample evidence of that fact. It was now a real war, with all the attendant nastiness.

The other thing to come out of the night's events was the assignment of Anglo marine guards to every Navajo soldier.

Redhawk shrugged. "If we'd been sent to Europe like some of the code talkers, we'd be left alone."

"In the dark and in their eagerness to slay the enemy," Jones said dryly, "our men grow a little too enthusiastic. If we don't assign bodyguards to vouch for the loyalty of our code talkers, we might as well just paint a bull's-eye on their asses!"

The brass agreed. A bodyguard was assigned to Redhawk and Johns, as well as the other Navajo marines on Guadalcanal. In the delicate balance between prejudice and acceptance, the two Navajo survivors of the fiasco on the Matanikau River had somehow tilted the scales of justice in their favor. Even Simms, the surly Texan who had given them so much trouble, was not as belligerent, though he didn't claim them as his buddies, either.

"Saved my life, I reckon," Simms muttered when asked about it. "And I'm damn glad to be here!"

It wasn't long before the marines began to doubt the wisdom of his last statement. Glad to be here? Not on the island, not when the Japs had decided to attack with renewed vigor. But it didn't matter to Simms, because he was shipped back stateside, with a Silver Star to his credit.

The bad news about the U.S. defeat at Savo was generally known now, and coupled with the ambush, morale was low. Some of the marines muttered that the island was nothing but a sitting duck without air support, and the opinion was shared. Radio communications relayed from Tulagi brought the news that all objectives on the island had been achieved. Marines leaving Guadalcanal to sortie on Tulagi had encountered an enemy sub in the channel between, giving them some tense moments, but had managed to land safely. On their return, they brought back ten Japanese prisoners and were met with hostility.

Redhawk and Johns were on the beach with their new bodyguard, a man by the name of Walter W. Weintraub, when the lighter carrying the prisoners bumped ashore. The sun was barely up and chow lines had already filed through the mess tent, when they joined members of their squad on the shoreline.

"Kill the sonuvabitches," one marine muttered tightly as the Japanese were unloaded onto the beach. Tension was high since the Matanikau incident. Redhawk remained silent. He had a job to do, and he would do it, just as he had done his job on the ill-fated expedition the night before. Just as the enemy would do theirs. It was a nasty moment for the prisoners as they shambled past the hostile marines, fright etched into their features.

There was a flicker of interest in the eyes of one of the prisoners who came face to face with Redhawk, and for an unguarded moment he paused to shout something at the marine. A translator laughingly supplied the information that the Jap prisoner had assumed Redhawk was a countryman who had defected to the Americans.

"Guess it's your uniform and sweet face that caught him off guard, Chief!" the translator said. Redhawk shrugged, but he wasn't certain he liked being compared to the enemy.

As if sensing their countrymen were there, enemy bombers appeared over Guadalcanal just before noon. The air raid alarm shrilled loudly, and men ran for the cover of their foxholes. Inevitably, the unfinished airstrip was the target, and there was a chain of explosions as the eighteen bombers flew in high. The ground shook as the bombs dropped into the water near Kukum, and the antiaircraft chattered back at them as they swung slowly, then disappeared into the northern sky.

Frustration mounted as the marines realized that they had little effective gun power to fend off the air attacks.

"What we need," Sergeant Jones growled as he surveyed the blistering fires pocking the camp, "is some fuckin' air support!"

The situation wasn't all bad, however. In the afternoon of the fourteenth, a coastwatcher appeared in the CP with a band of native police. He was one of the sixty-four men serving the Australian forces in the capacity of communicating the Japanese ship, plane, and troop movements. Most of his organization was composed of men quite familiar with the islands, men who were planters, gold miners, traders, or skippers of coastal craft. It was a tight-knit group and a very well organized one, though flung widely across the Solomon Islands.

"You are one of the Ferdinands, right?" Johns asked the tall, burly Scots major when he entered the communications tent.

A smile split Major Gibson's craggy face, and he wiped one hand across it. He'd arrived at the CP hungry and shabby, and the marines had immediately fed him a generous portion of their short rations. Gibson eyed the stocky Navajo. "Aye, laddie, I am at that!"

"I met one of your men aboard the transport," Johns said. "He told us how effective you are."

"And you're one of the native Americans who use that infernal code, am I right?" Major Gibson asked.

"You've heard of us?"

"Any man connected with Cactus has heard of you! You gave the boys up the coast quite a start with your talk not long ago. We thought the Japs had broken into our frequency and taken control!"

"There'll be a lot more of that when our equipment makes it ashore," Johns promised. "Be ready for it."

Interested, Gibson asked, "What are you using now?"

Sergeant Jones made a disgusted sound. "One of our men fixed up a Jap radio left behind, but it won't reach that far. It's only five hundred watts. We're doing a little 'Oriental Engineering' just to kibitz on what's happening out there. Any news?"

"None you'll like."

"So let's have it," Jones said, hitching up his pants and clearing his throat.

Gibson pushed his cap back and lit up a pipe. The fragrant tobacco smoke curled into the air, wreathing his blond head. "You did feed my men, didn't you, Sergeant?" he asked first, and when Jones nodded, Gibson sucked on his pipe before saying, "I've had a bit of trouble keeping the loyalty of some of the natives. They saw me on the run from the Japs and began to get a bit restive. These men I brought in with me, though, they're as loyal as they can be and have stuck by me. I retreated farther and farther back into the hills behind Aola as the Japanese advanced. I saw the U.S. planes a few days ago—the seventh—and heard the naval row kicking up out there in the sound. I picked up the news of the marines' landing on Tulagi the next day, so I headed on down here to offer my services." He lifted a foot clad in a highly polished black shoe. "Waited 'til the last moment to put on my shoes, so I'd make a good impression."

"Your opinion of enemy concentration in the area?" Jones pursued, and Gibson shook his head.

"Thick as thieves in Morocco, Sergeant." He leaned forward to say softly, "And there's more coming."

"Have you conferred with General Vandegrift on this?"

Gibson leaned back in his chair and shook his head. "No, I haven't been interviewed yet."

Jones stood up. "Well, that's about to change, Major."

Gibson ended up being attached to the D-2 section led by Lieutenant Colonel Judd A. Barkley, Gerard's successor. His communiqués were vitally important. The enemy held Rabaul firm—much too close to Guadalcanal and Tulagi. It was only a sea voyage of two days, and the Japanese forces could easily crush the marine occupation of the island.

Enemy aircraft hit the next day, dropping bombs at will on the marines as they lay grim and helpless, exposed and unable to fight back without air support.

"When is the fuckin' airfield going to be ready?" was the question on every marine's lips.

Coastwatchers and intercepted radio transmissions indicated that Japanese activity around Rabaul was escalating. And the news came in a partially decrypted message that destroyers were leaving Truk on the fifteenth—headed for Guadalcanal.

"Shit," a marine by the name of Kryzminsky muttered as he sprawled on his hard pallet smoking a cigarette. "We don't even know when or where they'll hit, for Chrissake!"

Redhawk didn't say anything. He waited and listened with a patience born of the centuries. His silence was soon noted and remarked upon.

"Jeezus, don't you Indian boys ever get upset?" one man wanted to know. An annoyed expression curled his features, and he smoked one cigarette after another.

Shrugging, Redhawk said, "Yes, but being upset does no good."

"What does? What do you do back home, Chief, when you get tense?" Kryzminsky asked irritably.

"Run."

Kryzminsky just stared at him in the gathering gloom of dusk. *"Run?"*

Redhawk smiled slightly. "It lets off steam, as you might say."

"If you took a run out here," one man ventured with a laugh, "you'd look like a fuckin' sieve when you got back!"

"If you got back," Kryzminsky said, flipping his cigarette butt into the air. It landed several feet away and lay there, glowing red in the shadows. He stared at it for a long time, and silence fell over the group again.

Tension was growing. Redhawk could feel it in himself as well as in Johns and Little Wolf Smith. William Brown, who had worked with them for a time, had been transferred over to another outfit to be used on the radio. They were all finally getting some time on the radio, as the officers became aware of their speed and efficiency. It had taken time, but it was slowly happening.

That did not, however, keep them from being used in whatever capacity an officer needed them. Many of the code talkers were used as runners as well, in spite of Sergeant Jones's feelings that they were more useful in a specialized team of communications.

And while they waited, they kept themselves busy.

The Navajos were sent out on detail with a squad of men to scout the area beyond the airfield. Marines armed with machetes had sliced down any vegetation big enough to hide a possible enemy, then dug deep connecting pits called spider-holes, cushioned the holes with sandbags, banked them with roughly cut sections of coconut tree logs, hid them with tufted squares of grass, then wove the entire concoction together with an intricate network of barbed wire. The approaches to the field were booby trapped with an ingenious method: Hand grenades were set up with their pins partially withdrawn to be tripped by the unwary; artillery was trained on trails the enemy was liable to use; fixed machine guns, on an interlocking system, were set for massed night firing, and metal cans of gasoline were arranged in forks of trees with a pre-fixed, pre-set rifle that would fire a bullet directly into the can to set it aflame. The marines were ready. Now all they had to do was wait.

Chapter Twelve
Flyboys

A routine of sorts had been established by marines and enemy alike. During the humid daylight hours, Japanese submarines, or I-boats, would cruise offshore like Sunday afternoon pleasure boats, and with as little risk. Particularly frustrating was the occasional shell that would be lobbed into the Lunga perimeter. At night, when the weary marines tried to sleep in tents, foxholes, and on the hard ground, planes whined overhead, dropping flares or bombs, both equally irritating. Most of the damage was confined to the frayed nerves of men who had little to eat, scant sleep, and a high degree of anxiety.

Redhawk had to admire the marines' manner of coping with stress. The submarines began to be known collectively as Oscar, a rather ludicrous way of referring to the enemy that somehow took some of the sting out of the occasional bite. The single-engined plane that droned overhead at night was a Zero floatplane that came alone or with company, and became known to the marines as Louie the Louse. As a group, they were called Zekes. A rougher sounding two-engine nocturnal bomber became Washing-machine Charlie, for the distinctive churning rhythm of its motors.

Except for the enemy visitors, the orphaned marines felt abandoned by the Navy and quite isolated. Tulagi just across the sound was the nearest neighbor, and unfortunately just as helpless. Radio contact was the sole means of reliable communication, and that was scant.

A second lieutenant was in charge of all communications with higher commands. The captured Japanese radio was his domain, and the only outside link with the rest of the world. Redhawk, Johns, and the ever-present Weintraub were assigned to the radio shack.

The radio Redhawk and Johns had lugged from the transport ship to the beach was bulky, heavy, and too short-ranged to be much good. In order to use the TBS it had to be on a secure surface, with the generator providing the necessary electrical power. Operating the TBS took two men, one to crank the generator and provide electricity to power the radio, and the other to complete transmission.

When Zekes, or Japanese Zeroes, made their daily run overhead, it was very difficult to transmit or receive. The first day after being assigned a bodyguard found Redhawk squatting in the radio shack, sending out a message. It was coming back garbled, but he was finally able to receive.

"How do you do that, Private?" Weintraub knelt down beside him to ask. He had helped Johns position the huge generator on a wooden bench and turn the crank, and was fascinated with the gibberish that the Navajos so easily understood. "Only one or two of the sounds were similar, and I know you have to repeat them sometimes."

A faint smile flashed as Redhawk shrugged and replied, "We were taught not to transmit for too long at a time, so the enemy could not determine our position. And we were also taught not to repeat common words or letters too many times. Then the enemy might begin to understand." When Weintraub just looked at him, Redhawk explained, *"Wol-la-chee* is the Navajo word for *ant,* and stands for the English letter *A*. But if I say it too many times when spelling out Guadalcanal, the enemy might begin to decode."

"So what do you use instead of *wollachee?"*

"Be-la-sana, or apple. And *tse-nhil* for axe. It works pretty good, huh?"

"Yeah," Weintraub said. "So is *A* the only letter with only one interchangeable code name?"

Redhawk shook his head. "The six most commonly used letters in the English language are *A, E, I, N, O, T.* There are three alternate code words for each of those. For *D, H, L, R, S, U,* the second-most repeated letters, there is one alternate word for each."

Grinning, Weintraub, a tall, skinny marine with a shock of brown hair that defied his every effort to comb it, said, "So spell out Guadalcanal . . . using letters I can understand."

"Goat-Uncle-Axe-Dog-Ant-Leg-Cat-Apple-Nose-Ant-Lamb," was the swift reply, startling the marine and making Johns laugh.

"You thought we did not pay attention to our training, right?" Johns chided.

"If I did, I know now I'm a *schmuck,"* was the prompt answer.

"Schmuck?"

Weintraub winked and nodded. "Ah, you guys aren't the only ones around who know code words!"

Sergeant Jones put in dryly, "Schmuck means dick, Johns, and you don't have to be Jewish to figure that out."

Johns still looked faintly confused, and Weintraub laughed again. "That's why I was assigned as your bodyguard, you know. Sergeant Jones figures we'll teach each other an entirely new code."

"Don't give yourself any ideas, Weintraub." Jones rose from his canvas chair beside the radio. "If you three guys just make it outta this war alive, I'll be surprised." His big grin erased some of the sting from his words. "Anyway, I'm just doing my best to keep my radiomen from being shot by their buddies, not teach them new insults." His grin faded a bit as his voice grew serious, and he looked at the two Navajo youths. "That's why it's hard for me to tell you this, but you're being assigned to Company A for the next few days. You'll get your orders."

Redhawk shrugged. He wasn't too surprised. The marines were always doing things differently.

Willie Johns and Redhawk were assigned to accompany troops through the jungles to the village of Matanikau. The ambush was still too fresh in the minds of the officers to allow it to rest much longer. Matanikau must go.

"You are in the capacity of guides and communications, and that is all," Jones instructed them. "Do not take any undue risks. Understood?"

Redhawk raked a hand through his hair. He knew that once out in the bush, it wouldn't matter what the sergeant wanted for them. Their orders would be up to the discretion of their commanding officer. Jones was to stay behind, while they were to be under the command of a Captain Ben Hardwick.

"Understood, sir," Redhawk answered. Jones smiled, and he knew that the sergeant was well aware of what would probably happen when they came under fire.

"Keep the lines open, Chief," was all the sergeant said by way of warning.

The plan was relatively simple: One company of troops was to set out early the next morning, make their way through the thick jungles to the rear of the village, then work into position for a land assault.

Another company was to advance along the shoreline toward Matanikau from Kukum, billet for the night, then be in an excellent position to form a strike from the east after the initial assault. The third troops were to go by water, make a landing from the boats far to the west of Matanikau—beyond the village of Kokumbona far to the west—then attack from the west along the shoreline. Simple and effective, Redhawk thought. If it worked.

The two Navajos were assigned to Company A, and Captain Hardwick led his troops from Kukum along the shore, marching them into the dense, humid jungle where they would bivouac overnight before the attack.

They pressed through thick foliage, hacking at it with the long, sharp machetes, following ancient trails that had been cut through the jungle eons before. There was an air of waiting as they marched across old wooden footbridges, past brilliant arrays of wild orchids, marched through coconut groves, past neat rows of pineapple plants and back into the vine-shrouded jungle. In the fetid air and gloom, visibility was cut to only a few feet ahead.

"Damn!" a marine muttered around the cigarette dangling from one corner of his mouth. "This place gives me the creeps!"

Redhawk agreed with him silently. There was an eerie quiet that pervaded the air, and all of them were tense. A sniper could be hiding in the swaying clump of palm branches overhead or behind a thick cluster of pineapple plants that somehow reminded him of the yucca plants in Arizona. The only identifiable sounds were of jangling dog tags, the metallic clink of rifles and canteens, and the harsh breaths of the marines. Everything else was alien.

"They'll hear us coming a mile off," Weintraub muttered to no one in particular. He looked around nervously, his head bobbing on his skinny neck like a ball atop a spring. "I bet they're hiding just ahead."

"Or above," Johns said softly, and everyone within earshot could not resist looking up.

Radio contact was forbidden until the actual assault began. No chances were being taken that the Japanese might guess their actions.

Just before dark, they made camp. There were to be no fires, of course, and the menu was C-rations. Every man had his own private thoughts, and none of the usual jokes and teasing went on.

Lying next to Johns that night, Redhawk listened to the shrill calls of the macaws in the trees overhead and was thought how different this part of the world was from what he'd always known. It certainly provided an insight into other races, and he felt as if he had learned a great deal since that day in Window Rock. That day seemed like years ago instead of only months before, another life, perhaps. There were times he didn't feel like the same person, the same young man who had been swelled with arrogance, pride, and resentment. He still had his pride, but the arrogance and even the resentment had faded into faint reminders of how he'd felt toward the white man. It was certainly a different world here, where men banded together for a common cause without regard to race or prejudice.

Several times that night, the marines were awakened by rounds of heavy cannonading in the distance. It was not close enough to endanger them, and they ignored it as best they could.

Shortly after eight o'clock the next morning, the troops reached a small clearing and halted.

"We wait here for artillery strikes against Matanikau," the captain said. Pushing back his helmet, he crouched down beneath the shade of a tree and took out his map.

Redhawk and Johns crouched close by. They were

to man the radio, receiving and sending necessary messages. No code was necessary in times of battle, unless vital secrecy was involved. Most of the messages were sent and received too quickly for the Japanese to be able to react.

A half hour after halting in the clearing, one of the men came racing in from the beach. He was panting for air, and his eyes were wild with excitement.

"There's a Jap destroyer out there!" he told the captain.

Cursing softly, Captain Hardwick muttered, "Damnit! If we had some aircraft, those Japs wouldn't sail these waters so fucking bravely!"

As he ground his teeth in frustration, Redhawk and Weintraub went down to the beach to see for themselves. Using his field glasses, Redhawk could see the Rising Sun flag flapping over the long gray line, of the enemy ship. Guns bristled from the warship's turrets. Slowly, it maneuvered its bow around, pointing toward the shore, then swung like a lazy pendulum until it was broadside of the beach. No shots were fired from either side.

"It must be out of range of our shore batteries," Weintraub commented as he took the field glasses and held them up. "If it wasn't, our boys would be firing."

Redhawk didn't answer, and behind them they could hear the first random shots of the opening barrage against Matanikau. Redhawk pivoted, then broke into a run. The guns boomed loudly, whistling softly overhead to land with loud cracks of rhythmic explosion.

Forced to halt, then move forward, then halt as the intensity of the barrage picked up, Redhawk lugged his heavy radio equipment on his back. The sighs of the shells and overlapping explosions began to blend together until it sounded like one long wave of undulating noise in his ears. They were still traveling the shoreline, and just beyond the thin line of trees was the beach. And in the water was the huge Japanese warship, blasting away.

But that seemed trivial in the next assault wave, as a chatter of submachine gunfire rattled the air from the left flank. Rifle shots punctuated the rising crescendo, and in the racket, Redhawk could make out the sharp crack of a Japanese .25 caliber. He remembered that sound, could not forget the distinctive noise it had made the night of the ambush.

Diving behind a thorny clump of bushes, he muttered harshly as his radio caught in the branches and he was hung up for a moment. He jerked free just as another .25 shot smashed through the underbrush, showering him with leaves and chewed twigs. Lying flat and still on his belly, with the weight of the radio holding him down, he could see only roots and dirt from his close proximity to the ground. Feeble sunlight filtered through the leaves overhead. As usual in the dense, fetid jungle, visual perception was limited to only a few feet.

Not far away, he could barely make out the soles of marine boots and wondered if it was Johns. He called out gruffly in Navajo and was answered in the same.

"It is raining bullets," Johns said cheerfully, and Redhawk grinned.

"Dah."

From not far away came the grumbling comment, "It's one hell of a time for idle conversation, especially when no one else can understand what's being said!" Ducking a shower of shredded leaves and tree bark, Redhawk managed to lift his head long enough to say, "Those are Gentile bullets, so perhaps they are not meant for you."

Weintraub's answering laugh was quickly smothered by another hail of gunfire.

With his face pressed into the dirt and bullets flying overhead like angry bees, Redhawk found himself effectively pinned down for almost an hour. When the gunfire eased, he cautiously lifted his head and met Johns's inquiring gaze.

"Is it over?" Johns asked in Navajo, and Redhawk managed a brief shrug.

"I don't know. There must be a sniper ahead of us."

The order came to move forward and the marines scrambled to their feet, spitting out dirt and leaves, looking behind and above them for more enemy fire. The jungle closed in around them on three sides as they followed the trail toward Matanikau. Redhawk shifted the heavy radio on his back to a more comfortable position. It was tiring lugging it, and he worried that enemy fire might put it out of commission.

Moving cautiously along the open side of trail, Redhawk heard the ominous burst from a .25-caliber machine gun again, and he ducked for cover. More .25's clattered into action just ahead of them, filling the air with noise and deadly missiles.

Once more lying on his belly, he heard the captain ask for radio communication. It was dangerous, but he managed to edge his way behind a rough-barked coconut tree and hook his unit around it. Tense with expectation, Redhawk jerked at the handle, cranking juice to power the mike for Johns. At any moment, he fully expected to feel a bullet slam into his unprotected back as the message was sent asking for information.

White flashes zipped overhead, one bullet whizzing past his cheek, and he felt the hot breath fan his skin as he ducked out of the way, holding onto the crank, his arm automatically turning.

". . . forward troop movement halted!" Johns shouted into the mike, then had to jerk aside as a bullet slammed into the trunk of the tree right by his head. His face crinkled into a grin as he sat upright again and calmly finished his message. Captain Hardwick shouted instructions, and the troop moved forward again.

With his arm aching from churning the crank, Redhawk moved the TBS from the tree. He had gone no more than five paces when a chain of bullets stitched the trunk of the tree where he'd been standing. He glanced back, his steps picking up. There wasn't much time for relief that he had completed his message before the enemy had zeroed in on his position. He'd be grateful later, when the battle was over.

Now there was only time for cursing the pouring rain that pounded down on them, that and the sniper fire. The noise of battle was mostly confined to random shots and erratic bursts of machine-gun fire from both sides.

Redhawk slogged over soggy, rain-soaked ground. The firing continued. Then, as suddenly as it had begun, the firing stopped at the same time as the driving rain. Silence pressed down as heavily as the humid air, weighing on them, making the marines glance around nervously.

In spite of his outwardly cool composure, Redhawk felt the sharp, fluttering pangs of tension. The heat didn't bother him, nor the rain, but the heavy weight of humidity drained him, making him feel as if each step was an effort. He shifted the bulky radio, noticing that his boots left deep marks in the jungle floor, the mud sucking at his feet with a fierce tenacity that was indicative of the entire island. Guadalcanal was not a place fit for man nor beast, he decided, then recalled how many times he'd heard that said about the flat, dry lands of Arizona.

But to Redhawk, the soaring sky over Arizona spread above a beautiful land, a land full of change and surprise. After an infrequent rain, small life would spring into being, with green twigs thrusting up from between barren rocks, aquatic life burgeoning into a short life span in fresh pools that the searing desert sun would soon dry. His throat tensed, and he realized that he had not let himself think about his homeland because of the sorrow he felt at being away for so long. Even in his conversations with Willie Johns, it had not been mentioned. It was as if bringing it up would give it substance, and neither of them wanted that. Redhawk was grateful for the sudden distraction of unknown movement in the jungle, and he obeyed the order to halt.

A marine appeared on the trail ahead of them, cheerfully bringing a Japanese prisoner with him. "Caught this guy trying to piece his buddies back together," was his light comment as he paused. Redhawk looked at the small man. He was obviously terrified, and there was a grayish pallor to his skin beneath the tint of ochre.

For a brief instant, the prisoner locked gazes with the young Navajo. There was something besides terror in his eyes, a flicker of emotion that was quickly gone, and then the man was pushed forward as his captor went to find the captain.

Redhawk stared after him. He was surprised at the surge of hatred he felt for the enemy. That man must have been one of those men responsible for the deaths of the Gerard patrol, and he could almost hear the faint echoes of the taunting jeers that had floated through the thick jungle night along with the acrid smell of gunpowder and death. He turned to glare after the Japanese. His thoughts were focused on the enemy, on the small yellow men who were determined to wipe out the Americans. It would never be. No, not as long as he could breathe would he allow the enemy to overrun his homeland! The Navajos had occupied their lands for much longer than the white man, but even he had never been able to truly conquer them. No, the Japanese would not succeed.

Three correspondents with the troops decided to return to headquarters, and they took the prisoner with them. Redhawk was not sorry to see him go.

The closer they got to the village of Matanikau, the fiercer the fighting. Bullets whizzed overhead, submachine guns chattered, and the endless whirr of the enemy's .25's sliced the air. Redhawk, Johns, and Weintraub were left at the rear, with a runner moving between troops and radio to relay messages. The TBS was hooked to a tree again, and the three men huddled close by it with rifles ready. The thickest fighting was to the front, as the village was only a few hundred yards ahead of them.

"How is it you Indians can always find cover where there isn't any?" Weintraub grumbled good-naturedly. "You leave me standing in the open and feeling like a prime target."

"You make a good one," Redhawk said as he stepped from behind a small rise near the trail's edge. "You're nice and tall, and you move so slowly the enemy must feel sorry for you."

"That must be it, 'cause the last sniper had a golden opportunity and let it go," Weintraub admitted. He tilted his helmet back and wiped his sweaty face with one hand. "I just hope they keep feeling sorry for me."

More shots rang out, and they all hit the dirt again as a bullet narrowly missed Weintraub. Redhawk fired back at the place where a puff of smoke marked a sniper, and was rewarded by a faint cry as his bullet found its mark.

"Damn good shooting, Chief," Weintraub said from his prone position on the ground. He spit out a mouthful of dirt and leaves, and brought his rifle up to take aim. "Thanks."

Redhawk grinned. "Your words interested the *chendi,* I think. They couldn't resist testing you."

"Chendi?"

"Evil spirits," Johns explained. "But in this case, I think it's the Japanese."

"Great. I just wish I had a Thompson instead of this rifle. I'd take out the top of that tree line," Weintraub said, then ducked. More shots battered the brush around them, and the firefight grew intense.

As the day wore on, the news from the front reflected a slim possibility for victory. Finally, Captain Hardwick sent the message back for the radiomen to notify headquarters in English that the villages had been taken. No sooner had Redhawk complied, than the order came to use his code.

"Captain Hardwick says you are to notify the colonel that we were not successful, repeat, not successful, but do it in code so the enemy does not intercept," the runner said. He was breathing hard as he crouched down beside Redhawk and Johns, and his eyes glittered with excitement as he grinned at them. "Hardwick thinks that if the Japs know we didn't make it, they might throw more at us. But if they think we already took out those villages, they might retreat."

Redhawk looked doubtful. "Do you think it will work?"

Shrugging, the runner said, "Who knows? But it's worth a try, I guess. At least the captain seems to think so."

While Johns cranked the generator, Redhawk grabbed the mike to relay the coded message that the objective had not been reached. The enemy was far stronger than expected.

As the troops slowly retreated, Redhawk and Johns were sent farther back to the rear. Captain Hardwick was battle-weary and angry that they had not been able to take the villages.

"Goddamn Nips," he muttered, wiping sweat from his brow with the back of his hand. "Where in the hell are our planes? We can't even hope to secure this island without fuckin' air support!"

"Captain!" a voice yelled, and a marine rushed up to tell Hardwick that the bodies of the ambushed patrol had been found.

"Repeat that, Marine!" Hardwick barked.

The Gerard patrol's remains had been found half buried in a sandbar. Hardwick followed the runner and surveyed the sandbar studded with bodies. It was in the open, and enemy snipers were sure to be in the jungle surrounding it on three sides. Redhawk was right behind the captain as he paused at the edge of the trees.

Pushing back his helmet, Hardwick said, in a reluctant voice, "Leave them here for now. There's no time to bag them and take them. We'll have to come back."

Redhawk looked away. Death was not to be looked upon by the Navajos according to the ways of The People, but this was different. These were men he had known, men who had joked with him, shared with him. Flies were swarming over swollen bodies half buried in the sand and shallow water. He could see arms and legs thrusting up from the sand like macabre seedlings. Then he saw the young corporal, Mullen, who had defended him to Simms. He was lying with his mouth half open, his eyes encrusted with flies and staring at nothing.

Unable to stop himself and ignoring the warnings of his ancestors, Redhawk stepped through the shallows to tilt Mullen's helmet over his face. It was the human thing to do for a comrade. Anger hit him like a bolt of lightning, and he had to turn away. He would not ever forget that night, the screams of the wounded and dying and the bark of the .25's that had cost thirty-five marine lives. And he would never forget the sickening *thunk* of bayonets being driven into a live body.

He could feel the eyes of the others on him, the nervous group of marines who stood on the beach in the open and watched. A marine began to gather dog tags, and they clinked in his hand with awful finality.

Hardwick said nothing. Scattered bursts of machine-gun fire rent the air, and they all left the area in a running dive, scurrying for the comparative safety of the dense brush behind them. Redhawk didn't look back.

The arrival back at the CP was not heralded with much gladness. The failure to take Matanikau weighed on all the men. It was an anticlimactic ending to an entire series of defeats.

Redhawk slung himself onto his pallet and took out a pack of cigarettes. He was lighting his first one when Johns joined him.

Surprise etched his features as he watched Redhawk blow out the match and take a deep drag from the cigarette. "Since when did you begin smoking?"

"A few days ago. W.W. gave me a cigarette and I liked it."

Johns said nothing, just sprawled back on his blankets with his eyes on Redhawk. After several minutes of silence, he said, "We are changing all the time."

Redhawk nodded. "I know. But if we didn't, we would not survive."

"Does smoking cigarettes help us survive?"

"Maybe. Maybe not. But right now, it doesn't hurt." Redhawk looked at his cousin through the thin gray swirls of smoke, and he smiled. "Would you like a cigarette?"

Johns held out his hand, and Redhawk lit one for him, then gave it to him. When W.W. Weintraub joined them, he made no comment about the two awkwardly smoking cigarettes, but acted as if everything were normal.

Several hours after the noon chow, they walked to the radio hut near the Fifth Marines CP. Little Wolf greeted them with a cheery grin and a wave of one arm. His bodyguard, a tough-looking corporal by the name of Reid, was stretched out on the floor of the hut, his helmet over his eyes.

"What's with him?" Weintraub asked, jerking his thumb toward the snoozing corporal. Smith grinned.

"He's tired from having to watch me so hard. I don't stay in one place, and Corporal Reid worries that he'll lose his stripes if I get shot by a trigger-happy dogface."

From the depths of the helmet came the sonorous retort, "I'd probably get a medal for relieving the corps of another mouth to feed."

"He likes me," Little Wolf said. "We've grown close."

"As snakes," intoned Reid.

Redhawk laughed. Enforced proximity made strange friends, indeed!

"So what are you doing over here?" Little Wolf asked, unhooking the earphones from over his head and slinging them around his neck.

"We just got back from Matanikau," Johns said, and there was no need to say anything else. The failed mission had been transmitted to Little Wolf. He nodded.

"You found the ambushed patrol, I heard."

"Dah. We are to go back for them when possible."

Reid pushed the lip of his helmet back from over his eyes and stared up at the two Navajos flanking the tall, skinny Weintraub. "Won't do you any good," he said.

"Why not?"

"If the Japs don't drag 'em away, the river will

carry 'em out to sea." He shrugged when they just stared at him. "I can listen good enough to know where you found them."

Redhawk realized he was right. The spot where the remains of the patrol had been found was too near the river for the bodies not to be washed away during the next storm. It left him with a feeling of impotent anger, which showed in his eyes.

Reid looked up at him curiously. "That's the way war is, you know. Nobody ever said it was fair."

"Did I say anything?"

"Chief, you don't have to. It's written all over your face, just like it is on every other marine's."

Some of the tension in him eased slightly, and Redhawk gave a short nod. "Yeah, you're right."

"Those are our boys out there, and all of us want them shipped back home." Reid sat up and hooked his arms around his bent knees, still looking directly at Redhawk. "But we all knew it was a risk when we shipped out for the Pacific, didn't we? That's why we're here."

Weintraub looked astonished, his bushy eyebrows lifting in mock amazement. "Is *that* the reason? I thought we were here for souvenirs!"

Whatever Reid would have replied remained unsaid. The unmistakable droning of airplanes overhead interrupted the conversation, and the men ducked outside.

"It ain't Tojo Time," Reid commented, looking up at the sky. Ragged cheers began to sound, and he turned to the others with a wide smile. "Hey, it must be our guys!"

By this time all four men were crowded outside the door of the hut, staring up at the sky. The planes circled the field, and when the first one touched down on the airstrip, Redhawk glanced at his watch. It was 1607. He broke into a run toward the airfield, newly named Henderson Field after a hero of the battle of Midway.

General Vandegrift was present to greet the flyers, and there was a festive air to the day as the marines laughed and shouted rude greetings to the pilots who climbed out of the cockpits. Redhawk counted nineteen Grumman Wildcat fighters and twelve Douglas Dauntless scout-bombers.

The planes bumped onto the airstrip one by one, rubber tires skidding as they braked to a rolling halt. The bubbles popped open, and grinning flyers clambered out. The marines laughed and cheered as the fly-boys waved long-billed blue baseball hats in the air. They all wore identical khaki shirts that looked sun-faded and worn.

"Wouldja lookit that!" a marine near Redhawk said in an almost reverent tone. "Cocky as hell, ain't they?"

"They have a right to be," someone else said in the same tone.

"Hell, I can't believe we don't have to dive into foxholes because we hear airplanes!" another marine said, adding in a dreamy voice, "I think they're beautiful!"

That comment generated laughter, and men were slapping one another on the back and joking. Even Redhawk, who was still not comfortable with the constant touching, allowed himself to be patted on the back and nudged. It was an occasion for celebration, and the air was thick with it.

"Hey, fly-boy!" a marine called out, cupping his hands around his mouth to be heard over the din. "Going to a ball game?"

Grinning back at him, the tall, lean man looked much too young to be an experienced pilot as he doffed his baseball hat and made a mocking bow. But he was already well learned in the art of marine banter.

"Fucking A," he shot back, earning a round of

laughter. "And we're playing the Nips at Henderson Field!"

The marines cheered, and the Pennsylvania farm boy gave another cocky wave as he leaped from the wing of his plane onto the hot landing strip. Waves of heat and humidity shimmered around him and the others, but they all acted as cool and comfortable as if standing in a brisk southeastern tradewind.

Redhawk was fascinated with the pilots of the silver-winged birds. They reminded him of his peyote dream and the white eagle that had carried him over the ocean. Could there be a connection? It seemed doubtful. And besides, there was no huge mountain of sulphur on Guadalcanal.

The celebrated arrival of the two MAG-23 squadrons meant two of the three factors necessary to keep Henderson Field in marine hands were in place, though barely. Air support was vital but so was naval support, and that was not yet in command. The Navy was doing its best to get essential supplies to the island, but a constant threat from the Imperial Navy of Japan made it slow-going.

That night, there was a jubilant air to the marines as they toasted the newly arrived Bastard Air Force with confiscated Japanese beer and saki.

"Here, fly-boy," Private Kryzminsky said, thrusting a warm bottle into the hands of a pilot. "Do you wanna drink or don't you?"

The watching marines laughed as the pilot upended the bottle and drained it in almost one swallow.

"Tastes like horse piss," he said, handing the empty bottle back to Kryzminsky.

"You Pennsylvania farm boys oughta know!" was the swift retort, and everyone laughed.

Not taking offense, Lieutenant Wayne Moose, who only a year before had been a boy fresh off a farm in the mountains of Pennsylvania, grinned back at the marine. "I don't mind drinking it, but who milked the horse, Marine, you?"

Kryzminsky could not keep his face from reddening, but he took it in stride as he said, "Okay, Fly-boy, you got me that time. I owe you one."

Moose grinned back at him so affably that no one could have taken offense. "So who keeps count? Hand me another beer, why don't you?"

In talking to him as they sat around foxholes and tents that late afternoon, Redhawk discovered that Lieutenant Moose was a well of interesting information. The talk invariably turned to the newly arrived air force.

"We started out in Oahu," Moose told them, chewing on a cigar as he talked. "Colonel Wallace was alerted by Nimitz back in June that he'd need two squadrons each of dive-bombers and fighters. A lot of the pilots were pretty green, and seeing as how our equipment was pretty old, the marines thought we'd be perfect." Moose grinned at them. It made perfect sense to the two Navajos, who were well accustomed to the marine mentality.

"So, if they notified you in June, why'd it take so long for you fly-boys to get here?" a corporal asked. "We've been needing air support since Day One!"

Shrugging, Moose said, "We spent the month of July in intensive training. We headed south on the carrier *Long Island* around the first week in August, but some of the boys just couldn't cut the mustard. There's a big difference between training and actual combat, and split-second decisions can make or break an entire mission. Anyway, McCain was yelling that planes were needed on Cactus now, and so some of the greener boys were traded to Lieutenant Colonel Bauer's New Hebrides squadron. It took us eighteen days just to get from Oahu to within flying distance of here."

"We're sure as hell glad you made it," Sergeant

Jones said. "Maybe we can kick ass and take names now."

Moose grinned and pushed his baseball cap to the back of his head. "No trouble, Sergeant, no trouble at all! It won't take us long to push those Japs all the way back to Tokyo."

Kryzminsky shook his head. "I just hope you flyboys are fortune tellers as well as pilots. . . ."

Chapter Thirteen

No Quarter Given

Redhawk thought about the pilots that night. He lay in his blankets on the hard ground and stared up at the sky overhead, wondering how men felt about flying among the clouds every day. He'd never thought about it much before, not when he was in Arizona, anyway. Then it had just been an occasional silver streak overhead, a shadow dancing across the flat ridges and striated buttes of the red rocks he called home.

The pilots seemed like different men than the marines who fought on the ground. More dare-devil, of course, but more confident, too. If they ever wondered about not making it back home, they certainly didn't let it show. Some of the Air-acobras' P-400 fighters had their noses painted with sharks' jaws, openmouthed and grinning fear-somely. It reminded Redhawk and Johns of the paintings their shamans and ancestors had brushed on cave walls, buffalo robes, and war shields. It was the same principle: Scare off the evil spirits with a show of ferocity and courage.

The lieutenant had told them rather sadly that

the Airacobras were only medium-altitude fighters and they couldn't climb high enough to effectively mix with Zeroes. That fact was frustrating to the Sixty-seventh Fighter Squadron, but not daunting. Nothing would keep them out of the air, and anyway, Moose had said, the Airacobras' nose cannons and other armament were formidable enough as close-support weapons against the ground troops of the enemy.

There were frustrations in every outfit, Redhawk reflected. He and Johns and the other Navajos felt the same bite of frustration at not being given enough responsibility on the radio. All their weeks of learning and training to use the code seemed to have been wasted. Not many of the officers were convinced that it was more effective than the old way, and only a few—like Jones—were willing to give them a chance at it.

What would it take before they could prove themselves, before they could prove that the code they had worked so hard to devise would be a good one? Johns voiced the same question aloud, his words floating softly across the dark space between them.

"Do you think they will ever give us a chance to show what we can do?"

Redhawk shrugged, then realizing that it was probably too dark for his cousin to see him, he said, "Who knows? If they do, we must be certain to prove how quickly it works. We may only get one chance."

"*Aiee,* we have shown them already that it works! In test after test, we have been faster and more efficient! And even on patrol, we are able to send messages more quickly than regular radiomen."

"Don't be discouraged," Redhawk advised, even

though he'd been thinking the same thing. "There will be a time when even the most stubborn officer will recognize it."

The chance came sooner than they'd hoped.

The next morning, Friday the twenty-first, started with a rumbling barrage in the distance. It seemed that the enemy, which had constantly been landing men and supplies beyond the marine perimeters, had advanced. Their new front line was the Tenaru River (actually mistaken for the Ilu on the first rough maps, but the popular name stuck, and the marines refused to correct themselves in conversation).

The message that had been decrypted a while before reporting that Japanese forces were headed to Guadalcanal was correct. Exact information did not reach Vandegrift, but the general did know that some more troops had reached Cactus a few days before. How many was any marine's guess.

The fact that the United States was successfully decrypting enemy radio transmissions was a highly guarded secret. Any intelligence learned from radio interceptions had to be handled very carefully. Transmission of information learned also had to be by the most careful, secret means possible. Hence, the code talkers were pulled into service.

Cryptological aids and the intricate devices that were used could not be brought to the Lunga perimeter for fear of capture by the enemy. The best alternative seemed to be their ace in the hole—the code talkers.

Woken early, before first light, Redhawk and Johns were hustled over to the radio shack. They were alert, and a current of excitement made Redhawk's eyes glitter.

"Do you men think you can send and receive messages in complete secrecy?" an officer demanded crisply, and Redhawk didn't hesitate.

"Yes, sir."

Along with other means of gathering information, the second lieutenant, Roger Harwell—who became the middle man for messages between Vandegrift and other authorized officers in his command—secured intelligence by ships that were equipped with the necessary crypto devices to successfully decode intricate messages, by special air couriers and even by visitors to Cactus. Those last were only of the highest rank, of course, including Nimitz himself. A select few were on a strictly limited distribution list for radio intelligence.

Redhawk, Johns, Smith, and Brown were among those select few, in positions of highest confidentiality. They were the team who would send and decode, and their messages would be relayed to the commanders.

The plan Harwell relayed to the code talkers was simple enough: A radio station was to be set up on a ridge south of the airfield, equipped with cryptological devices of a high grade. Along with those devices for decoding enemy messages, the code talkers were to perfect their training.

"Show 'em what you can do, boys," Harwell, an easygoing Southerner, said with a smile. "I've heard that you guys are the best, and that's what it's going to take to beat the Japs on their home ground."

"Sir, I understand that you have a key position here," Redhawk said, and Harwell's easygoing manner subtly altered to a shrewd study of the young Navajo.

"True enough," he said after a moment. "But my main function is to coordinate intelligence."

Redhawk nodded silently. He had heard that Harwell had been assigned as a special assistant to the chief of staff for *all* communications with higher headquarters, and that covered a much larger field than just intercepting intelligence. If anyone could see that the code talkers got their fair chance to prove themselves, it would be Harwell.

Early that morning, the Japanese made a brief, futile effort to take Henderson Field. The arrival of the Cactus Air Force was a dangerous threat to enemy troops, and they threw themselves at the marines with fierce energy. A quick response managed to repulse the enemy, but intelligence learned that a powerful enemy naval fleet was gliding toward Guadalcanal. It had been gathering strength for two weeks, and now the intent was to protect the landing of more ground troops as well as to draw U.S. carriers into a battle.

Then Sergeant Major Joshua Ganza staggered back into the CP with a chilling tale: He had been captured by an enemy patrol while out scouting east of the First Marine lines. After tying Ganza to a tree, the taunting Japanese soldiers had tortured him with their bayonets. Slicing ribbons of flesh from his body and inflicting deep cuts and gashes, they tried to force information about American defenses from the native scout who had recently rejoined Gibson's constabulary. When Ganza didn't talk, the enemy had vented their frustration on him, then left him for dead. After chewing through the ropes binding him, he managed to break loose and return to the lines to give warning that the Japanese movement had begun.

The earlier intercepted message that the Japanese had left Truk on the fifteenth had been correct; they were at their destination—Guadalcanal. Papers that had been captured by the Brush patrol of the First Marines did not contain detailed information as to where and when the enemy would strike. It had been a stroke of luck to capture the papers at all.

Captain Charles Brush had led a patrol east of the perimeter on the evening of August 19, after having learned from native scouts that fresh enemy troops were reported in the vicinity. Brush had been given a specific mission to search out and destroy an enemy observation and radio post, some thirty-five miles to the east. After crossing the Tenaru and heading east, the patrol—including four of Gibson's constables—spotted a large group of Japanese officers and soldiers near Koli Point. That was only five miles east of marine lines.

Stealthily laying out an ambush among the coconut palms near the beach, the patrol managed to surprise the enemy, killing all but one. Returning to the division CP with a huge booty of captured documents, the marines learned that the ambushed enemy was only the first of a much larger body of troops to follow. They were army, not naval troops, and the marines now knew that Colonel Kiyanao Ichiki was the commanding officer.

The First Marines were to man the defenses on the eastern side of the perimeter and had been ordered to extend the line farther inland. It was a tense situation. During the night the marine outposts heard the unmistakable furtive movements of enemy troops to the front. As they were just beyond the Tenaru, they were moved to the western side.

At 0300 hours, a company of two hundred Japanese soldiers attacked. They charged out of thick brush and coconut palms, with machine-gun and mortar fire as cover, screaming at the top of their lungs. In a frenzied mass that looked like one jointed wave, they rushed the sandbar.

The barbed wire that the marines had prudently

erected as a last line defense snagged most of them, but a few managed to fight their way through the lethal coils. Heavy barrages of gunfire drove the rest back to regroup. An hour before dawn, they charged again in a strengthened attack. Some of the enemy even waded through the shallows to circumvent the barbed wire, trying to get through the rear defenses at the sandbar. Once more, the Japanese were repulsed with heavy losses of life.

The enemy's front was the Tenaru River, running a rough north to south line. The shoreline ran east and west. It was the plan to take troops—and tanks, if possible—around the enemy's southern flank. Then a sharp drive northward would push the enemy to the sea. The marines already holding the line at the river were to prevent any further advance, thus boxing in the enemy from two sides.

Redhawk, Johns, and Weintraub were sent forward with the reinforcement troops around the southern flank. One of the communication lines had been put out of commission, and they were to repair it. The break in the line was between an advance post and Colonel Potter.

Sniper fire popped loudly as the marines moved through the brush and coconut groves. It grew louder the closer they got to the front, and the three men moved very cautiously. They had separated from the main body to find the break, and now they were more vulnerable than ever.

Walking low and bent, with their gear rattling much too loudly to suit them, they moved from tree to tree, pausing to listen before moving out again. Here the brush was thick and high, providing excellent cover for enemy snipers.

Redhawk stepped cautiously, looking for possible booby traps, the unusual leaf or twig jutting at an odd angle. It was dangerous even walking through the jungles. He was looking for a telltale sign that the cable—which was visibly strung for easy location—had been cut in two by enemy fire. A freshly chewed crater several hundred yards past the coconut grove gave him what he was looking for. Mortar fire had severed the thick phone cable, and they crouched in the dirt and dead leaves to repair it as swiftly as possible.

"Damnit!" Weintraub said, ducking as an artillery burst hit near them. "That was too close for comfort."

Looking up from splicing the thick cable, Redhawk asked him, "How close is comfortable?"

A faint grin quivered nervously on his face as Weintraub replied, "Somewhere up around Tokyo."

"Too close," Johns said without looking up. "Maybe near Berlin."

Weintraub acknowledged the joke with a tight nod and shaky laugh. "Yeah, maybe that's comfortable enough."

The repair job was completed in record time, with the three men listening to every sound. A rifle grenade burst nearby, spitting dirt into the air in an arcing shower that rained down on their helmets. They gathered up their tools and ran for cover. Rattling chains of piercing enemy machine-gun fire cut through the noise of the explosions.

They pushed ahead to rejoin their unit, waiting between the lethal rounds of gunfire until a pause, then moving forward again. Finally, they saw the glitter of sunlight on the river and the smooth curving wash of grayish sand that confined it before allowing it to run out to the sea. A grove of slender, shadowy coconut trees hid the Japanese just across the ribbon of water.

Diving for the cover of a newly dug foxhole as

another burst of machine-gun fire rattled, they just managed to keep from being "illuminated" as Weintraub called it.

"Don't you mean *eliminated?*" Redhawk had asked him, but he'd shaken his head.

"No, *illuminated* is the word. Once a man's been shot, it's illuminating, indeed."

"No argument there," Johns had said, and the discussion had ended.

Now they lay in the foxhole with dirt up their nose and their butts in the ground, grateful for the lack of illumination.

A Japanese had been taken prisoner, and Colonel Potter had him questioned. Seeming unafraid and composed, the colonel strolled calmly across the open ground, heedless of possible sniper fire. An interpreter interrogated the wounded prisoner, but the answers were less than satisfactory. The man seemed more frightened than hostile and evinced surprise upon learning he was on Guadalcanal.

"Apparently, the Japanese don't even tell their soldiers where they're being sent," Potter observed with a shake of his head. "And their front line is a hundred yards ahead of us."

Redhawk couldn't resist looking across the Tenaru to the coconut grove. Death lurked in its shadows. It came visiting in the form of .25's popping from the grove across the river. He scrunched down in the foxhole again, while the *ping* of bullets whizzed overhead.

"Where the hell are we, anyway?" Weintraub muttered a few moments later, and someone down the line answered him.

"Hell Point."

"How apt," came Weintraub's faint comment. "For us or them?"

"Them," was the laughing reply.

"Ah."

Redhawk couldn't help grinning at him. The serious-faced bodyguard looked slightly pale. "You are not enjoying this?"

Weintraub gave him a sick smile. "Having the time of my life," was his unconvincing answer.

"Me, too.

Redhawk ducked as another barrage of sniper fire cut through the air and chewed into a palm behind them. Bits of bark clawed into his back and showers of dirt from a tossed grenade pounded down in a rattling wave. When it cleared, he lifted his head again.

"That was close," Johns observed calmly. He shouldered his weapon and squinted along the sight, placidly picking out a target. He waited with supreme patience for a careless enemy to provide him with one.

"Wasting your time, buddy," a marine said. "They're out of our range right now." He hunkered down in the foxhole and fished in his helmet for a cigarette. His weathered face crinkled into what passed for a smile. "You guys look mean as hell and tough as nails. Except for your squeamish partner there." He gestured to Weintraub.

Affronted, Weintraub said indignantly, "I'm not squeamish, just careful!"

Shrugging, the marine said, "Since we're sharing quarters right now, I might as well tell you that rule number one is to stay under cover. The Nips play by the same rules sometimes." He lit the cigarette. "Take your time. When Crawford comes up from the other side, he'll flush those bastards like a good hunting dog flushes a covey of quail."

"Then it'll be like a shootin' gallery," another Marine said. "Give me a cigarette, Tarrant."

Tarrant, the marine who'd offered advice, shrugged. *"Semper fi,* buddy," he said, but dug into his helmet again and fished out another cigarette. The marine grinned back at him.

"Next one's on me, Tarrant. When we get back to the CP, anyway."

Tarrant gave a noncommittal grunt. "I hear ya."

Redhawk didn't have to ask what *"semper fi"* meant. He'd already learned that it usually meant "take care of yourself out here."

"Were you here last night?" he asked Tarrant.

"Yeah. It got pretty hot. Some of our men managed to make it up to the point of the sandbar last night when the Japs were pouring it on pretty heavy. Those bastards put up flares that were like the noonday sun, and we took some bad losses. Sonuvabitches." Tarrant shook his head, then ducked as a mortar hit close by, and dirt and leaves rained down on them. "Shit. My cigarette's out. And that was the last one."

Redhawk produced a pack from his helmet and offered one to Tarrant. He took it with a nod of thanks, and his eyes crinkled at the corners as he grinned. "You're with the Fifth Division, aren't you? What the hell are you doing out here?"

"We volunteered to fix some wire."

"And decided to stay for the festivities," Weintraub added, shifting position in the dirt.

"Regretting it?"

"Oh, no. I love getting shot at. I rank it right up there with a sharp stick in the eye."

Tarrant laughed. "You shoulda' been here this morning."

"What'd I miss?"

"Some of the Nips swam across the lagoon under cover of dark this morning. They hid in some abandoned tank on the river bank. Then those bastards set up a machine-gun position that nearly scoured us." His face was sober as he said in a soft tone, "Every man who tried to man the artillery piece on the bank got hit. We lost some damn good men this morning."

There was a moment of silent reverence for the lost men, then Johns tactfully changed the subject.

"How'd you know we were with the Fifth?" Johns asked him.

Tarrant looked at them for a moment without speaking, then shrugged. "I've seen you around here. Thought at first that you were mercenaries they'd paid to come in here, cause you look so damn mean. I asked around and found out about you hotshot communications experts a while back."

"We're not the only Indians on Canal," Johns pointed out, and Tarrant nodded.

"Yeah, but you're the meanest-looking ones."

"Only when you get to know them," Weintraub interrupted Tarrant. "Then you realize that unless they scalp their quota for the day, they just ain't happy. Why . . ."

A fierce barrage of withering fire interrupted the conversation, and an order came down the line to move forward.

"Here we go!" Tarrant said, heaving himself up and out of the trench.

Redhawk, Johns, Weintraub and the other marines were right behind him. They ran in zigzagging lines from tree to tree, crouching over and expecting at any moment to feel the hot slam of a bullet.

It was common knowledge that the enemy often hid in the treetops, and Redhawk spotted a slight movement overhead as he paused beneath a slender coconut tree. Without speaking, he gave a soft birdcall that caught Johns's attention. When Johns turned around, he pointed up to the branches bunched at the tree's top.

Lifting their M-1s', Redhawk and Johns took careful aim. Redhawk's heart was pounding, and his mouth was dry as he squinted along the sight and trained the barrel on the spot where he'd seen movement. When the tree fronds rustled again, ever so slightly, he squeezed the trigger. Johns fired simultaneously, and the enemy plummeted silently to the ground almost at their feet.

There wasn't time to savor their victory. A sharp burst of machine-gun fire came from the sandbar that closed the mouth of the Tenaru, and they were ordered forward.

"Men, there's enemy on the lee side of the sandbar," an officer said. "Hit them with mortar fire."

Curving gently toward the sea, the sandbar provided perfect cover for the Japanese. Steep shoulders thrust up like a graded road so that the marines could not see over to the other side. The enemy had set up a machine-gun nest and periodically raked the marines with a killing barrage.

In a fierce, pitched battle, Redhawk discovered, there were many distractions. Somehow, he and Johns became separated when they ran for cover, and he ended up beside Bobby Tarrant. They waited behind a coconut palm while mortars were trained on the sandbar.

"Fuckin' crazy, ain't it?" Tarrant asked without expecting an answer. It was one of those casual observations that seemed too true to be acknowledged, so Redhawk just nodded.

Caught between marine and enemy fire, they decided to stay in one place until it subsided. The world was filled with enough noise to shake the ground, and Redhawk swallowed hard. He couldn't recall the last time he'd heard nothing but silence.

It seemed too long ago to be able to remember.

To the right, a line of marines sprawled behind stacks of sandbags, firing out to sea. For a moment, he wondered why they were wasting ammunition, then he saw the dark speck frantically swimming in the water. Small waterspouts spewed into the air wherever bullets struck.

"They've got one of those bastards out there," Tarrant said. "That Nip better hope he's got fins, 'cause our boys mean business."

Redhawk looked past the swimmer to the wide expanse of sea. "Where is he swimming to? I don't see anyplace he could reach . . ."

Tarrant gave a short bark of laughter. "He's trying to swim up behind us. If he made it—as some did earlier—he'd toss a grenade and try to blow us all to hell."

Redhawk's attention was once more distracted by the successful hit of a mortar on the machine-gun nest dug into the sandbar. There was the distinctive *whump* of the piece being fired, the soft, whistling sigh as it sailed through the air, then the bone-jarring tremor of the ground as it landed and exploded. The action was repeated three times, and a shrieking figure jerked up from his hiding place and began to run. In a split second, there was no place for him to run. The shell made a direct hit, and the furiously fleeing man just disintegrated in a cloud of smoke and debris.

Flashes of bright explosions dotted the coconut grove beyond the river, and wisps of hazy smoke drifted eerily through the trees. At the rear of the grove, the heavy thunder of rifles and machine-gun fire shredded the smoke.

Breathing heavily, Redhawk and Tarrant made a run for more cover as machine guns began to chatter to their right.

"They're tryin' to cross the river again," Tarrant said when they paused. He leaned back against the curving trunk of the tree and wiped beads of sweat from his face. "Some kinda' shit, huh?"

Redhawk nodded wordlessly. His M-1 felt clumsy in his hands, and he felt the familiar fluttering in his belly that made him wonder if he were a coward or just smart enough to be scared. Was there a difference? Could he tell if there was?

When he and Tarrant ran to another trench and dove in, he found himself beside Johns and Weintraub again.

"Welcome," Weintraub said through white, set lips, then lapsed into tense silence. A faint trickle of blood slid down the side of his face, and Redhawk glanced at Johns.

"Tree limb."

Redhawk nodded. Even the land conspired against them. A simple tree limb had dug a nasty wound into Weintraub's cheek.

Word came down the line that Colonel Crawford was coming up behind the enemy.

"Keep your fire down!" was the order.

Colonel Potter stalked in front of the firing lines, repeating it over and over. "Keep your fire down. Those are our people coming in at the rear."

Sparing a moment of admiration for Potter, who walked as calmly as if on a Sunday afternoon stroll in the park, Redhawk crawled forward on his belly until he was able to bring up his weapon and position it. He could already see the shadowy figures of the enemy being pressed toward them by the advancing marines, and laid his cheek against the stock of his M-1. The enemy ran along a narrow strip of beach edging the coconut grove from where they'd inflicted such heavy casualties on the marines all day.

His finger tightened on the trigger, but before he could take aim, a rapid *bratt-bratt-bratt* mowed down the running men like green grass. They lay still and did not rise again.

"Hot damn!" someone crowed excitedly, "Crawford's circling the wagons!"

"I don't know what you're so fuckin' excited about," Tarrant drawled. "That means that those Nips are gonna give us hell as Crawford pushes them from the rear."

Caught in a vise, the enemy would likely advance in sheer desperation and attempt another crossing of the river. Red tracers streaked through the air, and more yellow explosions shattered the coconut grove.

"No firing unless you can hit your target!" Potter ordered, and word was passed down the line.

Rolling back to suck in a deep breath, Redhawk happened to catch Weintraub's eye. "Ambulances are behind us. Do you want to—"

"No," Weintraub cut in. "It's only a little scratch. Besides, what would you guys do without me? With all these Japanese running around, you might get blown away by mistake."

"And miss this?" Redhawk waved a hand toward the burning streaks of smoke from the tracers, the withering bursts of artillery fire, and the erratic thumps of the huge mortars.

Weintraub grinned. "Yeah. Some party."

Redhawk felt a surge of emotion he didn't understand. He wasn't used to feeling something for another man besides detachment or the affection of blood ties. This was different. There was a sort of dignified courage in Weintraub that made him feel close to him, made him want to protect him.

"Lookit our guys!" Tarrant shouted, and Redhawk's head swerved to look where he was pointing.

Huge tanks rumbled as clumsily as sea turtles across the ground, mowing down foliage and anything else in their path.

"They're headed for the sandbar," Johns said with rising excitement. "Look!"

After a brief pause on the sand spit, the monster machines rattled ferociously into the coconut grove. Their metal treads mercilessly shredded trees, while the guns pivoted in slow motion, spitting out flame and death. Tall palms fell slowly, almost gently, colliding with other trees in a domino effect. Screaming enemy ran from the tanks that would chew them up without effort, fleeing into the hands of the marines and fusillades of bullets. Some tried vainly to disable the tanks with grenades and rifles, but most died trying.

The canister shells of the tanks ruthlessly pounded the grove, and Japanese soldiers ran like frightened birds.

"Damn, I didn't realize there were so fucking many!" Tarrant breathed softly.

Redhawk silently echoed the sentiment. Swarms of enemy scurried like ants from disturbed hills, streaming out of hiding places in underbrush. Desperate bursts of machine-gun fire made little impact upon the mechanized beasts.

Then one of the tanks jerked to a sudden halt as a blinding flash of light exploded beneath its treads. It settled in a tilted motion, and the great gun stopped. One of the other tanks lumbered toward it, then another, and moved alongside.

"They're taking off the crew," someone said, and Redhawk realized he'd been holding his breath. The tank had looked peculiarly vulnerable once halted, like a crippled animal. The other tank roared on through the grove in a devastating rumble of fire.

It wasn't long before the tanks had flushed out more enemy and nearly leveled swathes through the grove. Without them, it would have taken the marines long hours and many losses to flush the Japanese, who had been very firmly entrenched.

Intense firing resumed on the front lines, and enemy soldiers began to grow desperate as the vise closed in on them. There was no inclination for mercy on the part of the marines. No quarter would be given. The enemy had proven that he had no mercy, and that is how he would be treated.

Fleeing Japanese were shot down, some before they could reach the beach, some before they reached the water, and some after they'd managed to dive into the sea. Swimming enemy heads made tempting targets, and the marines did their best to shoot them all. It wasn't easy. The tiny dark dots in the water were difficult to hit, but each man made a supreme effort to do so. After all, one escaped enemy could always be dangerous.

Redhawk advanced with the others, shooting his way closer to the grove that still held pockets of resistance. Japanese soldiers fought back with bayonets and samurai swords, slashing marines ferociously, hacking at them with skillful strokes that severed hands and heads. Redhawk used his bayonet to parry the swing of a sword and saw the faint glitter of light along its deadly curved edge. The weapon met his rifle with a solid clang and bounced away, and he took the opportunity to slide his bayonet into the screaming enemy with a cool, deliberate thrust that easily skewered him. He jerked his bayonet free. It was a terrifying yet exhilarating experience, and he had no time to think about dying.

It's a good day to die, my son.

Men beside him fell away at times, but he

couldn't stop to tend them. He had to move forward, over tangled brush and through the trees, aiming, firing, diving for cover, rising to fire again. It was a mechanical process, done without conscious thought, nothing but the sheer will to survive urging him on.

Finally, the artillery fire ceased and mortars began. The marines watched from trenches and foxholes as the huge orange flashes filled the grove like obscene flowers. It was too risky for those across the river to fire into the grove for fear of hitting their own men. Those at the rear were busily wiping out the enemy. Machine-gun fire was rampant and sharp.

Lifting his head to peer over the lip of the trench, Redhawk saw the pile of Japanese dead on the sandbar, stacked like cordwood with arms and legs flung out at odd angles. Across the spit of sand jutting into the Tenaru he could see Crawford's men cautiously advancing in groups, rifles held at the ready, tension written in each man's features.

"Heads down," came the order as Crawford's troops fired at wandering enemy soldiers. No one wanted to be hit by a stray bullet.

It began to grow quiet, with only occasional bursts of fire, and slowly Redhawk rose along with the others.

"Check out the dead," Potter ordered, and it fell to Redhawk, Johns, and Weintraub to do so. They moved along the spit of sand with rifles held at the ready, fingers curved on the triggers. Any sign of movement was the sign to fire. Taut as a bowstring, Redhawk stepped over dead bodies. Age-old warnings against dead spirits were firmly tamped down, and he refused to allow his mind to travel in that direction. This was different. He had to obey orders, and the orders were to check the dead. He swallowed hard and saw from Willie Johns's face that he was having the same thoughts. Weintraub was muttering something in Hebrew.

A strong stench permeated the area in the grove, an almost tangible wave rising in the air. It was the smell of burned flesh and scorched hair; it was the smell of death. The humid heat had already puffed some of the bodies into grotesque, glossy balloons. Bodies shredded by bullets and shrapnel looked as if they had been shoved through a meat grinder, and especially revolting were the enemies who had been run down by the tanks.

Occasionally, a body would catch Redhawk's eye simply by the unbelievable posture of death, the grinning head charred to a cinder, the eyeballs blackened by flamethrowers, and the hair completely gone. Flesh and bones peeled away and left hanging like half-peeled bananas; intestines drooping obscenely from body cavities; arms gone or splintered into unrecognizable masses of flesh; or, the most horrible to him, an unmarked body with no visible sign of a wound but the man stiff with death.

After the first shock of such horrifying deaths, it lost its ability to do so again. He merely glanced over them now, looking for signs of life. Life was dangerous in the enemy.

The muffled sound of movement struck Redhawk, and he turned just in time to see a "dead" Japanese half-rise from the pile of bodies and feebly toss a grenade. Firing in an automatic motion, Redhawk heard the thunk of the bullet strike the enemy. It was a peculiar sound. The grenade bounced harmlessly, its pin still in place.

"Good shooting," Johns said tonelessly. Redhawk nodded. They moved on, stepping cautiously, heads turning constantly to look for signs of life. Two more Japanese were found alive, their faces contorted in hatred and pain, their eyes glittering strangely up at their killers. M-1's fired almost simultaneously and they jerked, then lay still.

Tarrant came up behind them, his voice soft. "The dead are treacherous little bastards, aren't they? I've seen 'em try to stab a man as he passes, or shoot him." He lifted his rifle and began to methodically shoot each body. "Can't be too careful," he said when he paused to reload. "Potter said to make sure they're dead enough not to wound any more of our boys."

More marines solemnly joined those on the sand spit, firing into the bodies. Redhawk was reminded of how the enemy had thrust their bayonets again and again into wounded marines that night at Matanikau, and he did not let himself feel any sympathy for the Japanese. They had felt none for them.

The continuous line of fire and bullets, striking bodies and water, churned up the mud. It frothed in a reddish brown swirl. A fresh burst of fire from the grove indicated that more enemy had been found. Redhawk detected the telltale sound of the .25's the enemy used.

"Snipers," someone said, and they spread out on the sand spit so they wouldn't be such excellent targets.

The battle at the Tenaru was almost over. By the time the casualties were counted, twenty-eight marines had been killed and seventy-two wounded. But the Japanese had suffered the heaviest losses, with over eight hundred bodies counted and a few prisoners.

The attempt to recapture Henderson Field had been crushed. It was reported that Colonel Ichiki was not among the few enemy who had escaped to

Taivu Point. He had burned and shredded his colors, then put a gun to his head and committed hari-kari on the battlefield.

"Saved us trouble and a bullet," was Tarrant's pithy remark when the marines discovered Ichiki. Redhawk agreed.

Chapter Fourteen
Hot Air

The weather didn't cooperate with the marines or their newly arrived air support at all. It was too thick to offer much visibility, and the sky fighting was hot and intense.

Word came via radio that a formidable Japanese force was on the way to Guadalcanal—two cruisers, three destroyers, four transports. All commanders on land and air sweated over defensive plans for hours.

The dive-bombers sent out to intercept returned without having found any action. At dusk on the twenty-third, thirty more planes from the *Saratoga* landed, refueling hopes that a confrontation with the enemy would be successful.

"Ever get tired of waiting on the enemy to do something first?" Weintraub asked Sergeant Jones. They were sitting just outside the row of tents stretched over their shallow depressions scraped in the dirt, and for once were enjoying some leisure time.

Jones shrugged and stretched. "It's not always that way. Just sometimes."

"Seems like lately we are always hitting back, not hitting first."

"That'll change," Jones predicted, and Redhawk had the same thought.

"Are you bored with the waiting?" he asked Weintraub.

"No, but it's like waiting for the other shoe to fall."

"Shoe? . . ."

"Just a saying," Weintraub explained. "You know, like . . . uh . . . birds of a feather flock together."

"What?"

"Never mind." Weintraub shook his head, rubbing absently at the raw scratch on his cheek. "It doesn't matter anyway. When our boys decide to—"

The droning of airplane engines ended his sentence, and all four men jerked up their heads to look at the sky.

"Tojo Time's over for the day, and that don't sound like Louie the Louse," Jones murmured. "Better take cover."

Bombs whistled through the air and marines scrambled for cover, reminding Redhawk of a disturbed anthill. Bombs exploded at intervals, showering the area with dirt and metal fragments, chewing up portions of the airfield.

"That should make the Seabees happy," Weintraub muttered. "They love getting out there and patching up the airfield."

"They're very good at it," Redhawk commented, then ducked as another bomb hit close by. "They do it very fast and very efficient," he added when it had stopped raining dirt.

"It ain't like they haven't had enough practice," Jones said dryly. "We've been hit every day since we've been on this fucking island."

"Those Japs should have run out of bombs by now," Weintraub said, then ducked as another bomb came screaming down out of the sky.

"Damn! That was a bad one," Jones said when the huge explosion shook the ground with shock waves.

When the all clear went out, the marines found a huge crater near the CP. It was fifteen feet deep and twenty-five feet across, and hot metal fragments had peppered the CP and even the general's tent.

Redhawk and Johns were called to the radio, and they took off at a run.

"See if you can find out what's going on!" was the brisk order, and they began to crank the radio.

Ship to shore radio contact was made, and it took a while for them to piece together what was happening outside the small world of Guadalcanal.

The Japanese were attempting to land the rest of Ichiki's Twenty-eighth Infantry Regiment and a thousand troops of the Fifth Yokosuka Special Naval Landing Force. That force was on a transport, the other troops in four destroyers converted for their use. These men, Redhawk learned, were under the command of Raizo Tanaka. The good news was that the U.S. Navy was sending the first large supply ships to Guadalcanal since the marines had landed.

"Hot damn!" Weintraub said, his eyes lighting. "Three square meals a day instead of one!"

"More cigarettes," Jones said. "More rifles and ammo. More tanks, land movers . . ."

"Broads?" Weintraub suggested with a comical wag of his brows, and Jones shook his head.

"You're a degenerate, W.W."

"Yeah, well, I've got a lot of company!"

Company or not, supplies didn't get there quickly. Each side, Japanese and American, had a double goal: to give distant support to the supply and reinforcement runs, and to successfully engage the other's main naval fleet if possible. To accomplish this, the main striking forces of opposing navies remained within carrier-plane range of their convoys but did begin moving cautiously toward each other.

Redhawk received the information that the Japanese were approaching from Truk, as planned. American forces patrolled east of the Canal. Inevitably, they clashed.

American carrier planes found a small Japanese carrier, the *Ryojo,* and sank her. Two larger carriers, the *Zuikaku* and the *Shokaku,* were left to the enemy. On the American side, there were only two carriers, the *Enterprise* and the *Saratoga,* as the smaller *Wasp* had been sent south to refuel.

While American carrier planes were bombing the *Ryojo,* flights from the large Japanese flattops attacked American carriers. The *Enterprise* was heavily damaged by three direct bomb hits and limped toward Pearl Harbor for repairs. The remaining *Saratoga* didn't dare risk nighttime attacks by enemy battleships closing in, and steamed south.

While the carriers were battling two hundred miles from the island, marine fliers from Henderson Field intercepted raiders from the doomed *Ryojo.* They managed to bring down sixteen bombers and Zero fighters, losing three of their own planes to the enemy.

The following day, while the Japanese steamed down from the north, marine dive-bombers zoomed in for the kill. They hit and hit hard, sinking the huge transport-carrying naval troops. An added coup was crippling the *Jintsu,* Japanese Admiral Tanaka's flagship. As it floundered back toward Truk, Tanaka switched his flag to an escorting transport, but his luck ran out. An AAF

Flying Fortress from the New Hebrides sank one of his rescuing destroyers.

Finally, the marines were enjoying a run of good fortune mixed in with the bad. A naval squadron of dive-bombers from the *Enterprise* flew to Henderson Field. The Cactus Air Force, battle-weary and battered after only four days of hot action, celebrated the new arrivals.

A few days later, more new arrivals touched down on the runway, P-400's, the souped-up versions of the P-40's. These planes had fearsome teeth painted on the metal snouts, like the Flying Tigers, but were used mostly for reconnaissance since they did not have the needed high-pressure oxygen bottles for fighting.

Redhawk and Johns worked in twenty-four-hour shifts, manning the radio to establish contact with the carriers, trying to piece together the results of battles and enemy strength. It wasn't easy, especially when the Japanese seemed more determined than ever to step up their air raids.

Natives of the island brought the horrifying news of what had happened to Catholic missionaries living among the islanders. Japanese survivors of Ichiki's command had taken two priests and three nuns prisoners, then attempted to force them to enter the American lines and spread false rumors about the strength of the enemy. Refusing on the grounds that they did not engage in secular matters but only matters of the Church, the two priests were tortured and killed, as were two of the nuns. The torture lasted a week. . . .

"Goddamn them all to hell!" Kryzminsky snarled, and there wasn't a marine there who didn't share his sentiment. Hatred for the enemy was growing, and the marines were now spoiling for another fight.

"We smeared their asses on Tenaru, and we'll smear 'em again!" was the general opinion.

In spite of added air support, Tojo Time went on as usual. The familiar screech of the siren put Redhawk on edge, and he glanced over at Johns as they sat hunched over the radios in the communications hut.

"They're back."

Johns didn't bother to ask whom he meant. He'd heard the sirens, too. They were both tired, having been on the radio for hours without rest. Most of the information they gave or received was useless, but some of the news of what was going on was vital. It gave a fair indication of enemy strength and position.

As the droning of planes grew loud, Redhawk took off his earphones and stepped out of the hut to look up at the sky. His stomach lurched. It looked like the sky was full of them!

"Come out!" he shouted, half turning back to the hut, afraid that the enemy would aim for the radio. He was right. A low-flying plane managed to avoid the ninety-mm antiaircraft, buzzing low, almost brushing the tops of the palms. "Johns!" he shouted again, diving for cover into a trench dug behind a stack of sandbags.

Bullets chewed up the ground all around him, stitching across the sandbags in neat rows, spilling sand all over him as he lay with his arms over his head, wondering where he'd left his helmet. All around him, he could hear the *boom-boom-boom* of the antiaircraft, and miraculously, the Zero still kept flying. It rose, banked, and returned in another swooping dive. Redhawk heard the unmistakable sigh of a bomb being unloaded just as Johns stepped out of the hut in a running dive.

"Take cover!" he screamed, half rising, but Johns

was still too close to the hut and too far away from the sandbags and trench. The bomb hit, knocking Redhawk back into the trench and peppering him with pellets of dirt that stung like bullets. His ears rang, and a red mist hung in front of his eyes. For a brief, dazed moment, he wondered if he'd been hit, then remembered Johns.

Crawling back up, he saw Willie Johns lying beneath what remained of the radio hut. He was still, his helmet at an awkward angle and his arms flung over his head.

A wrenching gasp tore from his throat as Redhawk surged out of his trench and toward his cousin. Scrabbling over debris, planks, roofing, and the scattered framework of the hut, Redhawk managed to tear away most of what was on top of his cousin. He rolled him over and was relieved to see his eyelids flutter. Johns's normally dark copper complexion was a mottled gray, and blood smeared one side of his face. Redhawk gave him a shake.

"Are you hurt bad?" he asked in Navajo, and Johns blinked up at him. For a moment he didn't appear to recognize Redhawk, then he managed a shaky smile.

"Did I fall off a mountain?" he asked, and Redhawk realized that he was dazed.

"Don't move him," a voice from behind said, and he recognized Sergeant Jones's authoritative tone. "He could have a concussion. I've sent for a corpsman, and we'll get him over to sick bay."

"Great," Weintraub said. He looked as rough as Redhawk, with dirt and torn clothing. Redhawk looked up at him and saw the concern in his eyes.

The camp was frenetic with activity, men scurrying from blazes to bombed-out buildings. As they put Johns on a litter and ran him over to the sick bay, Redhawk trotting beside him, a Zero made a last pass. Antiaircraft knocked it from the air, and a ragged cheer went up from the ground.

The final score was one marine killed and ten wounded—with seven Japanese bombers and five Zeros shot down.

"Not too bad, huh?" Weintraub asked, and Johns looked up from the cot where he was recuperating and grinned.

Mosquito netting swung gently with the wind, and the blankets he was on were soft and clean. Sick bay was filled with men who'd suffered injuries or come down with malaria from the infested insects. Long rows of convalescents lined the open-air building. Just as many marines were down with malaria and dysentery as were with injuries. The bitter yellow Atabrine tablets they were given prevented some, but not all of them from getting it. Part of marine issue was Halzedone and salt tablets, to purify the water and keep a man sweating.

"I'm a statistic, right?" Johns joked.

"Right, but you're one of the ones who's gonna make it outta here," Sergeant Jones said. "In fact, I think you're just goldbricking, Chief."

Johns managed a soft laugh, and his dark eyes shone in a face that had regained its normal color. "I know what that means, and maybe you're right. They serve better food in here, and I don't have to sleep in the rain."

"No nurses, though," Weintraub pointed out, and they all smiled at his attempt at humor.

Redhawk said nothing, but his stoic expression didn't fool any of them. He could see their thoughts in their eyes and was grateful they didn't mention it. Johns's injury had been a blow to him. He hadn't considered how he might feel if his cousin were killed until then. It just wasn't something he'd given much thought. His own death, yes, but not his cousin's. That had seemed incomprehensible to him until the bomb had shattered his complacency. Even the Matanikau ambush had not made him think about it. Now he knew how quickly death could come to even his cousin.

"Hey, Johnny," Weintraub said, his voice soft with a concern that made Redhawk stiffen with agonized embarrassment, "he'll be okay."

"Thanks. I know he will." Redhawk paused and shuffled his feet, then glanced up at the much taller Weintraub. "We are like brothers," he offered in an attempt to explain feelings he didn't really understand himself.

"Hey, I know that." Weintraub looked suddenly embarrassed himself and wished he hadn't begun a conversation that had become more personal than either of them were comfortable with. Sometimes it hit too close to home to grow personal. It made a man think about his own feelings too much.

"Hey," Redhawk said, imitating Weintraub's manner of speech, *"semper fi,* Mac!"

Weintraub grinned with relief. "Semper fi yourself, Chief!"

Nightly operations by the Japanese—which were called the "Cactus Express" by the marines—made Redhawk wonder how strong the enemy was growing on the island. He wasn't the only one who wondered about it. Top brass had the same concerns about the night movements by fast destroyers heavily laden with enemy troops and supplies. They landed and unloaded east and west of the Lunga perimeters at night, almost always shelling the camp and airfield as a sort of parting gesture.

Unfortunately for the frustrated Cactus Air Force, their operating range was approximately two hundred miles. The squadrons of enemy destroyers ranged north about three hundred miles until mid-afternoon, waiting out the light. Then, when the bombers at Henderson Field would only be able to get in one shot at them before nightfall, they would head southeastward at high speed and come within range. It was a hit-and-miss operation of unloading and fleeing homeward before the sun shone on the Cactus planes and allowed them to go after them.

Enemy forces were gradually building up on both sides of the marines.

Chapter Fifteen
Bloody Ridge

The day dragged on toward noon, a hot, sticky day. Redhawk and Kryzminsky were crossing from the sick bay toward the airfield when the sirens began to shrill. They looked up at the sky, gauging the time they had before having to take cover. The air raids were so frequent and regular that men didn't drop everything and run as they once had. Now they knew about how long they had before the planes would be overhead, dropping their loads on the airfield and surrounding camp.

"Hey," Kryzminsky said, nudging Redhawk with his elbow, "it's Tojo Time."

Redhawk nodded. He strapped on his helmet and walked toward the sandbag-entrenched foxhole, with Kryzminsky at his side. Sometimes the percussion of the bombs left him with a nosebleed, and as he slid into the dirt trench, he tried to remember to lever his body slightly upward to avoid concussion. Kryzminsky dropped in beside him and assumed a similar position as the planes drew closer.

"This is the time I hate the most," Kryzminsky muttered when they heard the bombs falling from the planes. "You never know where the fucking things will hit!"

"We're not on the airfield, and the odds are ten to one that we'll get hit hard here," Redhawk pointed out. He put his head in the crook of his arms as he heard the familiar sighing sound of a bomb falling and rattling with a metallic clunk through the air. It was close, but how close would it hit? He could feel Kryzminsky duck, too, and then the bomb exploded and the world in front of the sandbags disappeared for a moment.

Showers of debris pounded down on them, and he felt a sharp *thwack* on his back. Sucking in a quick breath, it took him a moment to realize that he wasn't badly hit, that it had only been dirt or possibly a tree branch. As the clouds of dust slowly began to settle and he could relax, he glanced over at Kryzminsky, who still had his head buried in his arms.

"I think it's over for a while," Redhawk said. "They never have time for more than one pass before our planes are giving them hell."

Kryzminsky made a funny sound, and Redhawk looked at him more closely. A fine film of dust and dirt coated his uniform, and his helmet was slightly askew.

"Hey, are you okay?" Redhawk asked, and when Kryzminsky didn't answer, he put out a hand to roll him over.

The marine fell back with a peculiar thump, his eyes wide open and his mouth slightly gaping. A small, neat hole in his temple trickled blood. He was dead.

Redhawk took the last puff of his cigarette and flipped the butt into the air, watching as it sailed in a glowing arc to the ground and lay there, a tiny beacon of light in the gathering gloom that gradually died. Dying was like that, he thought, life sometimes fading into nothing but empty ashes, sometimes extinguishing quickly. He'd seen it happen too many times in too many ways lately.

Men died lingering deaths from wounds or malaria; men died quickly, not even knowing how or why. He'd found himself becoming fatalistic about it, more so than usual. It was all a crapshoot, Kryzminsky had said.

"Hey, if it's your turn and you're in the wrong place at the wrong time . . . phffft! You're dead."

Now Kryzminsky was dead, his body buried in the square of ground neatly hewn from the Guadalcanal jungle. There were long rows of markers for men who had died in fierce, pitched battles, men who had died from malaria, men who had died by accident. Or were they all accidents? Redhawk had to wonder, sometimes, how one man could survive the total destruction of a radio hut and another man would be killed by a tiny bomb fragment, leaving the man next to him safe and untouched. Chance? Maybe. It didn't make much sense.

But then again, nothing made a lot of sense lately. He was glad Willie Johns was out of sick bay now, much thinner than he had been but still a familiar, safe sight. It had made him too unsettled when they'd been apart, and that bothered him. He'd grown too dependent on Johns in an odd way, having the nagging feeling in the back of his mind that their lives were inexplicably entwined and that if one died, both would die. And even more oddly, he felt no fear for his own life. His fears were for his cousin.

Johns had always been the more passive of the two, the one who followed wherever Redhawk led. He wasn't servile, but just always willing to let his cousin take charge. And he'd never complained when they'd both landed in trouble because of Redhawk, though Johns's older brother had. Jimmie Johns had frequently argued that Willie should not be so agreeable to their cousin's plans, that it always got him into trouble. But Jimmie was eight years older than Willie, and after their parents had died, he'd gone to work off the reservation, leaving Willie in the orphans' home with Redhawk. The two had grown inseparable.

The first mail call was the following day, with marines crowding around the jeep where a beleaguered soldier called out names and handed out the precious letters from home.

"This looks like maggots around a carcass," Weintraub muttered as he stood back, waiting for his name to be called out.

Redhawk jerked around to look at him and saw the faint lines of fret on his face. Then he understood. Every man there was anxious to hear from someone at home, someone who cared about them and who could remind them of what they were fighting for. He smiled slightly. He didn't expect letters. Who would write him? His only family was Willie Johns.

"Don't be so cheerful," he told Weintraub.

"Yeah, right."

Shrugging, Redhawk folded his arms across his chest and stood back, watching as names were called and men reacted with unrestrained enthusiasm or tightly held control. Some went off by themselves to read the important news from home and others shared with anyone who'd listen.

Willie Johns was surprised and pleased to get a letter from his brother. After being wounded in Germany, Jimmie had been sent back to Arizona and had discovered that Willie was in the marines.

"Listen to this!" Johns said excitedly, and Redhawk smiled as he read aloud, " 'I am very proud that you are in the service and know that you will do well. For being wounded at a place I'd never heard of until I was sent there, I received a medal. . . .' A medal! Do you think I will receive a medal for being injured?" he looked up to ask Redhawk.

"I don't think so, not when you were too slow to leave your post," Redhawk teased.

"Maybe you'll get a medal for being the dumbest marine still alive," Weintraub suggested with a straight face. "But there's pretty stiff competition on that one."

"You have many letters," Redhawk said, looking at the pile strewn across Weintraub's lap. "All from your women, I presume?"

A sly grin squared Weintraub's mouth. "Most of them. Let's see, my Aunt Fanny wrote me, and my Aunt Letty, and my cousin Sarah—you should see her, she's twenty-two and has a body like a dead stick—and of course, I have three or four letters from my mother." His expression sobered slightly, and he cleared his throat. "And a box of cookies that are probably too stale and hard to eat, but I'm willing to share." He held out a cardboard box.

Too polite to refuse but not certain he wanted to eat the unappealing treats, Redhawk took only one. "They're good," he said after biting into it. "Are these kosher?"

Weintraub laughed, his eyes narrowing in amusement as he surveyed the short, dark Marine. "You better believe it, Chief! Kosher! You guys have a lot to learn, I tell you, a lot."

After Weintraub had read aloud from several of his letters, punctuating them with funny descriptions of the writers or asides as to why they must have written, he asked Redhawk, "Don't you have anybody who writes to you, Chief? A girlfriend, maybe, or relatives?"

Shrugging, Redhawk said, "No, but it does not matter."

"No women? A good-looking guy like you?" Weintraub snorted rudely. "I don't buy that shit for a minute! I mean, Tarrant was right when he said you look mean as hell, but most women go for that stuff, a real tough-looking guy instead of a skinny string bean like me. Hey, with that square jaw that looks like you're just waiting on some poor sonuvabitch to try and put a fist on it, you can get away with a lot. You've got some meat on you, muscles on top of muscles. Women go for that stuff, boy."

Another shrug lifted his shoulders, and Redhawk managed an indifferent smile. "I don't see too many women back home. We never stayed in one place very long."

"But wasn't there any one girl?" Weintraub persisted. "Not even one?"

After a moment of silence, Redhawk gave a reluctant grin. "Yeah, one." He could feel Johns's curious glance and knew what his cousin was thinking. He looked over at him, one brow lifted slightly and saw awareness flare in Willie's dark eyes.

"Dansie Lonehorse," they both said at the same time, then laughed.

"Dansie Lonehorse?" Weintraub repeated slowly. "That sounds as bad as Ophelia Onyx Fernstrom." He grinned. "My first girlfriend. Her mother was a fan of Greek mythology and cheap jewelry."

They all laughed, and the talk turned to other subjects for a while.

Within a few hours, Redhawk and Johns were

back in the new radio hut, enmeshed in high priority transmissions. Something big was happening, and news trickled in to Cactus in bits and pieces. That night, in the lantern light spraying around the small dugout where the radios were set up, the news came in regarding enemy movements. Men clustered around the radio tuned to inter-air frequency, straining to hear reports from pilots about the enemy's activities.

Word came in that the Japanese had ships landing troops on the island and that the Cactus Air Force was trying to bomb them before they succeeded. Flares were dropped, but the pilots still had poor visibility and could not see the enemy.

"Am down to one thousand feet . . . visibility poor," came a crackling transmission over the radio set.

"Control, come in control . . . cannot locate enemy position, over. . . ."

". . . cruiser heading due east . . . fifteen minutes ago . . . she was making twenty knots . . . cannot locate now. . . ." another pilot reported.

"Do you know how many miles east of the field?" Redhawk asked into the mike, and flipped over to wait for a reply enveloped in static to come in.

"Ah, maybe fifteen miles," came the reply a few moments later.

Redhawk was instructed to report to all planes that the enemy was landing troops at Taivu Bay, fifteen miles east of the landing strip. He could hear inter-air discussions between the pilots who circled the scene blindly, unable to locate the enemy.

"Listen to this, sir," he told the communications officer on duty, and handed him the earphones.

". . . go down to five hundred feet," a voice

crackled, "and see if we can find the enemy. They should be right under us at that point. . . ."

But the next transmission indicated no success.

"Damnit!" one of the communications officers swore, his fists knotted in frustration. "How are we supposed to hit them if we can't see them?"

"The weather's too soupy," a captain said, and his face was just as frustrated.

Redhawk kept sending and receiving transmission, but it was after four in the morning before any definite news was reported. One plane relayed the information that three large landing boats had been sighted east of Taivu Point and was immediately corrected by another pilot saying they were one mile *west* of Taivu Point. The weather was still uncooperative, too thick to provide decent visibility for the planes to intercept.

The enemy made a bombing raid before daylight, but no damage was done to the radio dugout. Redhawk and Johns kept to the radio set, doggedly pulling as much information as they could from the beleaguered pilots. Three large landing boats were strafed by the fliers, and an Army captain made a report that his patrol flight had found six enemy boats on the beach near Taivu. There was no sign of the Japanese, no sign of activity, and no sign of the transport ships that must have launched the boats.

"It's not looking too good," Johns said wearily to Redhawk when they were relieved of duty for a while. They lay, exhausted, in their tent. "Only three of the P-400's are still flying. All of the others have been damaged or destroyed."

"Not in the air, though," Redhawk pointed out. "Most of the damage has been mechanical or ground shelling. And our ground crews are good at taking a damaged plane apart and using the parts for others."

Rolling over on his cot to look at his cousin, Johns said, "What is really the most frustrating is the lack of radio contact with the army planes. They don't receive on the navy band, and the twin broadcast system we fixed up is not that great. They can't pick up at any range over twenty miles."

"We need radios with air forward observers. The heavy foliage prevents the planes from seeing our colored panels, and that's what the pilots depend on." He was silent for a moment, then said in a more cheerful tone, "At least more transports have landed at Lunga Point, and we have supplies for a while."

"You mean more food," Johns corrected, and Redhawk grinned.

"Dah, more food. I've grown tired of finding my own."

Johns looked at him curiously. "Have you done so?"

"Just a few days ago, while you were still in sick bay. I ran into Tarrant—do you recall him?—in the bush, and he was complaining about being hungry all the time since we are on short rations." Sitting up, Redhawk swung his legs over the side of his cot and said quietly, "I gave him a lesson in diet."

For the first time in two weeks, Johns really laughed. "I have a feeling that you do not mean coconuts."

"No—horse."

"Oh no . . ."

"Oh yes. I had gone to wash my clothes in the river, and Tarrant did the same. It so happened that on my way to the river, I had seen a young horse that must have been killed by rifle fire. It was still warm and I knew that it would not last long, so I marked the spot with a stick so I could find it again. On the way back, I stopped. Tarrant came by, and he stopped and asked me where I got the steaks . . . did I shoot the cow?"

"Did he really think you had killed it?"

"He still thinks so."

By this time Weintraub had stepped into the tent, and he was listening to the story. "So what'd you do then, Chief?"

"Cooked it over a slow fire," was Redhawk's prompt response. "And I did not tell him until he was full that he was eating horse."

Weintraub laughed heartily, slapping his knee and chuckling and saying, "I can just see that doggie's face when you told him!"

"Actually, he said it was the best steak he'd ever had. But he did look a little pale around the mouth."

Weintraub was still chuckling when he left the tent, and Redhawk lay back on his cot and folded his hands beneath his head. He looked up at the low canvas ceiling.

Johns said softly, "I think a large battle is being planned for very soon. I overheard some of the officers discussing it."

"Scuttlebutt also has it that Army troops are being sent to the Canal so we can ship out," Redhawk said. "I don't know what to believe anymore."

There was a brief moment of silence before Johns asked quietly, "Did you hear about the pilot who walked into camp today? He had bailed out of his plane on Cape Esperance and walked back."

"Cape Esperance? Isn't that on the northwest corner?"

"It took him a week to get back, and he ran into enemy patrols a time or two, the way I heard it. He had to kill the enemy with rocks or their own weapons, but he did it."

"He lived off the land," Redhawk said, "right?"

"They say he ate insects to stay alive."

"Is he Navajo?" Redhawk joked, and Johns laughed again.

"If he's not, he should be."

Nights were shattered by enemy shelling—the Tokyo Express—and days were punctuated with the shrill air alert frequently sounding. Two American destroyer-transports, the *Little* and the *Gregory,* had been caught off Lunga Point and sunk. Marine Raiders landed at Taivu Point and worked their way west, drawing fire from light artillery, mortars, and machine guns. Army Airacobras flew out from Henderson to bomb and strafe ahead of them, and early in the afternoon, marines swarmed the enemy's rear base in the village of Tasimboko.

The Division Command Post moved from the landward side of coral outcropping—an area growing increasingly popular with the Japanese bombers—to a spot the Japanese had named Lizard Hill. The marines thought it an apt name. The ridge humped out of the terrain, a squat reptile-shape with bent body, crooked tail pointing to the airfield, rounded snout to the mountains, and stumpy legs poking out into the jungle, with ridges jutting along its spine. The new CP was erected on the Lizard's left rear appendage. A jeep park was formed with a trail leading into the HQ area. On both sides of the "leg," thickly forested, brush-covered ravines bracketed the land.

Then word came from native scouts that several thousand Japanese had been spotted less than five miles away. The air was thick with tension.

On September 11, twenty-four Wildcats were

flown from Esperitu Santo to Guadalcanal. Cactus Air Force was in constant need of reinforcements and these were welcomed.

All experienced troops were pressed into immediate service. Redhawk and Johns went with the Fifth. Second Battalion was held in reserve on an inland line two thousand yards along the Ilu River.

The long, low ridge, like the slinky spine of a dragon, snaked through jungle-covered ravines. The ridge presented a good approach to Henderson Field from the south, as it ran roughly northeast and southwest. The stage was set.

Late in the morning of the twelfth, a vee of Mitsubishi 96's droned overhead. Redhawk, Johns, and Weintraub huddled in a foxhole and watched them appear in the cloudless blue sky. The decent weather made it clear for the antiaircraft guns, and they went into action. White puffs formed in the sky, and the *ack-ack* bursts missed the first planes in the formation. They still shone silvery and strangely beautiful overhead, death on the wing.

Then one of the big guns struck a bomber, and it exploded with orange fire and clouds of white smoke. Another antiaircraft shell hit, and another bomber made a peculiar whining sound as it nosed down in sheets of flame and thick, oily black smoke. Still sailing serenely on as if unaware that two of their planes had been hit, the formation passed on out toward the sea, leaving one behind.

The single bomber immediately engaged in a dogfight with a fighter. The smaller American plane darted like a hummingbird around the slower bomber, spitting bullets in a rattling wave until the enemy slowly rose, then dove in a deathly spin toward the waters of Tulagi Bay. It exploded upon impact, spewing flame and coils of black smoke in the air.

Rifle fire rattled on the front lines, and Redhawk sucked in a deep breath. He felt hemmed in, with enemy above, behind, and ahead, and the fact that he was also surrounded by marines didn't make him feel much better. Did it make any difference to an enemy bomb if he was in the midst of friends or out in the open? Not that he could tell . . .

"Private Redhawk!"

His head jerked up, and he saw Jones gesture for him to join him. Scooting up and out of the foxhole, he ran in a sort of crablike crouch and flung himself into the long trench beside the sergeant.

"Yes sir?"

"We've been ordered up on that ridge, and I want you and Johns to man the radio. There may or may not be a need for you, but I want you to be prepared."

Redhawk brightened slightly. He'd assumed that he and Johns would be just infantry, but now there seemed to be an opportunity to use their specialized training.

"Yes sir!" he said as he scrambled up and out of the trench and ran back to Johns and Weintraub. "We're to get our radio and pack it along with our gear," he told them. A smile lit Johns's round face, too, and Weintraub looked slightly bemused.

"I don't know what's worse," Weintraub said a moment later, his voice sighing, "the fuckin' war or the fuckin' brass."

"They do change their minds a lot, don't they?"

Weintraub looked at Redhawk. "You don't have to sound so damned cheerful about it."

"It's our chance to show how useful the code can be in battle. I made a promise to someone at Camp Elliott, and I'd like to be able to keep it."

"I'd just like to be able to get back in one

piece—preferably still breathing," Weintraub grumbled.

"Always complaining," the marine next to him said with a wide grin. "Don't you like anything over here?"

"Sure . . . what's not to like?"

Another bomb fell from the sky and they all ducked again, waiting for the inevitable shower of debris and dirt to bombard them. When it passed and the bombers had slowly faded out to sea, they scrabbled up and out of the foxhole.

"So, it's off to war!" Weintraub said with a forced grin and gaiety. "Gee . . . I can hardly wait."

"You won't have to, Private," a voice said, and they turned to see Colonel Harte behind them. "We're moving out right now."

Fighting their way through brush-tangled ravines, the marines dug in. Marine Raiders met with small arms fire on the southern edge; ducking down into the kunai grass of the open strip surrounded by jungle, they dug in to wait.

The Japanese did not let the marines grow comfortable. Twin-engine bombers bombarded the ridge with five hundred pounders and daisy cutters. Rising to the bait, Cactus pilots darted into the air like angry wasps, shooting down twelve bombers and three Zeros. The fight was on. . . .

Scouts reported that the Japanese general, Kawaguchi, had a battle flag flying on the Lunga River. As the marines dug in, they could hear enemy movements in front of them, moving from left to right across the river. And it was obvious the enemy knew they were there.

A rumbling chant rose into the air, and Redhawk stopped to listen. "What are they saying?" he asked the man next to him.

Leaning on his shovel, the marine's brow furrowed as he shook his head. "I ain't no interpreter, but Comstock told me they're hollering, 'U.S. Marines be dead tomorrow!' They keep shouting it over and over, the same thing."

Grinning, Redhawk listened carefully, then mimicked the singsong chant. Before two minutes had passed, the entire line of marines was doing the same thing. It became a game. The louder the Japanese would chant, the louder the marines would chant. It was pure bravado, and every man there loved it. Of course, there were marines who insisted upon adding their own colorful versions, and those were greatly appreciated as well.

"It's like a fuckin' circus," Weintraub observed with a wide grin. "Ain't we having fun now?"

"You're sick, W.W.," a marine said, but he was grinning as widely as Weintraub.

"Edwards took Taivu Point," the marine offered a few minutes later. "Even got a general's dress uniform. I hear he's gonna send it to the Old Man."

"That should make him happy."

"Fuckin' A," the marine said again.

Company A was in the dense jungle sloping down to the Lunga River, five hundred yards away. Company B was ordered to dig in with double aprons of barbed wire spiraling down the lines. Light machine guns and attached heavy artillery had been positioned to give interlocking fire, but that did not seem possible because of the thick terrain. Bullets could not veer to go around crested ridges or tangled ravines. Mortars had been placed for cover on the ridge, huge 81's and the shorter 60's, and ammo was stacked neatly beside them.

The companies were ordered to dig in and stay put. If they were overrun, they were to keep down.

"And for God's sake, don't let any overeager soldier get up to take a piss at night!" Edwards commanded roughly. "We don't need to lose any men."

As daylight faded into dusk, they came, Kawaguchi's soldiers storming the marine positions again and again. They screamed threats and obscenities in clumsy English, driving between A and B companies. Methodically, calmly, the marines fired their weapons as the Japanese came at them. Bodies began to fall, and more bodies fell on top. Still they came.

Sweat streamed down his face as Redhawk fired his M-1. He squeezed the trigger carefully, and had the satisfaction of seeing an enemy clutch his chest and wheel slowly to the ground. Sometimes there was no way to tell if he'd hit his target, and he always wondered if he was just wasting ammo. Enemy soldiers ran into the spirals of barbed wire and some of them died there, hanging like obscene flags on the sharp metal points. Corpses began to stack up.

When his position was overrun by the Japanese, Redhawk stood up and bellowed an old war cry, his voice mixing with the voices of the enemy. It stopped one man cold, his eyes growing wide and his own cry curdling in his throat. He hesitated just long enough for Redhawk to drive his bayonet into the enemy with a swift, smooth thrust. There was a peculiar resistance, and when he saw the man's mouth open soundlessly, he took a foot and kicked him free of the weapon. Turning, stabbing, shooting, Redhawk managed to fight his way back with the others. He saw Johns close by, fighting with the same grim determination, but did not see Weintraub.

Just when it seemed as if the Japanese would completely overrun them, they stopped. It was as gratifying as it was surprising.

"Shit, Johnny," Redhawk heard someone say, and turned to look up at Weintraub. "What the hell was that whooping you were doing?"

"A war cry," Redhawk said with a tired grin. "Haven't you ever seen a western movie?"

"Yeah, but I don't think they'll ever be the same."

Redhawk nodded. Somehow, he knew how Weintraub felt. He looked around at the ground littered with dead and dying marines. Cries of "Corpsman!" filled the air, and there was a bustle of activity before the next assault wave could begin.

"Do you think they'll attack again?" a baby-faced young marine asked. He was breathing fast and hard, in short, panting gasps, his blue eyes huge and his pupils dilated. "Again tonight, I mean?"

Redhawk didn't bother to answer, but took the young marine by the arm and told him to help a wounded man back to the medics. "Hurry, or he may die before you get him there," he added, and pointed the direction. The boy seemed grateful to be leaving the field of action with his burden.

"He looked too young to be here," Weintraub commented, sinking down to the stark comfort of a log. "I bet he wasn't over eighteen!"

Redhawk grinned. "How old do you think I am?"

Weintraub looked nonplussed. "I don't know . . . twenty-three or four?"

"Twenty next month," Redhawk replied, and jerked a thumb toward Johns. "Two months older than him."

Weintraub shook his head, muttering something beneath his breath. "Let's just sit while we can, gentlemen," he said after a moment. "I have a feeling when the sun goes down, we'll get it again."

"I have a feeling you're right. . . ."

The night was thick and black, with very little noise. Redhawk lay quietly, his muscles tense, his radio between him and Johns. It had not been used and was not likely to be, in his opinion. There was no place in a pitched battle for long communications. Short communications were more to the point and security was not vital. He'd hoped they would be able to use their code instead of runners, but the officers kept to what was tried and familiar instead of taking a chance. He couldn't blame them. This would be a decisive battle for the ridge that ran down to the airfield. If the marines lost it, they lost Guadalcanal.

Late that night an enemy cruiser and three destroyers shelled the ridge thrusting up out of the ravines, and enemy troops threw themselves at the barbed wire fortifications the marines had erected. An unmistakable droning filled the air, and Redhawk recognized it even before he heard a marine mutter, "Louie the Louse!"

A flare burst out and arced to the ground, lighting up the area like the Fourth of July. The marines hit the ground to wait it out. Naval bombardment added a booming accompaniment to the firefight to the south. Rifles, deep-throated mortars, shrill barking machine guns, and *kabooms* of grenades formed a deadly night medley. Searching lights from enemy ships scoured the shorelines like evil fireflies and Japanese flares timed the rhythms of ground attack. The continual droning of floatplanes wasn't dangerous, but they were too noisy to let the marines get their much-needed rest. At five-thirty in the morning when the air raid shrilled, wary marines huddled in foxholes and waited, expecting more of the deadly Betty Bombers. Thankfully, none came.

In the hours before first light, the usually hot, humid jungle had grown damp and chilly, with cold seeping into the bones. Redhawk shifted uncomfortably. The heat was no problem for him. He'd grown up with it and even welcomed it at times. But the wet cold made his teeth chatter, and he strove to still the reaction. He could see from Johns's miserable expression that his cousin was doing the same.

"Arizona!" someone shouted, and he looked up with a frown to see a man stumbling toward him. "You're needed at communications. Phone wires are cut, and Edwards wants to find out how the companies came out last night." The runner stopped to peer doubtfully at Redhawk's face. "You are the guys from Arizona, right?"

"Right." Redhawk replied, rising smoothly from his bed of blankets and dirt.

By the time they got to Edwards, the colonel was pacing the ground and chewing furiously on the end of his cigar. He swirled around to glare at them.

"Can you men get through to Companies A and D?"

Remembering that Little Wolf Smith was in the First, Redhawk smiled. "What do you want to say, sir?"

Colonel Edwards's rigid posture relaxed slightly, and his cigar stopped its agitated bobbing. "Ask them how they are," he said in a tone as pleasant as if he were making casual inquiries.

Redhawk and Johns cranked up the radio and ascertained that though enduring some losses, A and D were dug in. B and C had been shot up but were firmly entrenched. The enemy had managed to wedge in between them and the airstrip, however. A hole had been drilled through the right flank of the defenses flung up along the perimeters of the ridge.

Edwards stared at them thoughtfully. "It sounds like pure gibberish, but you boys pulled it off. By God, you boys aren't bad!"

Redhawk allowed himself only a moment's elation. "We were well trained, sir," was all he said, and Edwards's grim face softened into what passed for a smile.

"I expect no less of marines!"

All in all, it wasn't as bad as it could have been, though it was bad enough. Kawaguchi's troops had charged out of the thick rain forest from between the Lunga and the ridge. After breaking through Edwards's lines, they cut off one platoon and managed to force the marines to fall back to the second hump in the ridge.

"Jeezus," a marine groaned, "Edwards must be nuts! We already got Japs barkin' at our heels, and he tells us to pull back? Why don't we just fistfight the sonuvabitches?"

Redhawk managed a smile at the weary marine. He was just as tired and understood how the man must feel. They had sat through a long night, with shells bursting overhead and rifle fire shearing tree limbs and mowing grass and a few heads, and now they had to position mortars and lay out a field of fire for the supporting artillery.

"I think he has that in mind," Redhawk said, "only on our terms, not the Japs'."

"Fuckin' A," the marine sighed. "I wouldn't mind taking out a few Nips."

As they joined the reserve company, mortar fire rained down on them. Marine artillery fought back, their fire pounding the attackers mercilessly. Japanese infiltrators tried to worm their way through the choking jungle to set up sniper positions, and in the growing light of day, the marines delivered devastating fire. The enemy retreated.

Orders came down the line in the lull afterward: "Improve all positions," Colonel Edwards barked. "Dig in deep, wire up tight. Parallel all wire lines, get a hot meal. Then get some sleep; you will all need it."

"Those orders sound comforting," Weintraub said, and Redhawk laughed.

"I thought you'd be glad to hear them."

"If it had been a few days ago, maybe. Now? When half of Japan is at our doorstep and we've got Nips in our back pockets? No way in hell!"

"Whining again, Weintraub?" Sergeant Jones asked. He stood there with his hands on his hips, a grim smile on his face.

"Aw, Sarge, you know I just like to complain." Weintraub looked slightly embarrassed, and he cleared his throat when Jones just looked at him. To his relief, Jones finally gave a shake of his head.

"Hell, you wouldn't be a marine if you didn't! But there's a lot to do and not much time to do it. We need to get a move on."

Marines dug in on the slopes of the hump in the ridge. The reserve battalion shifted across the contested airfield to the northern edge of the long ridge. It was a day of fast, frenetic activity for the marines, and there wasn't a man jack of them who didn't know it had to be equally busy for the enemy.

That night, the fighting grew intense.

Redhawk and Johns were back in the lines with Weintraub and the other marines. They fired at the small, dark shapes of the enemy outlined in the night by bright flares and the explosions of artillery.

"It's like trying to hit a goddamn needle in a haystack," a marine grumbled, and Redhawk silently agreed with him. It wasn't easy to find the enemy, much less shoot him. Shells screamed through the dark, exploding in deafening bursts of thunder. A short distance in front, the sound of rifles and machine guns rattled the air, punctuated by the deeper rumble of grenades and mortars.

"Shit!" Weintraub swore softly, "they're so close I can hear the Japs talking!"

"Screaming is more like it," Johns disagreed.

"Where the fuck is that heavy artillery coming from?"

"Behind us," Redhawk answered briefly, ducking as a chunk of dirt torn up by bullets sprayed them. He waited a moment, then cautiously lifted his head again. His mouth was dry and his stomach churned, but there was a strange exhilaration thundering through his veins.

"Behind us?" Weintraub echoed. "Hell, *our* guys are supposed to be behind us!"

"Well, somebody ought to tell them they're shooting the hell out of us," Redhawk said shortly, then ducked again.

It was several minutes before a runner came up in a running dive, slamming his body down into the trench next to Redhawk. "Arizona," he said between gasps for air, his eyes large and staring in the dimly lit night, "Edwards needs you to get on the horn! We already tried, but our guys think it's the Japs radioing in to get them to stop shelling us. If they don't stop with those howitzers soon, we're gonna all be blown to fucking hell!"

"And he thinks they'll listen to us?" Johns put in.

The runner nodded. "He says nobody can imitate that shit you guys put out."

"Thank you," Redhawk said dryly, and rose to a crouch. "Lead the way." He glanced over at Johns. "Ready?"

Weintraub put in, "I think I'll sit this one out, guys. It's a little hot for me out there."

Grinning, Redhawk said, "If we get shot for Japs, it's on your conscience!" Weintraub grinned back.

"Use junior there as your bodyguard. He looks honest."

When they reached the colonel, he was red-faced and furious, his familiar cigar chewed almost in two. "Call those dumb bastards on the phone and tell them to change positions of those howitzers! A few more shells like the last ones, and we'll be strumming harps up here!"

As if on cue, a shell plummeted earthward, and they all dove for what cover there was. Colonel Edwards got up first, and his cigar was smashed to a flat pulp. He spat it out and said more calmly, "Ready, Private?"

"Ready, sir."

Johns cranked the radio, and Redhawk dialed the frequency and adjusted the earphones. Keeping one eye on the sky and the other on a slip of paper with the proper coordinates as dictated by Edwards, Redhawk finally managed to get through to Lieutenant Colonel Marsden's unit.

". . . you are bombing the wrong positions . . . change grid coordinates to 456739," he said in code, and received an answer from Little Wolf Smith.

"Will report changes immediately." There was a brief pause, then he added, "Hope no serious damage done."

"Only to our nerves," Redhawk replied, then rang off.

Edwards looked at him. "Well?"

"They hope no serious damage was done, sir."

Uttering a short, rude remark, Edwards pulled a fresh cigar out of his pocket. "Stay close, men. You're better at this than I ever thought about."

It was an accolade of sorts, and Redhawk nodded. When they returned to their trench, Weintraub waved them down.

"Hit the deck!"

Instinctively, Redhawk and Johns slammed to the earth on their bellies, hands over heads and resting on elbows. A shell exploded too close for comfort, and as soon as it was clear enough, they rolled into the trench beside Weintraub.

"They're still shelling us?" Redhawk asked. "I just talked to—"

"Naw, that ain't our guys," a marine said. "The Japs have gotten close, that's all."

Tracers zipped into the area, and firing seemed to be coming from all sides at once. Redhawk could make out the telltale *ping* of a Japanese .25 caliber weapon close by. He saw the spray of dirt kicked up by the thud of bullets into the ground, and he felt a tightening in his throat.

"Hey, there's a man in that thicket," he said to Johns, and gave him a nudge. "Cover me for a minute."

"What are you going to do?" Johns began, but Redhawk was already rising to his feet, his M-1 lifting to his shoulder as he took aim. Johns automatically began firing at the thicket, and when Redhawk saw the shimmy of branches, he fired too. A faint cry filtered out, followed by the violent shaking of bushes as the enemy pitched forward and lay still. Redhawk could barely see the shocked, pained expression on the man's face, but he felt nothing. There wasn't time to feel anything before the next rattling noise made him dive back into the relative safety of the trench. Another shell burst close by, tossing dirt and fragments onto the men, and he could hear pained cries.

Enemy soldiers surged out of the jungle, crying loudly, *"Totsugeki!"*

Rising to meet this new threat, the marines fought them hand to hand. Positions were overrun, forcing the defenses back in a U-shape. Redhawk found that the targets were no longer distant and no longer too dark to see. He fired his M-1, reloaded, and fired again, his movements swift and without thinking. Ignoring the bruising ache in his shoulder, he pulled the trigger until his finger was numb, and still the enemy kept coming in wave after devastating wave.

"Fall back!" came the order down the line, and the marines fought fiercely as they tried to retreat. Orders were shouted right and left: "Move more sandbags to that gun pit! Place more barbed wire on that position!"

Several 105 howitzers were trained on the Japanese, and rifle and automatic weapons were used in an attempt to stem the tide of enemy flooding over the marines. Enemy snipers still managed to slip behind the lines. Ammunition supply on the beleaguered ridge grew short, and more was sent up at Redhawk's radioed request. He was back with Edwards, along with Johns and Weintraub, and for a time there was concern the colonel's CP would be taken.

"Tell the 105's to drop it five-zero and march it back and forth across the ridge," Edwards ordered, and Redhawk complied. Artillery obliged and blasted away at the enemy.

"Now tell them they're knocking the teetotal shit outta the enemy!" Edwards barked with a pleased smile. He ducked as a bullet sliced through the folds of canvas tent very close to his head, and he kept his voice and manner calm. "I intend to take care of those snipers in the morning when it's light, Private Redhawk. Remind me."

The enemy offered one last dying attempt before dawn. They gave up quickly when marine artillery responded with fervor. 105's, 75mm pack howitzers rallied, and the Japanese retreated as daylight broke, along with the snipers.

Chapter Sixteen
Interlude

Sometimes, mistakes cost American lives. On a September afternoon not long after the Battle of the Ridge—becoming known as Bloody Ridge—a navy ship off the Lunga Point opened fire on a Douglas dive-bomber that was circling low overhead. Apparently thinking that the plane was Japanese and ignoring the stars easily visible on the wings, the antiaircraft guns knocked the plane out of the sky to the horror of the veterans on the beach.

Shouts went up from those who recognized one of their own, but the ships, of course, could not hear.

"No!" came a concerted agonized howl. "It's *our* boys! Don't shoot!"

But it was too late. The pilot attempted to crash-land on the beach and was met with more fire. The dive-bomber spiraled into the coastal waters, with all the crew but one lost. Men who had mistakenly cheered were silent as the Higgins boats raced out to the rescue.

Weintraub choked out, "How in the fuck do we expect to win a war when we're killing our own?" and Redhawk had no answer. He felt the pain of the others and the shame of the gunners as the lone survivor, badly shot up, was rushed to sick-bay.

There hadn't been very much to cheer about lately. The *Wasp* and the *O'Brien* had been sunk, and the *North Carolina* was out of commission for a while with a huge hole in her hull. That left the *Hornet* as the only U.S. aircraft carrier still in operation in the South Pacific.

The word went out on the number of planes shot down by marine fighters to date—one hundred thirty-one. Grummans knocked one hundred nine out of the air, the Army Pursuiters were credited with four of the enemy planes, and the newly-arrived Navy fighters accounted for seventeen of them. A dive-bomber and antiaircraft batteries knocked out six. Over half of the one hundred thirty-one Japanese planes destroyed were fighters or single-engined, and the rest were the swift two-engined Mitsubishi 97's.

And scuttlebutt had it that reinforcements were on the way to the Canal. . . .

Eight days passed without the "Tokyo Express" making its nightly run. The only fire at night originated with newly landed troops still not "blooded," as Redhawk liked to say. "They'll calm down once they see action," he predicted when seasoned marines cursed them. He remembered his first "blooding."

Changes in staff were made, with Colonel Harte being shipped out and Colonel Edwards given charge of the Fifth Marines. Tents had been erected for most of the troops, and comfortable cots with mosquito bars covered the marines at night. Luxury!

"Fuckin' A!" Weintraub sighed happily one night when it was quiet and tropical and a full moon shone serenely in the soft sky. "I could almost believe I was on a fuckin' vacation."

Rolling over on his side, Johns eyed Weintraub curiously. "You know, one of the things that has interested me is the way most marines use the word *fuck* all the time. Why is that?"

Redhawk stifled a laugh at Weintraub's stunned expression and stammered reply. "Uh . . . I don't know, Willie. Everybody just does it."

"But it's used to describe good things as well as bad, and happy as well as sad." Johns shook his head. "It seems like an all-purpose word."

"Yeah, I guess it does," Weintraub agreed, and looked over at their new tent-mate. Four men were assigned to a tent, and with Kryzminsky gone, they had drawn a new man. "What do you think, Milano?" he asked the newcomer, a young Italian who looked too fresh-faced to be a marine.

Milano looked as astounded as Weintraub had looked, and he just shrugged his shoulders. "I dunno . . . maybe because it sounds better than other words. And it's easy to spell."

They all laughed, then Weintraub asked, "Where are you from, Milano?"

"Indiana," he replied, and got that familiar look in his eye that most marines got when they thought of home. "A little town outside of Terre Haute. Where are you guys from?"

The conversation drifted from man to man, and Milano was faintly skeptical of the code he'd already heard about. "But how is it useful out here?" he asked. "I mean, from what I hear, there's not much time to be giving out vital info in the middle of a firefight. And who do you talk to that can understand what you're saying?"

"There were twenty-seven Navajos assigned to Cactus, six or eight to a division," Redhawk told him. "We are able to communicate very well, but you're right about not being needed in the thick of a fight. On the Ridge, Johns and I did most of the sending for medical help, ammo, and supplies for Edwards, because he didn't want to take a chance on the enemy knowing our weaknesses or losses. Some officers don't use us at all, and some do. It depends on the man."

Milano nodded slowly, his dark eyes lighting. "Well, I'd heard about you guys, but I didn't know what to expect." He grinned suddenly. "I wondered if I was going to get scalped when I got assigned to this platoon."

"Ah, there's still no guarantee on that," Weintraub said with a straight face. He leaned forward to add, in a soft voice, "Haven't you wondered why there's an empty cot in our tent?"

Milano looked uncertain for a moment, his grin faltering slightly, then shook his head. "You guys are fuckin' nuts!"

"Fuckin' A," Redhawk said, and Weintraub laughed.

"The honeymoon's over," Weintraub observed gloomily as shells lobbed the CP. "Well, it's been two weeks, I guess, so maybe they couldn't stand not being near us anymore."

Milano slanted Weintraub a sharp glance, his nostrils distended and his eyes wide with fear. "You ain't right, Weintraub, you just ain't right," he muttered. Another shell exploded almost directly overhead and he ducked again, his entire body trembling. It was his first air raid and he had hit the floor immediately, rolling under his cot along with Weintraub.

A few feet away, Redhawk had also rolled under his cot, and he felt a pang of sympathy for the fresh-faced kid from Indiana. Had he ever looked that young and that scared? He didn't anymore. His reflection in the river, when he washed his clothes out, showed a hard-faced man with an unsmiling face. He'd seen it in Johns but it had been gradual, a mirror image of how he was feeling, and he hadn't paid it any attention until the shock of seeing his own reflection. Now he saw the slow metamorphosis of Milano beginning.

"Keep your head down and rest your weight on your elbows," he heard Weintraub instruct Milano. "And always keep your helmet close by."

Good advice for any marine on Guadalcanal.

With the newly arrived Seventh Marines fresh on the Canal, things began looking up. More troops were promised soon, and the 164th Infantry Regiment of the Army was on its way. The perimeter was divided into ten defense sectors, with each commander of his sector given strict commands to learn it like the back of his hand—each ditch, hill, and clump of brush. There were twelve miles of front and less than a division to hold on to it, and the enemy was massing.

Marines worked throughout the night. Positions along the rivers were strengthened; coconut trees were chopped down to provide beams and abutments for bomb shelters, and wire spirals were stretched out to the water's edge to stop the Japanese. Heavy sandbags by the thousand were filled and stacked atop freshly dug gun pits.

The supply ships made dawn landings, bringing fresh supplies and new clothes for the tattered, weary, hungry marines. New combat uniforms were distributed, which had a moralizing effect on the troops.

"Hey!" Weintraub said, pirouetting in a clumsy circle in his new finery. "Aren't I beautiful?"

"Just like an albatross, W.W.," Tarrant observed with a dry chuckle. "Just like a fuckin' albatross!"

Redhawk had to laugh. The tall, gangly Weintraub with his long neck and skinny body did, indeed, resemble the awkward albatross, more commonly called a gooney bird by the sailors for its clumsy movements and disregard for danger.

Gathering his wounded dignity, Weintraub peered down his nose at Tarrant. "Anybody ever tell you that you have all the charm of a toad and the exquisite manners of a grizzly bear, Corporal Tarrant?"

Grinning, Tarrant said, "Only those who are no

longer with us."

"Yeah? Well, maybe . . ."

"Okay, cut it out," Sergeant Jones broke in, walking up to the group of gathered marines. "We're having a war today and I thought I'd invite you gentlemen to participate. Any arguments?" When no one spoke, Jones signaled to his men. "Lissen up—"

The general had been pushing his staff to the limit, and they had come up with Plan 2-42. It was simple in its inception: Keep the enemy off balance, hit where they did not expect it, and skillfully organize with supporting fire. Five of the division's nine infantry battalions were called in: the Second and Third battalions of the Fifth Regiment, the First and Second battalions of the Seventh Regiment, and the Third Battalion of the Second Regiment. Operative dates were scheduled for October 7, with joint efforts taking place the following day.

Sucking in a deep breath, Redhawk heard Jones tell them that two battalions of the Fifth would force a path through the jungle to a point one mile upstream on the Lunga River. That was designated as the left thrust. Another force would make up the right, and the main drive would be at the mouth of the Matanikau by two battalions of the Seventh as well as the Third Battalion of the Second Marines. A company of well-trained men in the art of jungle tracking was to effect a crossing, thrust down the coastal road, and take the now-abandoned village of Matanikau.

Matanikau. Redhawk and Johns weren't the only marines who flinched at the name and the harsh, burning memory of the August ambush. The general himself had been heard to curse the river, especially since only a fortnight before, three of his battalions had been trapped on the far bank.

Rain steadily pelted the marines as they trudged

through ankle-deep mud in the murky light of dawn. Redhawk found himself cursing the rain and the steamy tropical climate that made him feel like a sponge on wet days and a baked rock on sunny days. Were there no compromises on this island?

"The terrain is just another facet of the enemy's tenacity, but we will overcome it as we will all obstacles, men," Sergeant Jones had said when they'd lined up in the downpour. Redhawk hoped he was right.

Plan 2-42 was in progress, and even the general had come to watch the men march through the rain. Six thousand marines marched out to take both banks of the river from the enemy, and it was inevitable that the enemy would fight back with savage ferocity.

Remembering the radio transmissions by Tokyo Rose, the Japanese-American woman who spilled demoralizing propaganda into the airwaves, Redhawk wondered if she knew something the Americans didn't. She predicted that the Japanese Imperial Army would annihilate the forces on Guadalcanal, that the marines were already reduced to only a shadow of their former strength.

"Maybe she's talkin' about you guys," Milano had cracked with a wide grin, gesturing toward the thin bodies of his tent-mates. "After all, two months on this grub, and I'd be a shadow of my former self, too!"

"It ain't spaghetti, is it, Milano," Weintraub agreed with a sad sigh.

"And it's not kosher," Redhawk put in, making Weintraub laugh.

None of them looked too happy now, sloshing through the rain and mud with heavy gear on their backs. Hours passed, and still the rain pounded down. Redhawk shifted his pack and radio, and glanced toward the side of the trail. The jungle was wet and dense, looming in ominous silence around them. His leg muscles were already strained from the mud sucking at his feet, and his back ached in spite of the months of enduring much of the same. Did a man ever grow accustomed to it? Maybe.

"Hey, Chief," Milano began, walking next to him, "are we in for this kinda' shit a lot?"

"Do you mean marching in the rain?"

Milano shook his head, scattering rain from the lip of his helmet in a spraying arc. "Uh-uh. I mean hand-to-hand stuff, like you guys were talking about not long ago, when you fought the Nips with bayonet and swords."

"They had the swords," Redhawk corrected, seeing the fret in the young private's dark eyes. They were close to the same age, yet he felt much older. Maybe he was. War was a proven seasoner of men. "It's been done a few times, but more often than not the mortars or 105's get them before they get too close."

Nodding, Milano tried to put on a brave front, but the slight tremor in his voice gave him away. "Hell, I wouldn't mind a few fuckin' souvenirs to take back home to Indiana!"

"Maybe you'll get them."

"Yeah, it'd be—"

A shot rang out, the distinctive *ping* of a Japanese .25 caliber sniper, and Redhawk gave Milano a shove to the side of the trail, diving along with him for the protective cover of the thick underbrush.

"Snipers," someone yelled, and Milano muttered shakily, "A little late to tell us that, buddy. . . ."

Redhawk could hear Major Brown issuing orders and the sound of ammo being clicked into place. Gun pits had been dug into the sides of brushy hills, and the enemy was firmly entrenched and determined to stay there. Taking position behind a huge rock, Redhawk tossed a grenade into one of the shadowed openings and ducked. The explosion tossed dirt and rocks, but he doubted it had done much to deter the enemy.

"Damn," Weintraub muttered to Johns as they inched forward, "your cousin got a little too close to me for comfort."

Johns nodded tightly. "But it was only dirt. The enemy throws bullets."

"Well put, Chief."

More shots rang out, forcing some of the marines to stay down. But Redhawk and Milano were in a position to shoot back. Shifting his M-1, Redhawk kept a steady stream of fire aimed at the black hole where an enemy gun pit had been stationed. Milano decided to go around behind and try to lob a grenade into the pit again, at closer range this time.

"I'll do my best to keep them busy, but there are others out there," Redhawk warned him. "Maybe you should wait until we're in a better position. Sergeant Jones always warns us, 'Don't be a hero.' Remember that."

"I'll remember," Milano said with a grin that didn't quite reach his eyes. He was scared and Redhawk could see it.

Enemy fire was growing more intense, bullets zipping through the air like angry wasps, shredding leaves and snapping twigs, thunking into tree trunks. It had an entirely different sound than the dreaded solid *thump* of lead into the human body, and Redhawk tautly waited for it.

"Arizona!" came the cry down the lines, and he muttered a familiar marine phrase. Obeying orders was ingrained, but his buddy depended on him for cover, and Redhawk hesitated. His M-1 was hot to the touch, and he jammed in another ammo clip. "Arizona!" came another yell, and Redhawk took aim and let fly with a round of bullets, giving Milano the cover he needed to make it behind the gun pit dug into the steep slope.

When Milano reached the hump of the gun pit, he jerked the ring on a fragmentation grenade and hunkered down to throw it. As soon as he threw it, he pulled the ring on another, and then another, throwing them into the gun pit. A reverberating explosion chain sent him sprawling backward, and he rolled dawn the slope to a shallow ravine and lay still.

"Damnit!" Redhawk swore, and leaped up to run to him. When he reached him, Milano was getting shakily to his feet.

"I got those fuckin' Nips," Milano said, but his eyes were slightly glazed.

Redhawk shoved him toward a marine, saying, "Get him to a corpsman," then he broke into a zigzagging run toward the front of the lines.

"About goddamn time," Major Brown said without anger, flicking a glance toward the drenched marine. "Radio CP. Tell them we've run into enemy fire about seventy-five yards above the mouth of the river. Their position extends about one hundred fifty yards upstream and we estimate close to two hundred of the enemy. Got that?"

Redhawk was already cranking the radio. He relayed the message, but it took longer than usual because of the constant fire and the bad transmission.

"The rain's fouling up the transmission, sir," he told him, and Brown just nodded curtly.

"Do your best, Private. We don't need the Japs knowing any more than they already do." He paused, then added, "Tell them the Japs have to be forced out, that they're dug in like termites in this goddamn jungle, the sonuvabitches."

"Yes sir."

It was only mid-morning, and all the marines were having a difficult time forging ahead. The enemy was dug in to stay and had no intention of being easily routed. The only communication was the radio, and transmission was poor. The dense jungle foliage and thick clouds and rain made the wireless erratic. Frustration built as Redhawk tried to find a frequency that would transmit, static crackling in his ears and only snatches of voices coming through.

"It's not working, sir," he finally had to report. He jerked his headphones off, his face crumpled in anger. "The rain has interfered with transmission."

"Good job, Private," Major Brown said. "It's not your fault. Keep working at it. I'll send out runners until we can get a clear frequency."

Runners were sent out to give orders and receive information, wading through mud and deep puddles, some of them across the river that was swiftly rising. It was a wet and miserable afternoon as the low light swiftly deepened into the black jungle night. Marines who had lugged heavy weapons through the sucking mud and pounding rain—mortar base plates, mortar ammo, tubes, machine gun tripods, and belts of ammunition—dug in for the night, trying to find a few dry spots.

"I think I'm sprouting gills like a fish," Weintraub muttered gloomily, hunching his poncho-clad shoulders up to his ears. Rain dripped ceaselessly onto his helmet, and all that Redhawk could see was the faint sheen of his eyes in the dim light.

"Then we'll send you across the river first," Redhawk replied. "You should be able to swim." He pulled his poncho closer around him and thought about Johns, who was taking his turn manning the radio. They were all exhausted but doing their best to rest before the morning brought the intended attack against the enemy.

Before midnight, there was the muffled thunder of guns booming, and Redhawk woke. He tried to blink the deluge of rain out of his eyes, searching for the source.

"It's far away," Milano muttered sleepily, and Redhawk nodded.

He found it hard to sleep, and when Johns finally came to dig in beside him, he asked, "What happened?"

"Some of the enemy tried to fight their way out, and the Raiders stopped them with 81's and 60's. There was also some hand-to-hand combat close to the river. Not many casualties on our side."

"Are we still scheduled to attack?"

Shrugging, Johns yawned tiredly. "I don't know. If the rain keeps up, the mission may be scrubbed, but the brass doesn't want to give up yet. Especially not since we won the first round against the enemy."

Mid-morning of the following day brought a change in orders. The attack was put off until the next day, ruining the chance of surprise, but the heavy rains had caused a flooding of the Matanikau. Gigantic trees had been uprooted upstream and were being swept to the sea with vicious force. The small sandbar at the mouth of the river, where Gerard and his ambushed patrol had died, had vanished under the swift currents.

Redhawk took the message and informed the major that a huge concentration of enemy ships had been reported near Rabaul. "The coastwatchers reported strong enemy movements around Rabaul and the Shortlands. General Vandegrift has decided that Plan 2-42 should be altered, sir."

Brown, a short, stocky man with thick eyebrows meeting over the bridge of his nose, swore softly. "So the attack is reset for October 9? And now we just sit tight. Damnit! These men are already tired and soaked to the bone." His jaw worked, then he gave a heavy sigh. "All right, Private. Carry on. Tomorrow will be here soon enough."

As frequently happened, the next morning was clear and bright, with no clouds in the hot blue sky. The air had a distinct crispness to it, almost like autumn.

The marines made a successful upstream crossing, and the force marched northward toward the beach in columns forming a three-pronged attack. The Raiders surged downstream on the west bank, marching parallel and a thousand yards west. The Second Battalion, Seventh Marines pushed against stiff resistance to the base of Point Cruz, a bulbous spur of land jutting into the channel. Lieutenant Colonel Palmer's First Battalion, Seventh Marines attacked along the slopes of a ridge west of Second Battalion, Seventh, coming upon a large enemy force hidden in a deep, dense ravine that ran south of Point Cruz. Palmer swiftly called in artillery, ordering his own mortars to throw all they had into the ravine at the same time.

The thick jungle wasn't enough to hide the Japanese from the heavy artillery and mortars. The ravine exploded into a hellish fire of erupting mortars and murderous metal fragments, ruthlessly cutting men apart. Enemy fortunate enough to escape death in that form found it on the open slopes as they tried to run from the deadly barrage. Fire from automatic weapons and rifles cut them down faster than they could run, and when they tried to escape back down into the ravine, more shells and mortars disintegrated them.

By two o'clock that afternoon, the three-pronged attack had withdrawn east of the Matanikau. Marine artillery had used over two thousand rounds of 75mm and more than a thousand rounds of 105mm ammo, and the slaughter was one of the bloodiest yet.

Revised Plan 2-42 was a success.

Major Brown leveled a stern glance at Redhawk and Johns. "You boys were invaluable out there on the radio. Why wasn't I told about your new code before?"

Coughing politely, Redhawk said, "All officers were made aware, sir, but most of them have preferred using older methods in times of extreme duress." He tried not to notice the major's slowly reddening face and had the thought that like most officers, Brown had probably dismissed the Navajo code as an unproven fluke.

"Yes, yes," Brown said, "probably so! Harrumph! However, now that it has been brought to my attention that you are able to transmit and receive messages quickly and accurately without giving anything away to the enemy, I intend to take advantage of it. I've talked to Sergeant Jones and he agrees with me that you men are performing with extreme efficiency, so I am making arrangements to bring this to the attention of General Vandegrift."

"Begging your pardon, Major Brown," Johns put in, "but the general is aware of our positions. He has left that up to the officer in charge as to when and how to use it."

Shaking his head, Brown muttered, "What a waste! Most officers wouldn't recognize an advantage if it bit them on the ass." His brow furrowed in thought, then he looked back at the two marines. "I'd like to keep you in my outfit, but I think you men would be a great advantage in upcoming campaigns. I am recommending promotions for both of you."

Faintly stunned by the swift progression of the major's comments, Redhawk swallowed hard. "Sir? Promotions?"

"Yes. A corporal's pay isn't much more than a private's pay, but it will buy a few more cigarettes. And privileges. Dismissed."

As the major sat down at his table and began rifling through papers, Redhawk and Johns gave him a half-hearted salute he didn't see and pivoted on their heels, leaving his tent in a daze.

"Promotion?" Johns repeated slowly, as if not quite believing it. "But how? Why?"

Redhawk smiled. "Why? Because we're damn good marines, that's why."

* * *

On the night of October 14, a Japanese naval task force glided into "Sleepless Lagoon" near the airstrip and launched a series of devastating salvos. At such a short range, the mammoth fourteen-inch shells were accurate, tearing up huge strips of the runway, as well as mangling planes and marines with equal indifference. Gasoline drums exploded, and ammunition dumps added to the raging inferno as the shells continued mercilessly.

"Sweet Jeezus," Milano muttered in what was almost a prayer, "when are those bastards gonna stop?"

Huddled in a sandbag-enforced trench, Milano, Redhawk, Johns, Weintraub, Sergeant Jones, and two other marines choked on dust and fear. It was all around them, almost palpable, filling the shelter. Each man gripped his weapon tightly, and they all wore the same expressions on their faces, the look of fear. The bombardment went on until it was difficult to hear anything even when there was a lull. With each new explosion, they ground their teeth and waited for the next one, for the ominous whistling of the shell through the air, wondering where it would land and if it would be directly on top of them.

"Here, kid," Sergeant Jones said to Milano, and handed him a lit cigarette. "Take a drag and try not to think about it."

"Not think about it?" Milano shook his head in disbelief but took the cigarette with a shaking hand. "That's fuckin' hard, Sarge."

"Life's hard."

"Not as hard as dying," Weintraub observed gloomily. His face in the gray light was pale, and there were fine white lines bracketing his mouth as he stared at the dust-choked opening, watching the bright flashes of light.

"Don't be so fatalistic, W.W.," Jones said calmly.

His face was grave but not tight, and his voice didn't shake when he talked.

"You're not going to give me that shit about if it's my time and my number's up, then there's nothing I can do, are you?" Weintraub shot at him. "Because if you are, Sarge, I can tell you right now that I don't buy that."

"Its not for sale." Jones shrugged. "Think what you want to think, or what you've been taught to think. Out here, when bombs are falling and you're scared as hell, no one cares what you think or how you think." He paused as a shell burst close by, peppering the bunker with dirt and fragments. A beam of the bunker sagged, and a sandbag tumbled into the entrance and broke open, filling the air with dust and the floor with sand. As the dust began to clear, Jones continued calmly, "Every man has his own fears, W.W., and you know that. None of us are going to tell you what to do, because we're too busy praying ourselves."

A glance around the murky gloom of the bunker was proof enough that he was speaking the truth, for every man in there had the same tight expression and opaque look in his eyes that meant he was concentrating on something else—his higher power, his god, his hopeful clinging to life.

Weintraub managed a shaky grin and shrugged his shoulders. "Yeah, I guess you're right at that, Sarge. It's these damn bombs that are making me so fuckin' edgy."

"They're making us all 'fuckin' edgy,' " Redhawk said, then ducked as another bomb shrilled down. The explosion rocked the bunker and filled it with debris, and they all tried to shrink against the dirt walls as the interior was showered. Redhawk felt a hot stinging in his leg and could barely hear the shouts of the others in the bunker. The bomb must have made a direct hit, because the beams collapsed inward with a loud cracking sound, and he suddenly realized they were all in danger of being buried alive in the bunker.

Instinctively, he clawed his way toward the front, shoving hard against a coconut palm beam that barred his way, shouting for the others to follow. Sergeant Jones grabbed his arm.

"No! It's safer in here than out there! Just wait, Chief. They'll find us after those Nips have gone home."

Redhawk was shaking, his taut control gone for the moment, his eyes huge and dark in a face as pale as the white man's. He glanced toward the entrance, where only a small shaft of gray light pierced the gloom, and forced himself to take a deep breath of dusty air. "Yes, they'll find us after they're gone."

Jones nodded and released Redhawk's arm. "Now sit down and wait for the next one, Chief. Those Japs are giving us hell tonight."

Crawling over the collapsed beam, Redhawk made it back to his place between Johns and Weintraub. Johns looked up at him with a strange expression, his features drawn.

"What is it?" Redhawk asked quickly. "Are you hurt?"

Slowly shaking his head, Johns said, "No, but our friend is." He lifted a blood-covered hand from behind Weintraub's neck. "I think he's dead. . . ."

Weintraub's limp body sagged to one side, and his head rolled back. Blood smeared his jaw and neck, and he was too silent. Jones moved quickly to Weintraub and checked his pulse, then sat back and looked up at the others, who were staring at him.

"Yeah, he's dead. Funny, isn't it? I mean, we were just talking about it and now—now we aren't." Jones swallowed hard and covered Weintraub's face with his helmet in an uncharacteristically tender movement.

Redhawk couldn't speak, couldn't voice the pain he felt at losing Weintraub. And somehow, even being in the dark bunker with the dead didn't bother him. He felt no fear at the spirit of the dead, but rather an odd kind of comfort that at least Weintraub wasn't frightened anymore.

Johns looked up at his cousin, and his eyes were dark with pain as he said in Navajo, "May his spirit roam grassy plains forever and the sun always shine on his face."

Redhawk just nodded, unable to speak.

The shelling seemed to go on forever, but it was only for an hour and a half. Then the ships departed, leaving behind a wrecked airfield. Almost all the gasoline supplies were destroyed. Marines dug out comrades whose bunkers had been caved in by fire, and took care of the wounded, dying, and dead.

October 15 was even worse for the beleaguered marines. It was another bright day, and Japanese transports swung into Tassafaronga Point to unload fresh troops while the marines had to watch with fists clenched helplessly.

Gritting his teeth in frustration, Sergeant Jones said through tight lips, "Those fuckin' Japs have gone too damn far now!"

Hidden stores of gasoline were brought in from the jungle, and the fuel tanks of heavily damaged B-17's were drained. When more transport planes landed with aviation fuel, the marines gassed up the undamaged fighters and bombers and loaded them with bombs and machine-gun ammo. It was time to make Tojo pay, they vowed.

In spite of putting three enemy transports out of commission on the beach and chasing away the Japanese naval force, thousands of enemy troops had been put ashore on Guadalcanal with supplies, weapons, and ammunition.

"Where the fuck is our Navy?" Milano asked no one in particular, his eyes staring past his comrades to a distant point.

"On their way, Private, on their way," Jones said.

Redhawk and Johns were employed in the radio hut, sending out coded messages for more avgas and supplies. Tulagi sent two yippie boats over with two hundred drums on the night of the fifteenth, but spirits were still low. Marines felt the losses greatly, and morale sank even deeper.

The next night, a flight of fighters veed in to the damaged airfield and spirits rose slightly, though those on the ground watched uneasily until the planes were close enough to ensure they were U.S. Wildcats. Then ragged yells and cheers rose with the men's spirits.

Leaning against the sandbags around the radio hut, Redhawk lit a cigarette and watched with mixed emotions as the fighters landed. He felt Weintraub's loss deeply and could not even talk to his cousin about it. Willie Johns was so different, able to express his loss, but Redhawk could not make himself talk about it. To say it aloud would only make it more painful, though there were moments when he envied his cousin's ability to do so.

Tossing his cigarette butt to the ground, Redhawk felt only a moment's regret that he was different. He'd been taught in his youth that a man should never be ashamed of being his own man.

"Replacements are being sent soon," Johns came out of the radio hut to say, and Redhawk turned to nod.

"Dah, I heard that. But we're here until they get here."

Shrugging, Johns said, "Let's go get some sleep while we can. They're using us a lot now that Major Brown has talked to the other officers about the code. I heard him say that we were the only reason the Japs didn't kill us all out in the field."

"It's about time," Redhawk said without emotion.

"We've been here for three months, and they finally realize that we're on their side."

"I don't think it was that. I think they were just too used to doing things the old way to realize that the new way was better." Johns shrugged again. "Anyway, they are certainly using us now."

Raking a hand through his hair, Redhawk looked up at the quiet sky and replaced his helmet. The constant shelling had gotten to all of them. Some marines never ventured far from a shelter, and most of them wore the same anxious expression and stony gaze. He heard men cry out a warning at the first noise in the sky, and saw them run and leap into shelters when there was no shelling. It was getting to all of them, and he had to exercise iron control not to do the same things. Still, he knew that it didn't matter where he was or what he was doing. If he was to die, he was to die.

He'd lost a lot of weight since being on the Canal, as had most of the marines, and he knew he'd changed outwardly as well as inwardly. The sun had burnt his dark skin even darker, and there was a harder look to him. It wasn't until he looked at his eyes that he recognized any of his former features. They looked the same, calm and flat, regarding the world with a mixture of acceptance and cynicism. And, he thought with a slight smile that barely stretched his chiseled mouth, he was growing some whiskers, though not very many.

"Arizona!" came a shout, and Redhawk's smile widened. It had become a familiar cry lately, and he was finally getting his wish, finally keeping his promise to Philip Johnston. The code talkers were an important part of the Marines now and had proven their worth.

Part Three

Chapter Seventeen

1943-1944

After the success of the Navajo code on the Island, those involved in the program became aware of a new problem rapidly becoming apparent. New code words had been added to the original code, and it was necessary to inform and teach the newest recruits before they could be utilized. Back in the United States, now Staff Sergeant Philip Johnston finally got the go-ahead to begin a retraining school at Marine Headquarters in Oahu, Hawaii. Recruitment of Navajos for training had continued after the original group had shipped out. There were one hundred and ninety new recruits that had completed the training at Camp Pendleton in California. (Camp Elliott was no longer used.)

The battered marines from Fifth Division left Cactus in November, and it was a weary, soul-sick group of code talkers who arrived in Hawaii for leave and then a retraining session.

"Thirty days was not enough," Redhawk said, and Johns agreed.

"But now we have at least six more weeks of training to complete, so we won't be sent back to the front for a while yet."

Redhawk shook his head. "I don't understand that. Why do we have to be retrained? Didn't we perform well?"

"According to General Vadegrift, we performed much better than he'd ever thought."

"So, why are we here?" Redhawk persisted. "We should be with our outfit, fighting in the Marianas."

Johns grinned. "They'll wait on us. I heard Sergeant Jones say he doesn't intend to get replacements so they'll send us back to him."

"Yeah, but think of all the fun they're having without us," Redhawk shot back, and they both laughed. It had become a joke with them, and to his surprise, he realized that he really did miss the men of the Fifth. Fighting alongside a man formed strong ties. Even with Kryzminsky and Weintraub gone, he felt a strong pull.

Reaching around him, Johns pushed open the door to the classroom and they went inside. There were other code talkers there who had been in battle, most of them on the Canal but a few who had been on the transport or communication ships. Their stories were all similar, all revolving around the use of the code in action. And Redhawk was discovering that he wasn't the only one who had been mistaken for the enemy. It was a familiar story among the Navajos, and they all laughed. One man had even been pulled naked from a bathing hole after some MPs decided he was one of the Jap prisoners they had taken. It took his commander to rescue the Navajo, who, it was said, had been bored with the entire proceeding.

Most surprising of all was the fact that Redhawk was not the only one who had been discouraged by the slowness of his superiors to recognize the use of the code. The others had experienced the same resistance, and a few had not had the opportunity to use the code in the field. There were new recruits mixed in with the "veterans," and one of them was to assist in the instruction of new terms.

"All in all, gentlemen," the instructor, Staff Sergeant Jerry Bradshaw said, "the code seems to be working well. We have passed the actual field test with flying colors. My congratulations to all of you who fought so bravely on the Island." He paused to smile at them, his gaze flicking over men who were just beginning to recuperate from their three months of hell. "After the officers in the field on Guadalcanal finally realized the speed, efficiency, and accuracy of the code in extreme battle situations, I have had requests from every marine division for at least eighty-two talkers for each division. Unfortunately, that is impossible at this time. At present, we only have enough trained men for eight to a division. Barely enough. So, upon your reassignments, you will be used strictly in upper echelon communications. That is all we can do until more men are recruited and trained. Sergeant Johnston is now at Camp Pendleton, and he professes himself quite proud of the way you men have handled yourselves." Bradshaw paused to glance around the room again. "You will be notified of your reassignments before the end of your training session."

In April, U.S. intelligence experts managed to intercept a message concerning the Commander in Chief of Japan's Navy. Admiral Yamamoto would be flying to Bougainville in four days. Bougainville was in range of the P-38's at Henderson Field, and the Cactus Air Force seized the opportunity to rid themselves of a formidable foe.

On April 18, two P-38's took chase on the Betty bombers that would be carrying the admiral. They broke formation to escape, and the U.S. fighters swooped down with guns blazing, taking out both bombers. The one with Admiral Yamamoto crashed and burned in the jungles of Bougainville.

In May of 1943, a dual drive was commenced, with General MacArthur's forces advancing northwest from New Guinea and Admiral Nimitz's forces moving west across the central Pacific. Both routes were to be used in hopes of preventing the Japanese from knowing when and where the next strike would take place.

General MacArthur and Admiral Halsey worked out a plan calling for a series of attacks focused on Rabaul as the ultimate goal. MacArthur's troops were to capture Lae and other Japanese-held points in northeast New Guinea, leap across the Vitiaz and Dampier straits to New Britain. Halsey's forces were to be moving toward Rabaul from the opposite direction, the chain of Solomon Islands, taking a number of Japanese-held islands lying between Rabaul and Guadalcanal.

Operation *Cartwheel* was set for June 30, 1943, and employed the strategy of simultaneous landings by MacArthur's and Halsey's forces along the curve of islands southwest, south, and southeast of Rabaul. American forces landed at Nassau Bay on June 30, taking it from the enemy. By March 20, 1944, Rabaul was completely encircled. The maneuver had begun with the invasion of Guadalcanal eighteen months before, and now the 100,000 Japanese troops still on the base were completely isolated and virtually out of the war.

One fifth of the invading marines on Tarawa were killed or wounded in November of 1943.

Redhawk and Johns were among those lucky enough to survive with only minor wounds and a raging case of dysentery.

After another thirty-day leave, this time back in the United States, where Willie Johns had a reunion with his brother, they were reassigned to the V Amphibious Corps, Fourth Marine Division. None of the guys they'd known on the Canal or in boot camp were with them. William Brown had been assigned to another campaign, and Little Wolf Smith had been injured in the last days on Guadalcanal and been shipped back home.

Redhawk and Johns were sent back to Pearl Harbor.

Training of the units assigned to the V Corps for the Marianas operation began seriously during the second week of March and continued until the end of May. Although the Army and Marines trained separately, the maneuvers were the same. Emphasis was placed on individual and small unit training. There were day and night exercises, as well as those stressing cooperation between tank and infantry teams and naval and artillery support. And after participating in those exercises, the code talkers were drilled in the code.

It was exhausting but had its lighter moments. The instructors found it difficult to keep up with the Indians who were their pupils and, on occasion, resorted to disgusted comments about their own lack of ability.

The Second Marine Division conducted amphibious maneuvers on Maui in the last weeks of March, and the Fourth Marine Division followed suit in the last two weeks of April. On the seventeenth of May, there was a full-scale landing exercise, with both divisions participating at Maalaea Bay, Maui. Two days later, a similar exercise was performed at Kahoolawe Island, south of Maui. That time, the troops practiced under actual naval bombardment.

It was old hat to Redhawk, Johns, and their old friend from Camp Elliott, Bell Wood, and they all laughed as the new recruits cowered in their foxholes while shells whistled overhead and dropped with alarming accuracy.

"Ah, they won't actually kill anyone just to show us what not to do," Redhawk soothed one jittery marine. "It's all part of basic training."

"But do they have to use live ammo?" the marine shot back, wincing as another shell exploded close by. "What if I stick my head up at the wrong time?"

"Then the man beside you will learn not to do the same," Redhawk replied solemnly. The recruit blanched, and the veterans laughed. Had they ever been so new and raw?

The Navajo code was top secret. The marines who were not directly involved in the program were briefed in the necessity of secrecy. This was to be a classified project. They were counting on the Navajos as a vital part of the war effort.

May 21, 1944 rolled around, and the troops milled nervously on the decks of the ship. The slow-moving LST groups were loaded with the first assault troops, and were scheduled to leave Pearl Harbor with the artillery and LVTs on the twenty-fourth. During the loading operations, an explosion carelessly caused by a civilian cigarette blasted one of the LSTs, resulting in a raging fire that destroyed five other crafts in the harbor. In spite of heroic efforts to stop the fire from spreading to the other vessels, the damage was grave. None of the LSTs could be salvaged, and all of the equipment and supplies on board were destroyed. Ninety-five men of the Second Marine Division and one hundred twelve men of the Fourth Marine Division were killed while their comrades watched helplessly.

Though Admiral Turner was uncertain enough ships could be found to replace those destroyed, the marines managed to find and load replacements in record time, and the invasion of the Marianas proceeded on schedule. Saipan . . .

The Mariana Islands are made up of three main bodies of land: Guam, Tinian, and Saipan. All major Japanese defenses, these islands were part of a chain that led to the Japanese mainland.

For the weeks prior to the scheduled attack, Johns and Redhawk worked almost nonstop on the flagship's radio. They were to play a key role in the invasion, sending and receiving vital orders and information. The Navy used them as much as the Marines, and they worked in shifts.

"We've come a long way since those days on the Island, when we thought we'd never get to prove the code," Redhawk said to Johns late one night. Johns nodded wearily. He was just coming off duty, trading places with Redhawk, who had been below sleeping until it was his shift.

"It won't be long now—if we believe these last orders."

Redhawk grinned. "How do we know that? The Army, Navy, and Marines can't seem to agree on anything. Plans have changed so many times, I wonder if any of the brass can remember what the plan is."

"Maybe we should ask Tokyo Rose," Johns suggested, and they both laughed.

The night before, the admiral had come into the

radio room while Redhawk and Johns were both there, and he had put a hand on each of their shoulders.

"Men," he'd boomed, "I just want to tell you that your code is invaluable. These messages are vital, and you men are doing your job with a speed and efficiency that amazes me." Pausing, the admiral smiled slightly, then added, "And what I like best is that those yellow bastards have no idea what you're saying! Tokyo Rose's last transmission made mention of the fact that the United States Marines must be planning something, because they were giving a very poor imitation of the Japanese language in their radio transmissions!" He chuckled, then gave them another pat on the back. "Keep up the good work!"

After he'd gone, Redhawk and Johns had exchanged gratified glances. Appreciation was a very sweet tonic, indeed.

That night, Redhawk carefully transcribed the words of the fleet commanding officer. Some 530 warships and auxiliaries that carried over 127,000 troops were waiting off the coast of Saipan for the word. The first move would be made by the reserve regiments some four miles north of the Second and Fourth Divisions. This attack, however, was to be a feint, a ruse to fool the Japanese troops into believing that was where the main offensive would begin.

Redhawk listened carefully to all the messages being transmitted in code, and he was able to get a hazy picture of what was to take place. The island air base was vital to the Americans, being large enough for B-29's, the massive planes that required a lot more airfield than the smaller fighter planes.

A transmission crackled over the radio, and he

scribbled it down as it came in. ". . . good position for LVTs and LSTs to go ashore . . . must dynamite more areas . . . request protection from naval guns for at least two hours until mission is completed. . . ."

General Howlin' Mad Smith had ordered that the code talkers be used exclusively in ship to shore transmissions. Redhawk and Johns drew the ship assignment, transmitting orders and coordinates to the forward marine patrols in the first waves of attack on Saipan. It was June 15, 1944.

It was agonizing to sit helplessly on the ship after having been deeply involved in combat and take messages regarding the fierce fighting of their troops. For three weeks, until July 9, the marines battled against overwhelming odds to complete the capture of the island.

Code named *Forager,* the operation ended with high casualties on Saipan—3,126 U.S. dead. But the cost for the enemy was much higher—27,000 Japanese dead, virtually wiping out the entire garrison.

From July 9 to 24, the Second and Fourth Marine Divisions were reorganized for the coming assault on Tinian. Again, the Japanese fought fiercely, expending enormous numbers of men on suicidal counterattacks. By the thirty-first of July, the island had been cleared north to south.

By this time, the engagement at Guam had begun. The Third Marine Division and the Seventy-seventh Army Division were landed on the island, supplemented by the First Marine Brigade. Two landings had been made, north and south of the Orote Peninsula. After a struggle costing 1,400 American lives and 10,000 Japanese killed, the island fell to the U.S.

American ships were pounding through the Philippine Sea with enough steel and iron to sink the world. They did irreparable damage to the seapower of the Japanese and inflicted heavy casualties on their air forces. The dogfight in the air came to be known as the "Great Marianas Turkey Shoot."

The capture of the Marianas and the completion of the Solomons/New Guinea operation paved the way for the next action of the war. Nimitz favored a drive against Formosa or China, but General MacArthur insisted upon a move to free the Philippines. There were those who believed the general's motive was purely a personal one: Having been forced to retreat in 1942, he had vowed to return one day. President Roosevelt agreed with MacArthur, and plans were formed to make a move by both MacArthur's and Nimitz's forces against the southern Philippine island of Leyte. By December, enemy resistance had ended, and all Japanese shipping in Leyte waters was at a virtual standstill. Enemy casualties numbered over 70,000, while the American losses were 15,584. By the end of the battle of Leyte Gulf, Japan's seapower was shattered forever.

From the middle of 1943 to the middle of 1944, an advance of 1,300 miles had been made in the Pacific, cutting off more than 150,000 Japanese troops.

Now, the attention of the Commanders in Chief turned to the last leg of the Pacific ladder leading to the Japanese mainland—Iwo Jima.

Chapter Eighteen
The Beginning of the End

"Iwo Jima is part of the Japanese empire, gentlemen. On a straight line northward from the Marianas to the mainland, it is almost exactly halfway between Saipan and Tokyo." The general stopped to tap his stick on the large wall map. "It is vital that we secure this tiny island. For security purposes, it has remained unnamed until now."

On the front row, Redhawk listened carefully. He was fast becoming a battle-scarred veteran, a warrior who had made it through some of the heaviest conflicts. He no longer trembled at the sound of bombs falling, but rather cursed them as harshly as any seasoned marine. Bombs were a nuisance, to be endured until possible retaliation.

But listening to the general outline their strategy, he felt the first tremors of disquiet.

"Mount Suribachi—which stands for cone-shaped mountain in Japanese—is just that, gentlemen," the general said in a short, gruff voice. "Iwo Jima is a sulphur island, hence the name. You will find the smell quite strong and noxious, so be prepared."

Redhawk's throat tightened and he glanced at Johns, who remembered the peyote dream as well as he did. Sulphur? In his dream there had been a strong smell of sulphur and blood all around, running in rivers. . . .

"So," the general was continuing, "be certain you take your Halzedone tablets to purify the water before you drink it. And of course, take your own water supply and hope it lasts." He cleared his throat again and tapped his pointer against the small teardrop-shaped island. "Iwo Jima is only five miles long and two and a half miles wide in the middle. This neck gradually flares out for more than a mile north of the base of Suribachi, and then widens to the east to give us the wide center. This northern part of the island is high ground, forming about two thirds of the area. A rocky plateau rises almost three hundred feet above sea level. The middle of the island is fairly level, with only occasional hills. It is a volcano island and was formed by two volcanoes rising from the sea. There are two craters, one inactive, the other still smoldering. Watch it; sulphur bubbles extremely hot in places. Suribachi rises five hundred fifty feet into the air, and there is a civilian village at its base."

As the general gave them the lecture on the topographical features of the island as well as the strength of the enemy and the importance of the two airfields, Redhawk thought about the recent fighting they'd done. He wondered if it had all been just to prepare him for this. He and Willie Johns, Bell Wood, and other experienced marines were to go in before the invasion, reconnoiter, and radio back vital information. It was a dangerous mission, and it was more than likely they would not return. The island was already swarming with Japanese, and General Kuribayashi had a firm foothold. The enemy realized the importance and were prepared to defend it to the last man.

There was no jungle on the island, only barren ground, tuft grass, bean vines, cultivated fields of lemon grass, small swales of sugarcane, and a small forest of oak trees to the east of Motoyama, the main village. There was also a small sugar refinery and huge vats for the sulphur processing.

"No jungle?" Johns muttered. "No jungle rot or festered feet? We won't know how to fight. . . ."

Redhawk laughed softly. "There will be other problems to make up for the lack of jungle. There always are."

"And don't kid yourselves thinking we've got an element of surprise on our side," the general turned to say. "We don't. The Japs have been waiting on us for eight months."

Twenty-five code talkers were to be in the Fifth Division. There would be ship to shore communications as well as division to division. By now, Redhawk and Johns had been used in many capacities. The past two years of battle had formed them into fighting men of the finest caliber, and they had both received medals, with Redhawk receiving the Silver Cross for a leg injury on Guam.

"Tell us," one of the newer recruits said after the debriefing had ended and they were on the ship's bridge, "have you seen much action?"

Redhawk and Johns exchanged glances, and both of them smiled slightly. "Our share of it," Redhawk said in a quiet voice. "You will, too."

The young Navajo looked at Redhawk and saw a composed man not much older than himself, but with eyes as old as the red buttes of Arizona. He was quiet, a respectful quiet that was shared by the other new recruits.

Redhawk shifted uncomfortably, not quite certain he liked being the object of so much curiosity. Clearing his throat, he said, "Taking the island will not be easy, but none of them are. The ones who make it are the ones who are careful."

"Didn't you ever take any risks, Corporal?" the young man asked.

Corporal. It still startled Redhawk when he was called that. He appreciated the promotion more than he did the medal.

"Yes, and I survived them. Not everyone does, but not everyone survives even when they're careful." He couldn't help but think about Weintraub and Kryzminsky, who had not died heroes' deaths but had died quietly, hiding in trenches from anonymous enemy bombs.

Later, when Redhawk and Johns sat quietly on their racks, Redhawk said with a note of fierceness in his voice, "I would rather die fighting than to die hiding!"

Johns just looked at him. He didn't have to feel the same to understand what his cousin meant. "You may get your wish if the brass has their way," he said after a moment.

"What do you mean?"

"You know, the reconnaissance we're going to do."

"Oh. Yes, you may be right."

A final rehearsal was conducted by the fleet off Tinian. The assault forces—the first ten waves—were placed on board LSTs. Having been trained for invasion by descending over the rail of the much larger attack transports—APAs—and clambering down rope nets into furiously bobbing landing craft bumping alongside the ship, they now learned they would be making the assault in a much different manner. The troops were to board amphibian tractors (LVTs) that were lined up in the dingy holds of LSTs, then roll through opened bow doors and descend a metal ramp to the sea. It was easier and not nearly as difficult as trying to land in an erratically moving boat from the rail, but the small LVTs plunged so deeply in the water that it left more than a few marines with heaving stomachs.

During the last invasion training maneuvers, the marines were not actually landed ashore on Tinian, but made a run toward the beach, then veered away. The men were drilled and drilled again, dusted with DDT, and exhorted not to salute or address officers by their titles in combat. The latter had a simple purpose: The enemy would be searching for high-priority targets, and any reference to an officer would immediately draw their fire.

They were now on their way, heading to the small island in the Pacific on February 15, four days before scheduled D day. Loaded LSTs carrying the marines of the Fourth and Fifth Divisions bore down on Iwo Jima. The main body of vessels were to follow on the sixteenth, bringing the rest of the men of the Fourth and Fifth, and a regiment of the Third that had joined the convoy from its base on Guam. On February 17, transports carrying the remainder of the Third Division and its attached units would bring up the rear. They were the floating reserves.

B-24 and B-25 bombers had been shelling Iwo Jima for sixty-nine days when the reconnaissance patrol was sent in under cover of darkness. Some fifty men were sent out, with instructions to seek out the enemy and report their strength and position. The estimates were that the enemy numbered over twenty thousand.

It was dark, and the Higgins boats bearing Redhawk and the others chugged in close to the faintly glimmering shoreline. The beach was gray with volcanic ash, and the marines had smeared soot over their faces to reduce visibility. Armed with Browning Automatic Rifles, as well as a working knowledge of Japanese—*Koh-sahn seh yoh!* meant "Surrender!"; *Boo-kee oh steh roh!* meant "Drop your weapons!"; *Koh-roh-sah-nah-ee-yoh!* meant "We won't murder you!"; *Koh-chee koh-ee!* meant "Come here!"; and *Dah-mah-reh!* meant "Shut up!—the Marines were as prepared as they were going to get. They split up into squads after splashing through the shallows to the beach.

Redhawk squatted briefly in a clump of brush, men pressing close around him. He was his squad's leader, and was responsible for gathering information, radioing it back, and getting as many of them out of there as he could. The feeling of responsibility weighed heavily on him.

"The shelling has slowed so that we might reach our objectives," Redhawk said, "but it will pick up again. The frogmen are also employed on the beach and in the surf, so watch who you are shooting at." He paused, his gaze flicking from one taut face to another. Most of the marines were white, with only a few Navajos among them to secure the code. Though they had been drilled repeatedly, the Anglo marines were not as adept at reconnoitering enemy territory without being seen or heard. Brought up in a land where there were no streetlights or city lights, the Indian marines were accustomed to traveling in the dark. It was not going to be easy out here, and he appointed one Navajo to every two Anglo marines.

"Stay close and stay quiet. Remember what we are here for, and do not try to engage the enemy yourself."

The gunfire support vessels off Iwo had begun a slow, heavy barrage intended to cover the landing of the frogmen on the eastern beach, while the reconnaissance patrols were put ashore farther up. Mortar shells exploded with booming violence along the gray sandy beach.

Ducking as a particularly close shell exploded, showering them with fragments of metal and island, Redhawk swore softly, then motioned for the squad to follow. They had split up as they landed, with squads heading in five different directions to scout out the enemy positions and make estimates of their strength. Navajo code talkers aboard ship were waiting to receive these important messages . . . messages that were vital to the Americans.

"It looks like those fuckin' Nips are dug in pretty good," Bell Wood muttered, and Redhawk gave him a quick glance.

"You're right." Blockhouses had been built along the beach, and the enemy had dug in deep in the mountains and caves of the island. Pillboxes—machine-gun pits built of concrete in the shape of a box—were firmly entrenched on the beach as well as at the base of Mount Suribachi.

That first night was spent in tense silence for the most part, with the marines trying to make themselves invisible to the enemy. With long slender sticks in hand to check for possible traps, they made their way carefully around the outer edge of the thick forest of oaks. It fringed the eastern edge of Motoyama, now just a collection of debris and twisted sheets of metal, crumbled buildings, and an air of desolation. Canteens clanked softly against their legs, and their weapons were kept up and ready.

As they reached a peculiarly shaped outthrust of rocks and dirt, Redhawk gave the silent signal to halt. Their own artillery was still coming down in a blizzard of shells, the noise deafening and the explosions shaking the ground. Carefully parting the sharp-edged blades of grass, he peered through them to the unusual hump of ground. He sat still for several minutes, trying to figure out what it was, and then he felt a nudge in his back. It was Whitworth, the marine he'd met in boot camp three long years before, and he was grinning at him.

"Tank camouflage," Whitworth mouthed silently, and at last Redhawk recognized it.

He nodded briefly and grinned back. The Japanese had cleverly hidden their tanks with mounds of dirt and brush to resemble the terrain. He noted the position and moved back. An hour's search turned up two more tank positions, thirty pillboxes, seven coast defense guns, fifteen dual-purpose guns with five-inch bores, and nine large blockhouses.

Redhawk radioed back to the ship, directing the artillery fire where it would do the most good. The Navy was quick to respond, and shells began bursting around them with deadly accuracy.

"Damn!" Whitworth said, lifting his head for a moment to glare at Redhawk. "Did you have to tell 'em to get us, too?"

Redhawk didn't answer. He was on the phone busily calling the ships again. ". . . 0130 hours

. . . put a cork in the whale's spout . . . some of our men getting wet in quad eleven. . . ."

"I don't know what you said, Chief," Whitworth muttered as the shelling altered course slightly, "but it seems to be working."

"It better," Johns put in grimly. "We lost a man with that last shell."

The squad was down to nine men, and Redhawk directed the covering of the dead marine with his poncho, marking the spot for later retrieval. There wasn't time now, and it would endanger the entire operation if they were to try to take the dead back.

A scouting of the caves on the hillside resulted in the grave discovery that there were thousands of the enemy dug into the formidable strongholds. Johns took a message from the ship telling them to move back so that artillery fire could be directed at the caves, and as they did, they were spotted by the enemy. A withering barrage of *ack-ack* sprayed across their position as they clung helplessly to the side of the hill, exposed and unable to retreat.

Bullets stitched the ground and brush, and there was an agonized cry as one of the marines was hit. Redhawk pressed his face against the rough scraping of rock and waited for a pause in the fire, then threw himself back and down the slope, rolling like a beach ball until he reached bottom. A moment later, six other men followed suit, half rolling, half sliding down the hill and out of range of the gunners.

"Move it," Redhawk shouted, "before they shift position to get us from the other side!"

Helping the wounded marine between two men, they ran in a zigzagging line while the enemy tried to get a fix on them. U.S. salvos began to fall again, the shells tearing up the ground in chunks and giving them a smoke screen as they ran.

"Are they trying to help or hit us?" one man screamed, and Redhawk wondered the same thing. At the moment, it was a toss-up.

Grabbing his radio, he called in code for more smokers to hide them. ". . . Am taking heavy fire, repeat heavy fire. Have hawk drop eggs two hundred yards east, two hundred yards east. . . ."

"Hey, I think they've got some anti-tank guns up there," Whitworth rasped, and Redhawk looked where he was pointing.

"Yeah, it looks like it." He jerked at the radio again, barking into it, "Four anti-tank guns in cliffs over East Boat Basin, possibly more . . ."

Scrambling toward a line of underbrush with the wounded marines in tow, Redhawk and his squad dug in for the night. They were in the very shadow of the enemy.

By the end of their reconnaissance, the patrols reported a huge increase in the number of pillboxes dug into the island—from less than fifty in the fall of 1944 to over three hundred. Concrete-reinforced blockhouses had grown from only two to almost forty. Out of the fifty men in the original patrol, twelve had been killed. The Japanese were, indeed, ready for them.

Chapter Nineteen
Thirty-Six Days Of Hell

February 19, 1945. Iwo Jima thrust darkly from the sea, a grim specter against the grayish horizon. From the ships, the island looked stark and barren, with nothing living on it . . . no trees, no trace of human beings. Thin wisps of clouds hid the top of Mount Suribachi from view, and the cliffs along the shoreline stood in curling seafoam.

By 0630, all transports were ready and in position. Less than ten minutes later, the naval bombardment began. In spite of the past seventy-two days of heavy bombardment this was to be the heaviest yet, a rain of fire and death on the enemy to ease the marines' landing.

Two battleships on the west coast and five on the east opened up with seventy-five rounds each within the first hour and a half. Cruisers blasted away with one hundred rounds each in a withering barrage, and clouds of smoke and dust rose above the writhing island in obscuring drifts. Not a single foot of the island from Mount Suribachi to Airfield No. 2 was to be left free of fire.

Naval bombardment was lifted from the beaches at 0857. Marine Corsairs clawed through the air in metallic streaks, screaming over Suribachi to drop their bombs. The oval missiles fell end over end, dropping into the volcano crater and destroying gun positions bristling along its sides. Gigantic balls of flame and thick clouds of smoke belched high into the air when the bombs exploded.

"Ready?" Redhawk asked Johns after sucking in a deep breath. Johns shrugged.

"Is anyone ever?"

Shaking his head, Redhawk went over his mental checklist of things to be done and supplies to be taken: The top of his canteen was tight, pins on his grenades bent just enough to keep them from being accidentally pulled, but not enough to slow his pulling them when necessary; his rifle was free of dust and ready, his radio in superb working condition. He carried two heavy packs of gear, a gas mask, a rolled blanket, and the inevitable poncho, as well as extra clothing and toilet supplies. His steel helmet was covered with a camouflaging brown cloth cover like the other marines, and he wore the official insignia of the Corps on the left breast pocket of his olive-green fatigues.

Because of their dangerous scouting mission, he and Johns were to go in the third assault wave. It suited him just fine. He had no burning desire to be a hero, nor did he want to sit and wait for death to find him. It was a contradiction of sorts, but his being here was a contradiction if it came down to that. What was a Navajo boy from Arizona doing out here? What was a Pennsylvania farm boy doing out here, or a young man fresh out of high school in Tennessee, for that matter?

"It's time," Johns said as the order came down to "Land the third wave."

There was a surge of men into boats, and from their position on the rail, Redhawk could see the churning waves of boats steering for the beach. Iwo had been divided into seven landing zones on the two miles of ebony sand curving from Mount Suribachi to the northern cliffs around a stone quarry. Green Beach—at the base of Suribachi—Red Beach I and II, Yellow Beach I and II, Blue Beach I and II, were the commonplace names. Not exactly stirring names like Omaha or Normandy, but for the men storming toward them with their hearts in their mouths and determination and fear in their faces, they were the most important names at the moment.

Amtracs pawed their way through the sea to reach the shore, making it with little trouble and only erratic enemy fire. But when the machines tried to claw their way up the steep fifteen-foot terraces on the shifting black sand, it was a different story. Remaining on the beach would mean certain death, and the wave of marines coming from behind had to have room to maneuver. There was an immediate choke-up of amtracs, while some tried to reverse gears to back offshore a few yards. Those poured on howitzer and machine-gun fire as a cover. It didn't get better. The amtracs up ahead snarled through the sand, but were heading straight for a concentration of pillboxes and blockhouses.

Marines spilled from the amtracs as the rear ramps thudded down onto the sand, running in ragged lines along the two miles of beach. Only a few sporadic small arms fire greeted them as they hit the beach in a dead run. The first few steps were easy enough, but then the men found that they were bogging down in the shifting, sucking grains of treacherous volcanic sand. Still they pushed on, leaving behind huge mammoth-size footprints as they struggled toward the terraces.

After the first few minutes of chaos, the marines began to organize themselves into squads, platoons, companies, and battalions. At least the beaches were free of enemy fire—for the moment. Three waves of twelve hundred marines stormed ashore.

Hummocks of sand that looked as innocent as anthills suddenly sprouted deadly machine-gun fire from tiny openings barely visible above ground level. Mortars as thick as hailstones poured down from hundreds of hidden pits. Antiaircraft guns and heavy artillery raked the beaches with devastating fire. Land mines that had been cleverly stitched into the terrain of the terraces exploded with sickening *ka-booms* as unwary marines stepped on them, and fifteen-inch coastal defense guns blasted from Suribachi's base, sides, and crater.

Watching from the ship, Redhawk felt his throat tighten with tension. It looked like hell, it was hell, and he was about to join them.

It is a good day to die, my son. . . .

There was no main defenses for the marines to overcome. Every inch of the beach was honeycombed with pits of death. The Japanese had over six thousand men pinned down on a pitifully small three-thousand-yard ribbon of wet sand, with more boats still trying to land.

Fourth Division headed for the far right of the beachhead. It was a dangerous, almost suicidal push to capture a heavily fortified hill surmounting a rock quarry studded with enemy pillboxes and concrete blockhouses. Devastating fire awaited that first wave. A naval gunfire liaison team was to pinpoint targets for the ships, radioing back the exact positions. As marines struggled up the steep terraces beside the quarry, heaving bulky loads of radio gear through that treacherous terrain, they were pounded with mortars.

And on the ship, the third wave was being sent in. Redhawk and Johns clambered into the landing craft and grabbed hold as it rumbled down the ramp to splash into the sea. It was hard to hear anything but their own voices ringing back to them. The noise was immense—the explosions onshore, the ship to shore firing that made their ears ring, and the shouting and yelling of men wound so tightly they had to release their tension.

Redhawk's mouth was dry and his throat tight. No matter how many times he was part of an invasion force he would never grow used to these first few minutes of terror. Once on land, with the shells falling haphazardly and small arms fire spitting around him with indiscrimination, he could function, but now he was at the utter mercy of the enemy and fate. He had no control over anything, but was an excellent target as the Higgins rolled toward the smoky shoreline.

It had been less than an hour and the dead and dying were already being evacuated in droves, rows of poncho-draped forms lying still on the beach, men crying and moaning, adding to the cacophony of sound assaulting the ears.

"Dear God," a man beside Redhawk said as they stumbled from the boats and into the shallow waters, where bodies bobbed aimlessly like lost fishing corks, "this is a scene from hell!"

Redhawk agreed. He'd always visualized the white man's hell as a place of fire and brimstone, with mountains of evil-smelling sulphur, and now he was there. It was the white man's war and it would be the white man's hell, he thought distractedly, then had to hit the wet beach as a shell screamed down. The man beside him disappeared in a froth of blood and smoke, and Redhawk blinked in surprise. There was nothing left but a shallow depression in the sand and part of a leg. His ears rang and his vision was blurred, but he did not dare stay in one place.

Lurching up, he saw Willie Johns and Bell Wood a little farther up the beach, and not far from them was Whitworth and their commanding officer. He tried to run through the sand that sucked at his feet like clutching hands, finally making it to the firmer terrace with the others.

"We're to push to the quarry and take the enemy defense positions," Captain Ron Frederickson shouted, waving the men forward. "Piss on the fire and call the dogs!"

"Get down!" someone else yelled, and they all dove for any cover they could find, some trying to dig holes in the shifting sands of the beach and finding it impossible. The sand just oozed back into the hole as quickly as it was dug out.

Mortars whooshed down, some as big as 320mm, nearly three times the size of the largest U.S. mortars.

"They look like fuckin' garbage cans flying through the air," Whitworth observed gloomily, then ducked as one landed a few hundred yards away. Even at that distance, the explosion rocked the ground, spewing out huge fragments of metal that chewed up a human body with an indescribable effect.

"Arizona!"

Redhawk surged upward again, pushing doggedly through the sand, hearing the cry that was his motivation.

"Arizona, send a message," Frederickson ordered.

Heavy static crackled on the radio as Redhawk fell into a foxhole and called the ship. "Catching maximum from the quarry," he radioed in code, the Navajo tongue guttural and sounding even harsher with the noise of battle all around him. *"Be-al-doh-cid-da-hi . . . a-knah-as-donih ah-ha-tinh . . ."*

"Tell them mortar and machine-gun fire is heavy," the captain broke in, and Redhawk nodded.

"I did."

The men under Frederickson huddled in a huge crater and waited for the next lull in the battle, waited for the next move forward.

Sherman tanks roared up the shoreline a short time later, giving Redhawk mixed emotions. Having the tanks was comforting on one hand, but they drew immediate enemy fire. An armored bulldozer preceded the rumbling giants, and the thirty-six-ton steel monsters waddled clumsily along the terraces. One tank was taken out by a land mine that left it crippled enough for shells from anti-tank guns to completely destroy it.

Landing zones for the Fourth Division stretched north from halfway up the shore to the high, pocked cliffs above the East Boat Landing, the area where Redhawk and his patrol had discovered the huge guns only a few days before. He knew that there were masses of concrete blockhouses armed with the coastal defense guns and artillery, as well as a veritable maze of bunkers, caves, and pillboxes. The entire area was riddled with anti-tank and heavy machine guns on the steep, seemingly impenetrable slopes. The high vantage point of the enemy allowed them to turn the beaches into a death trap.

Pinned down under devastating fire, Redhawk looked over at the few men in the crater with him. The captain, Johns, and Whitworth sat hunched over their weapons, faces gray and taut, lips compressed into tight lines.

"This is like a fuckin' turkey shoot," Whitworth said a few moments later, "and we're the turkeys!"

He was right. There was no place to hide, no place to escape the blistering fire they were getting. At least on the other landings, there had been some sort of cover, some sort of shelter where they could pause and recoup. Here, on this barren volcanic island, there was nothing and nowhere to hide.

"Arizona," Frederickson said after another shell had landed close by, "send another message. We've got to have some relief, and our men are being cut to pieces. Have them shell the cliffs, quadrant fourteen. . . ."

A pelting of rocks bounced off their helmets and rattled on their packs as Redhawk struggled to bring his radio up again. Not far away, someone had stepped on a land mine, and a bare foot dropped into the crater from the sky. Redhawk ignored it. His attention was focused on the radio and his message.

". . . 1140 hours, 4/25. Need artillery at quadrant fourteen, men are being shelled hard . . . 1140 hours . . ." he said in rapid code, using the Navajo term *be-al-doh-tso-lani,* or "many big guns for artillery." It was translated quickly on the other end, and he told Frederickson, "They should react soon."

"Are you sure this code can't be broken, Chief?" the captain asked worriedly. "I'd hate to have the Japs blowing our asses off just because we told them where we were."

"It hasn't been broken yet," Redhawk replied calmly. "I do not think it will be."

Minutes later, a withering barrage of artillery hit the cliffs above the trapped marines, enabling them to make a run for better cover. And to make it even better, F6F Hellcat fighter bombers zoomed in to drop bombs on Japanese positions just ahead of the advancing Fourth.

"Hot damn!" a marine cried as he leaped up from his foxhole and dashed toward better cover. "Just what the doctor ordered!"

Fierce small arms fire and grenades pinned them down for a few more minutes, but the marines wouldn't stay.

Third Battalion surged forward, determined and desperate, fighting back as viciously as the enemy. Whitworth ran up behind a sand-covered pillbox barring their way and tossed a grenade inside, then ducked as it exploded, effectively silencing the men within. He looked at his squad with a pleased expression and proceeded to the next pillbox. While Johns or Wood directed a stream of machine-gun fire at the small gun slits of the pillbox, Whitworth went behind to toss in his grenade. The muffled explosions and flying debris made him smile as delightedly as a child.

"Come on, Whitworth!" the captain yelled. "You're pushing your luck and we need you over here."

Regretfully, Whitworth joined his platoon on their trek up the rocky slopes. The marines were rapidly discovering that though it was unsafe to remain in the open, it was just as dangerous to take cover in trenches or huge craters. As soon as one of the likely refuges was filled with marines, the enemy would plaster it with shell and mortar fire, killing or wounding most of them.

The good news, Redhawk discovered as he listened to the radio transmissions, was that B and C Company of First Battalion had made it across the island to the western side only ninety minutes after landing. They had suffered heavy losses but had managed to inflict losses on the enemy as well.

On the beach behind them, Seabees probed for mines and destroyed those they found. The Seabees were busily trying to unload supplies onto the beaches and were being hit by heavy fire at the same time. Officers with bullhorns directed the landing and unloading of troop and cargo vessels, their voices carrying for five hundred yards or more. The Seabees, too, suffered greatly as they carried ammo over the hills and struggled to free bogged vehicles with a Caterpillar. One Seabee encountered a grisly dilemma as he unloaded a heavy Cat from the hold of an LSM. Upon reaching the ramp, he saw that the sand in front of the ramp was littered with dead marines. Torn between the great need for getting the Cat ashore and his abhorrence at abusing the dead, he finally ground his teeth together and drove the heavy machine over them, rationalizing that they were beyond feeling and the men above needed his help.

The Twenty-fifth Marines finally mounted the ridge they had been pushing toward all day under blistering fire. They discovered concrete bunkers that had been battered by the navy shelling, as well as pillboxes, caves, and trenches swarming with determined enemy. They fought fiercely, their bayonets flashing in the late afternoon light, hand to hand at times, slashing and shooting the enemy with ferocious energy. It wasn't until they were allowed to withdraw a hundred yards to the rear to recoup and exchange places with relief troops that they realized how weary they were and how many of them were dead.

By 1630 hours, the quarry was in American hands, and the order went out to consolidate positions for the night and expect the worst. The marines fully expected the enemy to come at them in screaming *banzai* attacks, their favored method of warfare in the past.

This time they were wrong.

Darkness fell swiftly, twilight lingering for only thirty minutes. Redhawk dug in with Johns and Whitworth and waited for the inevitable. Nearby, he could hear men complaining about being cold, but somehow, they had managed to find a crater heated by volcanic warmth just below the surface.

"All the comforts of home," Whitworth sighed, hugging his blanket around him.

Redhawk found it hard to enjoy any humor. His mind was focused on the harsh realities of war, the terrible sights that had assaulted him that day. The front lines were not even close to what had been expected; the only objective now in marine hands was the quarry, and that was tenuous.

In the thick darkness around them, every noise was magnified a hundred times. Men jerked nervously at any sound or movement, seeing things that weren't there. Bursts of machine-gun fire and rifle fire sliced through the night in orange and yellow spurts. Tracers zipped through the dark toward the enemy, leaving vapor trails behind. Star shells burst high in the sky, descending slowly under silk parachutes and giving off brilliant yellow lights that allowed the marines to see better. It was both a boon and a curse, for many of the distorted shapes of rock, tree, or bush were mistaken for the enemy and fired upon, sometimes resulting in the wounding of their own men.

Enemy mortars and artillery fell constantly, not as much as during the day, but enough to keep the men on edge and kill many more marines. The wary men strung heavy cord between foxholes and hung empty tobacco or C-ration cans along its length to warn of enemy infiltration during the night.

Up on the ridge, Redhawk could look down and see the frenetic activity on the beach. Destroyers illuminated the area with parachute flares fired at close range, and bulldozers roared and clattered through the night, pulling pallets of supplies further inland and slicing terraces and roadways for the incoming trucks and tanks. Revetments were scraped out by the massive machines to protect ammunition, fuel, and medical aid stations.

The field hospitals and corpsmen were hit just as often as the rest of the men, killing doctors and wounded with impunity. Although more than a thousand of the casualties had been evacuated before nightfall, hundreds still lay on the beaches on stretchers or ponchos. Many of them would die before they could be taken to hospital ships.

"When will it stop?" Whitworth demanded of no one in particular as the shelling battered the slopes of the quarry and the weary marines.

Redhawk didn't reply; there was nothing he could say. This had been worse than anything he'd yet seen, worse than Guadalcanal, Saipan, or Guam, and he knew there was a lot more to come. The radio messages had been flying thick and fast, battalions begging for help, pleading for corpsmen and reinforcements. Third Battalion's CP was hit by enemy mortars, and the colonel and captain were killed. Lieutenant Crane had taken command of the battalion, and Redhawk had radioed the news back to the ship.

Ron Frederickson had stepped on a land mine and, in an instant, disappeared from view in front of his astonished battalion.

"Did you see Frederickson get it?" Johns whispered, his eyes huge in the light of explosions and tracers.

Redhawk nodded tightly. "Yes."

Johns hand shook slightly as he twisted the top off his canteen and drank deeply. He'd replaced the water in it with whiskey and he offered it to Redhawk, who shook his head. He wanted nothing to cloud his mind and affect his judgment, but he understood why Johns did.

A huge explosion shook the ground, and Redhawk grabbed his phone. "A shell hit the ammunition and fuel dump," he said a few minutes later. "It's the Twenty-fifth's supplies."

Raging fires and a series of rumbling explosions lit up the night, bringing down heavy enemy fire, and they all crouched in their holes and hoped the sandbags would absorb the fragments. As the dump exploded in a chain of racketing booms, tracers zipped overhead and belts of machine gun ammo *pop-popped* like fireworks on New Year's.

Dawn finally dragged in, cloudy and bringing the clarity of disaster and desolation with it as the marines saw the awful destruction on the beaches and slopes. But they had made it through the first night on Iwo Jima.

Digging out the last bit of food from his C-ration can, Redhawk looked up at Johns and said calmly, "This is the place in my dream."

Johns was quiet for a moment. They had not spoken aloud about the dream of the sulphur, and since they had first heard about the island, they had both been acutely aware of the connection.

"Yes," Johns said at last, "I thought it must be."

"The rivers of blood are all around us, flowing in every direction." Redhawk paused for a moment and glanced around. "It's just like the dream, but I still do not know the end."

"You will soon, I think," Johns said after a moment of shell-rocked silence.

Redhawk's mouth twisted in a wry smile. "That's what I am worried about."

Johns smiled, too, unconvincing but undaunted. "So why are we worrying? We've made it this far, and I think the enemy is regretting being here as much as we are."

"Probably."

"Hey," Whitworth said, stepping over to them and crouching down, "talk so I can understand you!"

Unconsciously, Redhawk and Johns had talked in their native language, and now they looked at Whitworth and grinned.

"Got a guilty conscience?" Johns teased him. "Do you think we're talking about you?"

"Naw, I think maybe you found the way home and are trying to keep it to yourself." Whitworth's open face was wreathed in a grin, his blue eyes sparkling as he regarded them. "Well . . . we made it this far!"

"Before you go slapping yourself on the back,

Marine," a voice interrupted, "haul your ass up and off this ridge. We've got more to do before they let us go home."

Rising to their feet, they hefted their gear to their backs and followed Lieutenant Crane.

Artillery, naval gunfire, and air strikes for a northward drive and assault on Mount Suribachi had already begun, and the noise racketed all around them. Company assault squads moved forward with demolitions and flamethrowers. Cover was thoughtfully provided by machine-guns and mortars, and promptly returned by the Japanese.

Fighting on the Fifth Division's right, pushing up the center of the island, the Fourth's left wing kept abreast. Its objective was to push through to the north end of the first airfield. Some of the Japanese retreated, taking cover in the maze of tunnels dug under the ground and running like gopher holes.

Fourth Division's right wing was already facing the cross-island defenses when the artillery attacks began that morning. They were caught in a dangerous vise.

"Shall I radio back that this is impassable, sir?" Redhawk asked the lieutenant, and experienced a qualm when he shook his head.

"No. We'll push on."

Redhawk stared doubtfully at the terrain. At the water's edge huge rocks thrust skyward, rising in a cliff line to the flatter table at the top. The lower shore area boasted pockets of caves, small canyons, and fixed enemy strongholds, but atop the cliff, the terrain was virtually impassable. Trees and vines coiled tightly over an area where erosion and enemy excavation had formed cuts, dips, and pinnacles that made direct progress impossible.

There were mounds of rocks and dirt in all directions, with no one certain which held enemy positions and which were void.

"Yes sir," Redhawk said after a moment, and Crane shook his head.

"Call in for artillery to shell the crest," he said, and Redhawk brightened.

"Yes sir!"

"Have 'em walk those bastards across that ridge a few times, then we can advance a few yards." Crane hunkered down beside Redhawk as he got on the phone, his brows lowering so much that his helmet almost hid his entire face. "Sure sounds like gargling to me, but I hear you guys do it right," he muttered as Redhawk got the *Henry A. Wiley* on the line and gave his instructions and position. The destroyer obliged a few minutes later, and Crane looked back at Redhawk and grinned as dust rose in a choking cloud around them. "Not bad, Chief, not bad!"

Flamethrowers and satchel charges were employed to rid the Fourth of the deadly pillboxes, and many marines were lost in the effort. Redhawk watched with a curious detachment as a marine he'd been talking with only a few hours before lobbed a charge through the small aperture of the pillbox. A yellow arm flicked out almost lazily in that split second before the charge exploded, and a grenade took the marine along with the enemy, cartwheeling him into the air in a slow motion. He landed only five feet from Redhawk, his body a chewed mess. Redhawk looked away, his face revealing nothing.

He'd seen so much in such a short time that the power to shock was gone. He worried more about Johns than himself or anything else, keeping a sharp eye on his cousin and never allowing himself to be very far from him. In a way, it was a way to save his sanity by focusing on something else, on something he could control. The rest of the blazing hell and fire and death he could not hope to stem.

They moved forward very slowly, trying to blast a Japanese gun emplacement into oblivion. Two men stepped on land mines and virtually disappeared, while the others ducked the flying debris of metal fragments and human parts. One by one, in single file, the marines cautiously made it across a mine field and approached the bunker. The huge gun protruded evilly in the gray light of hazy day and sulphur-laden smoke. The approaches to the gun were guarded by machine gun nests that sprayed the marines with rounds of bullets, chewing up the ground, packs, and a few men. One marine stood up, his Thompson submachine spewing back at them, taking out a few of the enemy before his inevitable death.

Do you want to live forever? echoed in Redhawks mind, a cry from Guadalcanal. It had begun with a gunnery sergeant who had been in World War I at Belleau Wood, and he could not keep the refrain from circling over and over in his mind.

Redhawk called in for direct shelling, and the marines took cover while a destroyer blasted the bunker with heavy mortars. When the smoke cleared a bit, they moved forward again and circled to the rear, filling the ventilator openings with satchel charges until the bunker was a smoking ruin.

It had begun to rain, and the miserable wet combined with the thick volcanic ash jammed some of their weapons. Cursing, shouting, and sweating, even in the chill, marines desperately tried to clean out their rifles as a shower of hand grenades rained down on them. Only a few exploded, and those did no harm except to make them even more scared and miserable. Moving to the front of the bunker, they found some of the enemy who had been wounded. Glaring hatred up at them, they were feebly trying to pull the pins of grenades.

Crane tried out the elementary Japanese they had learned on the cowering men. *"Boo-kee oh steh roh! Koh-sahn seh yoh!"*

The Japanese replied with shrill screams of defiance and hatred, and the marines let their rifles loose . . . those that weren't jammed with the sticky mud of Iwo. After stuffing a C-2 charge into the grim muzzle of the big gun, the marines scampered away over the rocks almost gleefully. Any accomplishment was like a reward in this horror.

"Where the fuck are the reserves?" Lieutenant Crane muttered to no one in particular when the fighting grew intense and they were pinned down in an area that gave them little shelter.

Redhawk grunted as a fragment tore into the pack on his back, and after making certain he wasn't hit, he looked at the lieutenant and gave him the bad news.

"The ducks bringing the 105's swamped and sank, taking some of the men of the Fourth with it. Those that weren't hit by enemy fire are sitting in the ocean, and out of twelve, there are only two guns left."

"Great. Just fucking great! What else do you hear on that phone. Chief?"

"The Fifth managed to land some 155's on Red Beach and get them across to the west coast. Three battalions of the Twenty-eighth, Fifth Division are on a line across the neck, facing Mount Suribachi. The Twenty-sixth and Twenty-seventh of the Fifth are fanned across the southern end of the airport."

Crane just looked at him for a moment, then grinned. "Fuckin' A, Chief, fuckin A! Keep those phone lines open and we may get outta this alive yet!"

The second night on Iwo was a carbon copy of the first. Star shells glimmered in the sky and cast distorted shadows across the island, while artillery barrages kept everyone on edge and definitely awake.

Sitting in a deep foxhole that kept refilling with sand, Redhawk tried not to think about anything. He kept his mind on nothing, staring straight ahead. It was Johns's turn on the radio, and he was supposed to be sleeping. That was a joke, for sleep would not come to a man who had the constant roar of rockets and mortars in his ears, the heavy thump of landing shells, and the *ack-ack* of machine-gun fire and popping of grenades all around him.

Leaning back, Redhawk tried to make himself comfortable—or as comfortable as he could get with his pack and weapon at hand. Another star shell burst, rising high in the night sky and sending out streamers of light in a peculiarly beautiful pattern. It illuminated the area around him, and he glanced up to take a look.

A movement just beyond the crater where he

was bedded down for the night caught his eye, and Redhawk froze. It had the distinct shape of a man, a small man with a rifle and fixed bayonet. The shadowy figure turned and charged toward him. Reacting instantly, not waiting to see what he might do, Redhawk snatched up a hand grenade and pulled the pin, tossing it directly at the enemy.

To his horror, the grenade bounced harmlessly off the man's chest and rolled away. It was a dud. Still sprawled back against his pack and the side of the deep crater, Redhawk just had time to bring up his rifle to ward off the slashing thrust of the enemy's bayonet. He had no time to wonder why the man didn't fire but fought him hand to hand. The rifles were useless at this close range. They grappled, rolling around in the sand, both breathing harshly. Nothing was said; there were no sounds between them other than grunts and pants.

Finally wrapping his hands around the enemy's throat, Redhawk started to squeeze. The Japanese brought up a knife somehow, and Redhawk caught the glimmer of light along its wicked blade as another star shell burst overhead. Instantly, he increased pressure and threw himself to the side at the same time so that the knife blade glanced off his helmet, knocking it askew but doing no damage. Tightly, grimly, he dug his fingers into the yielding cord of the enemy's throat until the man's struggles slowed, then stopped altogether.

Breathing hard, Redhawk sat back on his heels and looked down at the dead enemy for a long moment. His breath was coming short and fast, and his heart was beating so rapidly he could almost hear it over the thunder of naval shelling. The enemy's face was contorted and suffused with blood, giving him the appearance of a wax dummy instead of a flesh and blood human being.

"Chief!"

Redhawk turned slowly, looking up to see Whitworth briefly outlined in the ghostly light of a flare. "Yes?"

Whitworth slid down into the crater and looked at the dead Japanese. "You got one."

"Yes. I got one."

Whitworth grinned suddenly. "Way to go! It may be a little slower killing them like this, but it's just as sure, Chief, just as sure.

For a moment, Redhawk just looked at him, then he said slowly and distinctly, "Fuck you!"

Whitworth collapsed with laughter as Redhawk glared at him. "I knew there was some emotion somewhere inside there, Chief, I just knew it! By God, I did get a rise out of you at last, just when I thought you were made of stone."

A reluctant smile flashed, then Redhawk sighed and said to the still-laughing Whitworth, "Help me get him out of here. I don't want to spend the rest of the night sleeping beside him."

The Japanese was dragged out of the crater and to one side, then they searched the body for papers or anything of interest. There was nothing, only a tattered photograph of a smiling woman and a small, dark-haired little girl.

Redhawk felt a moment's disquiet. The enemy had family, too, wives, children, mothers, and fathers. They were human beings and were caught up in a slaughter just like everyone else.

"Don't go soft on me, Chief," Whitworth said when he noted the expression on Redhawk's face. "He wouldn't have cared if you had family. He'd have cut your throat quicker than you could blink. Or shot you if he hadn't been out of bullets."

"I know." Redhawk shoved the photograph back in the man's pocket and stood up. "One must never allow thoughts of the enemy to affect them."

"Right. And by the way, the lieutenant wants to hear your sweet voice over the radio again." Whitworth looked at Redhawk and grinned. "I don't know why. It sounds like dishwater going down the drain when you make all those sounds."

"Only to the untrained and uneducated," Redhawk retorted, and Whitworth laughed again.

Like the night before, American landings were harassed by mistakes and accidents, as well as by enemy shelling. The beachmaster on Yellow I worked through the night to handle the unloading of cargo and troop boats, and to get the wounded evacuated. Expecting Japanese swimmers to slip in with demolition charges designed to blow the cargo boats to hell and back, marines were assigned to watch.

The activity never stopped—up in the rocks, on the shoreline, out in the water—and the night dragged on.

Chapter Twenty
Mount Suribachi

D day plus two, and the marines were still struggling to secure their landing. Both fronts were mustering to renew the attack, with artillery being called in to hit the rear and blistering missiles zipping overhead on the front.

Redhawk, Johns, and Wood were never far from a radio. Crane directed artillery at the hot spots where enemy fire was the worst, paving the way for the marines to advance slowly but surely. The young lieutenant had taken some shrapnel in his legs and was bandaged but still functioning at top speed. He wouldn't allow a corpsman to give him any morphine, saying it would slow his reflexes and endanger his men. Redhawk felt a burgeoning respect for Crane, and it was shared by the others.

"We have to keep pushing," Crane ordered, "so call in more of those—what do you call them in Navajo, Chief?"

"*Be-al-doh-tso-lani*, or 'many big guns,' " Redhawk replied with a grin. "Artillery, right?"

"Yeah, and mortars, too. The gun that squats, right?"

"Right."

"Colorful, Chief, fuckin' colorful," Crane said,

heaving himself up to hobble painfully toward the front. "Now let's go get 'em!"

If Fourth Division was finding it slow-going, the Fifth was finding it hell. American lines were now only about two hundred yards from Suribachi's main defenses. A pre-attack bombardment utilized a forty-plane strike against the base of the volcano, rockets slamming into rocks and brush with such force that marines were temporarily deafened.

Unable to wait for the stranded tanks to support them, the marines finally forged ahead along a seven-hundred yard line, some casually walking, some moving cautiously from hole to hole. Artillery kept up its shelling.

Though slow to react, the enemy made up for it quickly with intense rifle fire and machine-gun sweeps. Mortars began *whoomping* through the air, scattering marines to the four winds. Death-dealing shells landed with careless design, sending up blistering spirals of steel and sand as well as good men.

On a ridge far back to the rear, Redhawk had an excellent view of what was going on. The island was so small that it was hard not to see unless a man was down in the midst of it or in a ravine. But clinging to a rocky precipice and waiting for the shelling to take out as many of the Japanese as possible, he had a panoramic view.

The radio crackled constantly as commanders screamed for more artillery, more mortars, more cover. Men were cut off from reinforcements. Where were they? Where were the tanks? There were few messages sent in English; most of them were in the Navajo code, and the reasoning was simple: Any hint of a platoon or battalion in trouble brought instant fire on the unfortunate men, and they knew the Japanese were monitoring every frequency they could from their positions inside the volcano and caves.

Dug into the slope and waiting out enemy shelling, Redhawk heard Crane begin swearing. He lifted his head cautiously and saw the lieutenant crawling toward him. When he half slid, half fell into the crater where Redhawk was lying, Crane grimaced painfully.

"Those stupid sons of bitches are shelling us!"

Redhawk looked at him. "Yeah, the enemy has a bad habit of doing that. . . ."

"I don't mean the fuckin' Japs, I mean our artillery is hitting us!"

"Ours?"

Crane swore again as a shell whistled ominously through the air and landed a hundred yards away. Cries of pain rose immediately, and the lieutenant blanched.

"Look, Chief, we've already tried radioing those dumb bastards, but they keep shelling us! Send 'em the proper coordinates, or we'll all buy it!" Redhawk got on the phone as Crane added, "Those dumb-fucks thought we were the Japs calling off the shelling, and if they don't hear one of you guys, they intend to keep bombing the shit out of us!"

Crane wiped a hand over his soot-streaked face as Redhawk got the *Wiley* on the line and gave them a series of what sounded to the lieutenant like grunts and groans. But in spite of how it sounded, the shelling ceased abruptly, and he shook his head with relief.

"From now on, Chief, I think we should stick to using you guys. It would save us a lot of shells and a lot of our own men if we did."

"Do not, repeat *not* use any radiomen but those assigned to your company," came the command, and the officers were only too glad to comply. They'd recognized the invaluable service the code talkers rendered, confounding the enemy and getting vital information from shore to ship and back.

"Chicken in a hole," Redhawk radioed ahead, and the men on the front line blasted a foxhole holding enemy soldiers. It was quick and simple under the best circumstances, but it got hot at times.

As marines of the Fifth Division utilized tank crews, infantry, and demolitions experts to pound wedges into the connecting bunkers and pillboxes of the enemy, they slowly began to crumble. 37mm guns and 75mm half-tracks were operating up and down the front lines, and rocket trucks at the rear were lobbing missiles overhead, further battering the enemy.

At great risk to themselves, corpsmen ranged up and down the lines, treating the wounded and dying, arranging for them to be evacuated to the beach, sometimes dying beside them. Men unselfishly gave their lives for comrades and, in spite of great personal fear, kept forging ahead, bound by a driving instinct to win, to beat the enemy, to take that volcanic island.

In early afternoon a huge gain was made, and Redhawk watched it through his field glasses. After strafing the enemy's bunkers, a platoon advanced to one of the largest still being used. It had thick concrete walls and heavy artillery, as well as a machine-gun that raked the marines with devastating consequences. A tank tried to breach the bunker and failed, and bazooka and 75mm took over. The men tossed grenades and finally managed to position a flamethrower. The bunker became a raging inferno, and as the enemy tried to escape, they were picked off.

All along the front the companies of east and west beaches were moving across the volcano's flanks, taking out defenses along the way. The marines quickly discovered an effective method of dealing with the enemy: They attacked with hand grenades, sprayed the caves with flamethrowers, and then sealed them with bursts of explosive. It worked beautifully.

"Not bad," Lieutenant Crane conceded as Redhawk apprised him of the situation, "but those guys are just now getting the cross-island defenses that we've been bucking since we got here."

"According to reports, we now hold one third of the island," Redhawk said a few minutes later, the radio crackling badly with static and making it hard to hear. The shelling was as bad as the phone lines.

"Well, let's make it all or nothing!" Whitworth said, and they all turned to look at him. He shrugged. "Just an idea, guys, just an idea."

When the day ended, a cold rain was falling and it looked as if Suribachi's conquest was at hand.

It was still raining as the sky lightened on D day plus three. Shreds of fog obscured the top of Mount Suribachi, settling down into cuts and fissures. Rain pattered down and low-hanging clouds amplified the thunder of exploding shells, demolitions, and grenades. Machine-guns and rifles spit erratically, the *ack-ack* sounding oddly muffled by the wet sand that occasionally clogged barrels and jammed the weapons.

As the Fifth renewed attempts to take Suribachi, the Fourth was still fighting fiercely. Crane ordered Redhawk to call in rocket support against a hill on the front. He was on the phone immediately, and two rocket trucks jerked forward. The heavy trucks rolled to a halt, jockeying to the right position, then launched their missiles.

Fleeing enemy streamed from hillside defenses as the rockets tore into the hill with devastating fire, churning up ground and bodies. As Japanese fled, machine-guns chewed them up and marines gave out ragged cheers as they fell in huge numbers. More than two hundred littered the hill or limped away as machine-guns stitched patterns along the ground. Blood trails glistened in the gray light.

Redhawk's Thompson was hot to the touch, and he put it down when Crane came limping back, ordering more fire to be poured on the positions ahead.

"We've got 'em on the run now! Let's get those bastards outta here!"

Rain pelted them as they knelt on the rocky slope and called in more artillery, pounding the few remaining enemy bunkers with withering fire. Mortars *whoomped* overhead as Redhawk crouched in a deep trench and gave coordinates and quadrants. Things were finally looking up for Third Battalion in spite of heavy losses.

A drenching rainstorm made it hard to see, and the men were shivering inside protective ponchos as they tried to peer through the curtains of rain.

Redhawk found his hands shaking, more from exhaustion and chill than from fright, but Lieutenant Crane paused to peer at him closely. "Take a breather, Chief," he said, but Redhawk shook his head.

"I'm needed." He said it simply, without arrogance or conceit, and Crane nodded.

More supplies were still being landed on Yellow I, in the surge of high surf and beating rain. The wounded were being gradually evacuated, and stretchers lined the beach. Crane sent Redhawk and Whitworth to the Fourth Division hospital that had been set up at the north end of Airfield No. 1.

"I've got a badly wounded man who needs immediate help and we can't wait on corpsmen," he told Redhawk. "Take him in his poncho if you have to, but get him out of here." Slinging the poncho between them, they dodged shells as they carried the wounded marine down the slope.

"So why in the hell are *we* doing this instead of a corpsman?" Whitworth grumbled.

"Because all the corpsmen are busy or dead," Redhawk replied in his usual imperturbable tone.

Grunting, Whitworth flashed him a sour glance. "Great. You really know how to make a guy feel secure."

"That's not my job. I talk on the radio."

"Why is it we're about the only ones left without any wounds?" Whitworth asked a few minutes later. He was breathing hard, and they had paused to lower the stretcher for a moment. The occupant was unconscious, having passed out just after they'd bumped down the first ridge. "I mean, look at this guy, Riggs. He was standing there beside me one minute, all good cheer and ass, and the next he's four feet away, his clothes smoking and his hair on fire."

"Just lucky, I guess."

"Who—him or us? I mean, this guy's going out

of here, and while we're humping over rocks and Japs, he's gonna be lying in a clean bed eating steak and watching movies."

"You complain too much." Redhawk stood up and motioned for Whitworth to lift his end of the stretcher. "Crane said for us to double-time down there and back."

"And that's another thing," Whitworth complained as he lifted the stretcher, "always in a hurry!"

"Would you be happy if you weren't complaining?" Redhawk could not resist asking, and Whitworth grinned.

"Nope!"

"Then you ought to be the happiest man alive."

"Aw, admit you think everything I'm saying, Chief. You know you do."

"Maybe, but I don't say it. Come on. We're almost there and this guy's getting heavier by the minute."

When they reached the Fourth Hospital, they lowered their human cargo to the ground in a long line of men waiting to be taken out to the hospital ship. The weather made it extremely dangerous for the smaller landing craft to pull in and out in the churning surf, but the larger craft were doggedly ramming their bows up on the beach to disgorge cargo through their huge doors.

Down below, on Yellow I, thousands of marines wandered on the beach, some shell-shocked and confused, others awaiting orders or avoiding the hot slopes. Enemy fire still struck the beaches, but not as heavily as before. The worst impediment to getting the wounded off and the supplies on was the driving rain that soaked through raingear and drenched the skin.

"Damned if I know why we were in such an all-fired hurry to get Riggs down here," Whitworth observed. "He's gonna have to wait for hours to get on a boat going out."

Redhawk flicked a compassionate glance over the long rows of wounded. Many of them would die before receiving necessary aid, but it was unavoidable. There were not enough corpsmen to go around, and casualties were mounting every minute. Some LSTs were drafted into service as makeshift hospital carriers, but equipment was elementary and it was only a stop-gap measure.

Redhawk stumbled, then caught himself, looking down at the stretcher he hadn't seen in the pouring wet. After muttering an apology to the stretcher's occupant, he started to move on, but the man grabbed his trouser leg.

"Hey, Chief," came a weak voice, "got a smoke?"

Jerking around, Redhawk stared down at the man, trying to recognize him. The voice was familiar, but even as he dug into his helmet for a cigarette, he could not figure out the face. It could have been because it was mostly gone, with part of the jaw shot away and blood crusted over one side. His eyes were drawn to the bloody lumps under the blanket, and he saw that one entire side of the marine was pulpy flesh that looked as if it had been shoved through a meat grinder.

"Here you go," he said in a shaky voice, and when the marine took the cigarette between two fingers of the hand he had left, Redhawk saw the name on his shirt. *Jones*. He swallowed hard. "Hey, Sarge, how'd you guys get along without me?"

Sergeant Jones managed a feeble grin. "Bad,

Chief, real bad. We didn't have anybody to do our war dances. . . ."

His voice faded, and Redhawk knelt down beside the stretcher, trying to talk past the lump in his throat. "I missed the Fifth, too." He paused to clear his throat. "You guys have done a damn fine job out there, I hear."

"What's your lash-up?"

"Fourth Division, Twenty-fifth Regiment, Third Battalion." He drew it out, carefully spacing his words as the morphine Jones had been given made his eyes droop. "I'll tell my cousin I saw you," he said finally, awkwardly, not knowing what else to say. What did one say to a dying man? "We talk about you a lot and how you took care of us on the Canal."

The cigarette had burned down almost to his fingers, but Jones didn't seem to notice. He drew it shakily to his bloody lips, inhaled, and let it back out slowly. The rain had all but killed the fire on it.

"Me? Take care of you?" Jones mumbled. "Hell, Chief, if it wasn't for you guys, we'd of been wiped out a lot of times. Still jabbering in code?"

Redhawk managed another smile. "Sometimes."

"Keep it up, Chief."

"You, too, Sarge," Redhawk said, then stood up when the cigarette dropped away and Jones closed his eyes. "You, too," he said again, softly.

He pulled the edge of the poncho over Jones's head, then turned to see Whitworth standing silently to one side, the rain still beating down on him, his eyes full of sympathy.

"It ain't fair," Whitworth said, and Redhawk nodded. He couldn't answer. "Come on, Chief, let's get some coffee out of those selfish navy bastards."

After grabbing a cup of coffee from a sympathetic crewman aboard one of the LSTs, they humped back through the sticky sand toward the quarry.

"Come on, let's get back," Redhawk said, and they continued making their way up the slopes.

It was February 23, D day plus four, and the weather was finally cooperating. The skies were clear, and the sun rose in the east with benign assurance. It wouldn't last, but at least it was a break.

Two miles of beach looked like a rubbish heap, filled with marines and supplies, heavy equipment and weapons. Twisted wrecks of jeeps and tanks littered the shoreline, and ruined howitzers dotted the ground like charred sticks. It amazed Redhawk that without the slightest shred of shelter, the marines were still on the beaches of Iwo Jima. How had they done it? Dogged determination alone was not enough. It took a lot more than that to keep a man going forward when common sense told him he was about to die. And it occurred to him now, when it hadn't before, that the marines and the Indian had a lot in common.

Shortly after 0800 hours that morning, Redhawk heard on the radio frequency that a patrol was moving out from the base of Mount Suribachi with a flag to be erected atop the crest.

"Think they'll make it?" Johns asked as he peered through field glasses toward the volcanic mound thrusting skyward. "It looks pretty steep, and there's got to be lots of enemy resistance still left in some of those caves."

"They'll make it," Whitworth said, and Redhawk looked at him.

"Why do you sound so sure?"

"Because they're marines."

"Yeah, I guess I overlooked that fact," Redhawk said with a grin. "Death before dishonor."

His expression sobered as he realized that it was true. That was the heart and core of the marines, their unwillingness to let one another down. How many times had he witnessed supreme acts of sacrifice for a buddy? Or the determined push up a hill when men knew they would never make it down? It wasn't just for their country or even for themselves; they fought for the man next to them in the foxhole, the man they might have been quarreling with earlier but didn't hesitate to die for when needed.

He almost cringed when he recalled how he'd once said it wasn't his war. Well, if it hadn't been then, it sure was now. Maybe he should tell Johns that. There were times when his cousin doubted him, and he wanted him to know how he really felt. He looked over at him, but a man came running from crater to crater, bellowing for a radioman.

"Hey Chief!" came the familiar cry, and Redhawk and Johns both rose to go. Johns paused, his babyish face crumpling in a weary grin.

"Go ahead. You're faster than I am."

"You're just saying that because you want to stay here," Redhawk shot back, and Johns nodded.

"*Dah*. Good guess."

While Redhawk radioed messages from Crane to the front, then to the rear, directing fire on anti-tank, anti-air, and pillboxes, the marines on Suribachi toiled ever upward. It took them two hours of hard climbing, sometimes on hands and knees, before they reached the lip of the crater and paused to look warily around. No fire had impeded their progress, except for an occasional lone sniper, and they stood there uncertainly for a moment.

Then someone ran up with the flag, and the marines began to look for a pole to erect it at the summit.

"Those men should get flight pay for climbing that high," Whitworth commented, and Redhawk agreed with him.

All attention was focused on the important event on the far summit, and Third Battalion had a bird's-eye seat for the show. Even the enemy seemed to be in limbo, watching the scene play itself out, firing sporadically at the cliffs on the north.

"Wouldja lookit that," a marine breathed softly as the small flag was slowly raised, unfurling in a stiff breeze.

Shouts began to circulate on the beach, up in the cliffs, and down in the ravines as the marines saw their flag being planted atop Mount Suribachi. Ragged cheers rose and whistles blew, bells rang and foghorns bellowed loudly.

For a few minutes, there was no challenge. Then one of the enemy ducked out of a cave and took a shot at a news correspondent and a marine. He missed and was killed for his efforts. After that aborted attempt, a Japanese officer emerged waving a broken sword over his head and screaming defiance. He, too, died in a volley of bullets.

Now the summit exploded with action—hand grenades, machine-gun fire, and flamethrowers.

"Give 'em the hotfoot!" Whitworth shouted as if his words would carry that far. He danced around the slope until Crane told him not to be a fool and get shot.

Cave entrances on Suribachi were sealed shut with demolition, and more marines advanced up the slope to begin the mopping up. In just under two hours, another, larger flag was raised on Suribachi, flapping beneath an overcast sky for all the marines to easily spot.

"We've won," Whitworth said with a sigh, sinking down on a rock beside Redhawk.

Redhawk just looked at him. "Tell that to the Japs," he said as a mortar exploded not far away and they dived for cover. Whitworth looked indignant.

"We just have to convince 'em, that's all."

Lieutenant Crane lifted his head and glared at Whitworth for a long moment.

Chapter Twenty-One
Main Attack

"Hey, just because we got a flag on top of that hill don't mean we've won yet," a marine commented.

Redhawk turned his head toward him. That seemed obvious. The Japs had them pinned down with deadly fire, the bullets, tracers, and mortars flying overhead so thick it looked as if none of them would make it out of the ravine alive. A solidly entrenched bunker loomed ahead, barring their progress, death spitting out of the apertures with fatal accuracy. Already, three of their squad had been hit in less than a minute, and with the rest of them tightly pinned down, it looked as if they wouldn't be making much of an advance.

Between the tenuously held front and the northern sea lay General Kuribayashi's main defenses, stone fortresses of volcanic rock and caves. To Redhawk, it looked like a dark copy of Arizona wastelands, with the same barren rocks and plateaus, jagged cliffs chewing at the sky, deep cuts and gullies pleating the landscape, and choking brush that hid the enemy as well as the marines.

Turning his head again, his cheek scraping against the rock he was hugging, Redhawk looked for and found Johns. His cousin was in the same position, clinging to the ground as if it were about to be snatched from under him, head down to keep from getting hit between the eyes, rifle stock wedged between his legs to protect whatever he could from stray shells.

"Arizona," Lieutenant Crane shouted, edging close to Redhawk, ducking as a volley of bullets flew at him like a swarm of wasps. "Arizona, call out for artillery. And tell them we've got big trouble up here . . . blockhouses, bunkers, pillboxes"—he paused to duck a shell, then lifted his head and continued calmly—"caves, tunnels, trenches, some mortar pits, a few rocket pits, about fifty machine gun nests, spider traps, dual-purpose antiaircraft positions, stationary tanks, anti-tank ditches and mine fields, and those fuckin' booby traps. . . ."

"Is that all?" Redhawk muttered as he pulled at the bulky radio set. Beside him, Whitworth laughed.

"Ain't that enough?"

"Stow it, Whitty," Crane said, turning back to Redhawk. "Tell them anything you have to tell them, but direct some heavy artillery up here and we might get to advance another few yards."

"You mean inches," Whitworth put in.

A barrage of fire from their rear put an end to any casual conversation or radio talk, and they huddled in the ravine and prayed it would stop. All around him, Redhawk could hear men being hit, shells exploding next to them or bullets finding them somehow amidst everything else. Cries and sobs were common, and he wondered when he would do the same. It wasn't likely that he would get off this island in one piece, without suffering some sort of injury.

"Hey, Chief," Crane said when there was a brief lull in the firing, "tell 'em we're getting hit from front and rear."

It took several tries because of the intense firing, but finally Redhawk was able to get a message through to the ship. The reply, however, wasn't that encouraging.

"They say we've got our own men too close, but they'll try to walk some artillery up the ridge," Redhawk told the lieutenant, and Crane swore softly.

"That means we're likely to be blasted by our own guns as well as the fuckin' Japs, then."

"Yes sir, that's very likely."

"Killed by friendly fire," Whitworth commented. "That seems a contradiction in terms, doesn't it?"

"Whitty, *you're* a contradiction in terms," Crane said without glancing at the grimy marine. Pushing up, the young officer worked his way back to a group of men being held down by fire, shouting orders for them to retreat and move to the left flank. "Give those bastards a hotfoot!" he yelled to men who'd found a cave filled with enemy. "Then blast 'em with frags!"

The platoon had been reduced to twenty-two men, and it looked as if it would be reduced even more before help came to relieve them. Redhawk could see them spread out around him—Whitworth, Crane, Johns, Wood, Wiley, Madsen, Lowe, Roberts, Plotnik, and others he knew by first name, religion, and state. It was odd how quickly a man came to know those he fought with, ate with, slept close to at night. He knew, for instance, that James Plotnik had a wife and two little girls at home in Wisconsin, and that soon there would be another baby. He waited anxiously for word. Jerry Roberts was from Tennessee and had just celebrated his twentieth birthday a week before. He missed his mom, and had a sister that was blond and beautiful. Wilbur Wiley was of Indian descent, with high cheekbones and dark hair, but time and intermarriages had bred out all but the memory of his Cherokee heritage. Madsen and Lowe tried to pretend they hated each other, but they were inexplicably bound together by the ties of having endured boot camp and a campaign on Guam. Now they were here, squabbling good-naturedly most of the time—when the Japs were quiet.

The rest of the platoon were also men who had fought together for a while before hitting Iwo. Johns had remarked about the closeness of men who had gone through so much and developed a bond, while he and Redhawk had been moved from company to company. Meeting up with Bell Wood again had been a pleasant surprise. In spite of being relative newcomers to the platoon, the code talkers had quickly become a very important part of it.

There were hours when neither of them could break away from the radio, taking and receiving vital messages that sent the platoon up a hill or around the flank of the enemy dug into a cave. They were used during the hottest of the fighting as well as before and after, to receive orders and send back reports of casualties and progress.

By the end of the day, Fourth Division had managed only a few hundred yards, and the enemy was still dug in with all intentions of staying.

"We'll sleep good tonight," Johns said wearily, and Redhawk gave a startled laugh.

"Yeah, with Japs all around us, waiting on us to close our eyes, we should be able to rest easily!"

"Hell," Whitworth said from a few feet away, "I'm afraid if I go to sleep, I won't wake up!

Those little yellow bastards sneak up on a man during the night to cut his throat, and I've grown partial to mine without the perforations."

"You're too particular, Whitty," Wiley commented. "I don't intend to let those Japs cheat me out of my beauty sleep."

Whitworth grinned. "Yeah, well in your case, you need it worse than I do. I'm already pretty enough." He jerked a thumb toward Redhawk and Johns and Wood. "Now, if you were like these guys, you'd never need sleep. I don't think I've seen either of them sleep since we've been on this fuckin' island!"

"We sleep," Redhawk said. "We just know when not to."

Whitworth made a rude noise. "Like hell! Every time I roll over, you're looking at me."

Smiling, Redhawk said, "I'm a light sleeper."

Wiley shrugged. "Well, I don't think I'll miss my sleep, so if you see anybody, Chief, wake me up."

But some of the marines fell asleep in spite of all their efforts not to, and some never awoke. The enemy infiltrators slipped through the tangled brush in the ravines and over rocks, sneaking up on the unwary to plunge a bayonet into him or slice his throat with a knife.

Redhawk, lying only a few feet from Whitworth, fell into a light doze, his weapon in one hand, a knife in the other. He felt safer that way. Johns was several feet away, and the lieutenant was trying to catch some sleep in a small crater dug out by a Japanese shell earlier in the day.

He never knew later what woke him—some small sound that was different from the shelling and occasional small arms fire or the *rat-a-tat-tat* of machine guns—but Redhawk was suddenly alert, his eyes opened to narrow slits and his muscles taut. Crane and Whitworth still lay in exhausted slumber, but he knew from the posture of Johns's body that he'd heard the sound, too, and was awake. They made no signal that they'd heard it but just lay there, waiting.

They didn't have long to wait. A twig snapped in the charred, broken underbrush studding the rocky slopes, and a faint shadow stepped quietly forward. Redhawk's fingers curled more tightly around the hilt of his long knife, and he waited until the figure drew close enough to touch before he came alive.

Rolling to a crouch, Redhawk silently threw himself at the startled Japanese, his knife plunging into the man to the hilt, then twisting and jerking out. The man went down without a sound louder than a soft grunt, his curved sword dropping to the grainy floor of the crater.

Redhawk looked up to meet Johns's approving gaze, and nothing was said. Johns lay back down, tilting his helmet partially over his face so that only his nose and lips showed. Redhawk picked up the samurai sword of the enemy and placed it carefully beside his pack, then lay back down with utter disregard for the slain man a few feet away. The *chendi* that attended the dead no longer bothered him as they once had.

In the morning, when Crane and Whitworth woke, there was a loud yell.

"Sweet Jeezus!" Whitworth screamed, clawing at the sand of the crater as if trying to dig himself out. "Lookit what came to visit!"

Crane was not as vocal. He glanced from the dead Jap to Redhawk and Johns, and a small smile touched his mouth.

"Not bad, gentlemen," he said, "not bad."

There were no papers on the dead man, and he

looked pitifully small and scrawny in the gray light of day.

"Looks like he ain't had nothing to eat for a while," Plotnik said, gazing down at the body. "Maybe we've got 'em on the go."

"Yeah, Jimmy, and maybe they've got us where they want us," Jerry Roberts muttered. He wiped at his brow, smearing dirt across his forehead. "I just wish to hell we were off this fuckin' island!"

"Think about this before you lie down to sleep tonight," Crane said sharply. "Who was standing guard last night?"

His gaze moved to Lowe, who looked embarrassed. "I never heard him, sir. Hell, I never even heard the chief there kill him!"

"He came very quietly," Redhawk said, and pointed to the spot where the Japanese had first appeared. "I think there is a tunnel there, Lieutenant."

Upon investigation, an opening to a small tunnel was discovered, and the marines happily went about the task of sealing it. First, grenades were tossed inside to dispose of any Japanese rash enough to still be lingering, then a flamethrower was used, and finally a C-2 charge to seal it from being used again.

"That ought to take care of that one!" Madsen said with a gleeful rubbing of his hands, and Whitworth shook his head.

Rather gloomily, he said, "Yeah, but who's gonna take care of the other two thousand spider holes and caves they got on this fuckin' place?"

"Come on," Crane said, "let's move forward."

Fourth Division found that to be easier said than done. Its coastal flank was enmeshed in a terrain that defied their efforts to advance. Doggedly, the marines shot, blasted, burned, and fought their way forward, step by painful step, sometimes over their own men but slowly moving forward.

There were so many casualties that Redhawk called in for phosphorus mortars to hide the evacuation of the dead and wounded.

Wedged between two large rocks, he took a swig of water from his canteen, peering through narrowed eyes at the carnage on the field. He dragged a sleeve across his mouth and picked up the phone again, directing mortars as calmly as he could. He couldn't see Johns and had been cut off from the rest of the platoon by enemy fire. Bell Wood had been transferred to another platoon that had lost their radiomen, and losses were heavy everywhere. The Fourth had been ordered to take Hill 382.

The enemy defense system was comprised of Hill 382, a shallow depression called the Amphitheater, and a bald rise known as Turkey Knob. This was the area the marines were to take and hold, an area crawling with enemy and death.

The line of Fourth units facing the "Meat Grinder," as the area came to be known, had Hill 382 on their left, and the Amphitheater, Turkey Knob, and Minami Village in a group on their right. The shallow bowl of the Amphitheater was about three hundred yards long and two hundred yards wide, the rim pocked with caves and bristling with pillboxes. Marines attempting to advance to the far rim were met with devastating fire that flew across the depression. On Turkey Knob, the blockhouse that dominated it was studded with big guns. It was also an observation post and communications center, and the marines considered it vital to destroy it. Nothing seemed to affect it, not shelling, nor artillery.

"Gawd," Ted Madsen moaned, "ain't we never

gonna take this fuckin' island?"

"Don't be in such a hurry," Lowe shot at him. "What are we gonna do with it when we get it?"

Redhawk listened to them with only half his attention. He'd seen one of the pillboxes open up and spray a squad in front of them with fire, and the corpsmen couldn't reach the wounded. They lay there in the open, some of the men calling for help, their buddies helpless to give it to them.

His throat tightened. This was the true hell of war, the feeling of helplessness and frustration that so often afflicted the men. How could they hope to take the hill? It was riddled with the enemy, who seemed to have an endless supply of ammunition and weapons.

He glanced around at his comrades and saw them for the first time with the eyes of reality. Most of the men were filthy, not having even changed their socks since landing, and they were all crouched hunched over, shoulders up as if to ward off bullets. None of them had shaved, and beards darkened jawlines. Huge circles bagged beneath eyes that sometimes stared blankly ahead, and lips were cracked and dry, puffed, and black as if dehydrated. Hair was matted beneath the helmets, and lines etched the faces of every man there, making them all seem much older than their years.

Rubbing a hand across his own jaw—no beard, just a suggestion of one—he had the rueful thought that he looked just like them except for that.

But when the fighting began again, each man underwent a metamorphosis, his face hardening, the eyes becoming cold and steely, lips tightening into a grimace, pulled back from teeth in a snarl. And they would yell at the top of their lungs as they charged forward. Nothing on the island was as it seemed to be. Ridges that looked barren of the enemy suddenly sprouted machine gun nests and *"banzai!"* screaming Japanese. Empty ravines mushroomed with lids of spider holes flung back and dealing death, and mounds of earth that looked like part of the natural terrain began to growl and roar to life as tanks moved forward, dirt falling from tops and sides and gun turrets blazing.

Marines answered these challenges with bazookas, M-1's, Thompson submachine guns, and flamethrowers. Redhawk called in for artillery and mortar to be launched, and he directed planes with twenty-mm fire to take them out.

Combat strength of the Fourth was reduced to fifty-five percent, but they still forged ahead, gaining only in inches at times, but gaining. Artillery and naval gunfire paved the way in the front, but hand-to-hand combat and small arms fire was required to take it. Companies used hand grenades, rifles, sixty-mm mortars, demolitions, and the bazookas and flamethrowers to gain ground.

Lieutenant Crane employed Madsen and Lowe to blow the caves. Japanese were killing them by remaining underground, with only occasional deadly forays aboveground, and he wanted to seal the tunnels, trapping them below.

"Madsen, you take the charges to the entrance and toss them in, while Lowe directs fire for cover."

Madsen shrugged. He had boasted many times of his swiftness as a runner, and now he would get the chance to prove it. Lowe lined up several men with BARs and M-1's, arranging them in a semicircle to direct fire.

While Madsen hefted satchels of C-2 explosives,

then broke into a zigzagging race toward the entrance, the marines let loose with a fierce volley of fire. Bullets kicked up around the runner, enemy as well as friendly, and he burst into greater speed, pausing at the rocky mouth of the cave to fling the satchel in with both hands, then diving backward and rolling down the slope heedless of the tearing rocks.

A loud explosion shook the ground with a rattling *ka-boom!*, and rocks showered down for several hundred yards. The resulting landslide sealed shut the mouth of the cave, sealing in the Japanese.

"They've got connecting tunnels," Crane warned, "and are liable to pop up somewhere else, so get 'em all!"

Night fell, and the Fourth realized they were sharing Hill 382 with the enemy. They'd not secured it but had only borrowed ground for the time being, and they sat nervously.

"Shit," Ted Madsen muttered, his eyes constantly shifting from left to right, "those bastards are likely to sneak up on us during the night and blow us all to hell."

"Naw, they'll probably just cut us to pieces with those samurai swords they carry," Whitworth disagreed, and received a baleful glare for his comment. He shrugged. "I think we ought to let the chief stay on guard. Hell, we're liable to wake up tomorrow with the whole fuckin' Nip army dead if we do!"

"You have a lot of faith in me," Redhawk said. His shoulders lifted in a shrug. "I'm just the radioman."

"Yeah, be modest," Whitworth scoffed. "You're the only one here with a souvenir!"

"I try harder."

They all laughed at that, an uneasy laugh spiked with anxiety. The night was punctuated with the noise of shots, grenades, and artillery, and occasional shouts of pain could be heard from some distant—or close—ravine. It was unnerving.

"The damn Japs don't have to worry about being killed in their sleep like we do," Wiley said softly. "They're all hidden underground, and they know damn good and well that we're not likely to leave our foxholes."

"Maybe we should," Johns said, but no one agreed. Too many sleepless nights were behind them, with more ahead. No man felt particularly brave, just weary.

During the long night hours, men of the Third slept fitfully, waking with a start sometimes, hearing noises that weren't there, seeing shadows that weren't there. The platoon was camped in an antitank ditch, with brush on one side and a rocky slope on the other. It ran east to west, cutting along the hill in a jagged line. They were down to only fourteen men.

D day plus eleven came early, and Third Battalion heard that two marines of the Fourth had suffered saber cuts the night before, the infiltrators swarming down on them in the dark. Though the division summoned their energy and managed to overrun the entire hill that day, surging over a hundred yards beyond it, the casualties were high. Officers fell as quickly as enlisted, with one unit losing five. The attack on the blockhouse on Turkey Knob was effected by eight tanks, some of them using flamethrowers. After pouring on dozens of seventy-five mm shells and using thousands of gallons of fuel for the flamethrower, the frustrated marines saw the blockhouse revive. Its occupants had merely retreated to the safety of tunnels below until the fury had subsided.

D day plus twelve brought only minor changes to the Fourth's lines that moved in the Meat Grinder. Another fifty yards had been advanced, and the hill was finally declared secure for the day. The Amphitheater, Turkey Knob, and Minami Village still held out. And the strength of the Fourth was now down to fifty percent.

D day plus fifteen brought a welcome respite from constant battle and advances. The Corps commander set aside the day as a day of rest, reorganization, and resupply. It was met with relief, and except for a few skirmishes, no assaults were launched. Marines napped in their foxholes or swam in the sea, and some received mail from the Fourth Division's post office on the beach. Replacements were sent in and received with relief.

The smell of sulphur was especially strong that day. Redhawk could almost feel it soaking into his skin, and he thought of his dream. It had been real then but had still not prepared him for the grim reality of Iwo Jima. This was worse than any nightmare. There was no waking, no coming out of it to the safety of home. The days and nights were an endless nightmare.

March 10—D day plus nineteen—marked the fall of Turkey Knob and the Amphitheater. The Fourth Division rolled past the hard lines at last, after two weeks of being held up on the front. Some units pushed ahead hundreds of yards, drawing close to the sea, while patrols marched through ravines to the beach without meeting resistance. The door was about to close on the enemy, at the cost of many marine lives.

And death wasn't the only threat on the island. Marines unfortunate to be taken alive were frequently tortured, then killed, and it was that they dreaded most. A wounded man was helpless, and every effort was made to get him when he fell. Still the marines slogged on, determined to win, determined to go home alive.

Just before dawn on Wednesday, the fourteenth, the enemy managed to score a direct rocket hit near the northern end of the Fourth's line. It hit the CP, and the communications chief was killed and most of the battalion officers wounded.

That day and the next, the Fourth found the enemy unusually quiet. They prepared one of the few major maneuvers the volcanic island had allowed. The Twenty-third and Twenty-fourth drove east, swinging slowly south, forming a hammer head to bring down on the anvil of the Twenty-fifth, smashing the enemy between. For the only time during the campaign, the Twenty-fifth was able to form defensive lines, plugging in mines and stringing barbed wire, digging machine gun nests, and seating thirty-seven mm cannon and sixty mm mortars. They sat back and waited for the Japanese to be driven in like cattle in a gate.

The general had given out the order for the marines to capture the rest of the island, and they were going to do their damnedest to oblige him. Six days of battle had cost the Fourth Division 833 casualties. . . .

On the sixteenth, a Friday, Third Division troops captured a Japanese from the One hundred forty-fifth Regiment east of Kitano. The prisoner offered with quiet dignity to send a letter to his superior officer, proposing surrender. The marine general thought it might be worth a try, as Colonel Ikeda might be able to convince General Kuribayashi to accept surrender.

After giving the Japanese private a letter to Ikeda and a marine walkie-talkie, they allowed him and one other prisoner to pass safely through marine lines. After a long delay of several hours, the mission was reported a failure.

"It's almost over, Chief," Lieutenant Crane said in a soft voice. His face cracked in a smile, and he sat down on a rock beside Redhawk. "We've got 'em on the run now, and they don't have to surrender."

Whitworth slumped down beside Crane, resting his head against the side of the rock. "So, what are you going to do when you get home, Lieutenant?"

"Kiss my wife, walk down Main Street without worrying about bombs landing on me, and go into Pantene's Drug Store and order a cheeseburger loaded with onions," was Crane's prompt reply. "How 'bout you?"

"Go to see a ballgame, I think. The Yankees aren't doing too badly, I hear." Whitworth slipped off his helmet and scratched his head, then replaced it at a jaunty angle. "What about you and your cousin, Chief? You going to do some war dances?"

Shrugging, Redhawk said, "I can't speak for my cousin, but I intend to go into the mountains and find peace."

There was a moment of quiet, and in the distance they could hear the racketing of shells and *ka-boom* of mortars. Though it was near the end, it wasn't over yet.

"Yeah," Whitworth said after a moment, "maybe you've got the best idea."

Redhawk stretched, then got up to step into the bushes. "Yeah, maybe I do," he agreed, half turning back to speak.

A soft whistling alerted him, and he jerked his head up to see the mortar descending. There was no time to call out or warn anyone, no time for anything. The rock where Crane and Whitworth were sitting disintegrated as Redhawk stood a few yards away, immobilized by the sudden bite of fear at his vitals, the sight of marines vanishing the last thing he was to see for a while. Blood was everywhere, running in rivulets, splashing over him as the percussion knocked him through the air.

Navajo words filtered slowly into his brain, finally beginning to make sense, and Redhawk opened his eyes. There were only gray shadows above him, and he blinked.

"Direct artillery to quadrant eleven!" he shouted in Navajo, surging up, panic welling in his breast. "The enemy is around us, send in tanks. . . ."

Johns gripped him tightly, repeating in Navajo, "You are alive. You are hurt. Lie still." He said it again in the same calm voice, until finally it penetrated Redhawk's brain that he was not in battle but on a stretcher.

He lay back and blinked again, trying to bring Johns into focus. "Where am I?"

"On board a ship. We're headed for Hawaii," Johns said, and when Redhawk stared up at him in hazy disbelief, he said, "The war is over for us."

Grasping at Johns's hand, Redhawk said in an urgent voice, "I was wrong! It *is* my war!"

Johns smiled, his smooth baby-face crumpling in commiseration as he tried not to cry. "I know. It's your war, and my war, and the war of every American. It's over."

Redhawk closed his eyes. It was over for a lot

of good marines. They came to mind, names conjuring up images of faces, some smiling, others grave, but all dedicated men.

Gerard, McIntyre, Mullen, Kryzminsky, Weintraub, Crune, Whitworth. . .

Putting a hand over his eyes so Johns would not see his sudden tears, Redhawk knew there were too many names to recall, too many men who had died. And more would die in the days to follow, in the taking of that cursed island of volcanic rock in the Pacific.

"They're still fighting," Johns said into the gathering silence, where the ship's engines could be heard churning seawater.

Licking dry lips, Redhawk managed to croak out, "Where?"

"In a place called the Gorge. The Fifth is taking out the last of the enemy." He paused, then added, "Japanese radio has broadcast that Iwo Jima has been lost to the American marines. The premier of Japan said that as long as there was one Japanese living, they would fight, and they're doing that. The marines won't stop until the Japs are dead or prisoners."

"May all the gods be with them," Redhawk muttered, then turned his face to the steel wall by his bunk. "May the gods be with all men who go to war. . . ."

Epilogue

Granulated red sandstone, crushed charcoal, white sand, and yellow ocher poured through the fingers of the medicine man, making a sand painting on the floor of a high plateau. Redhawk watched tensely, his arms folded across his chest and his dark eyes narrowed on the figures slowly taking form. His throat tightened.

There, on the scoured ridge above a deep valley, the medicine man was painting a huge white eagle atop a high cone-shaped mountain. Red sandstone dribbled down the sides of the mountain, blurring into crimson rivers.

The dream, the peyote dream, with the white eagle and the rivers of blood . . .

Redhawk's face remained expressionless, but his muscles involuntarily tightened. How had the medicine man known? He had not told him about the eagle; certainly Willie Johns never had. This was the third and final day of the Enemy Way ceremony, a purification rite to blot out the memories of what had happened.

The samurai he had brought back with him was wrapped in a cloth and rested on the plateau floor beside the medicine man. It lay, a grim reminder of the war, a war he wanted to bury along with it.

On the first day, the diagnosis had been made that his mind suffered ill effects from the war, which was why his vision was still blurred. The herb man had prescribed herbs to cure his body and mind, and the last phase of the ceremony was now being performed—the draining away of the illness.

One of the assistants executed several oblong shapes and drew a stick figure of a man with slanted eyes. Other shapes took form, geometric in design, all with a purpose. Finally, the medicine man sat back, his old eyes studying the painting he had made. Then he turned to look up at Redhawk and motioned him to come forward.

Slowly, Redhawk stepped into the center of the sand painting and sat down facing the old man. His face was solemn, his mind suddenly racing back over images that came to him without being summoned—the faces of dead men, of men under fire, of old comrades—and he shut his eyes.

As the medicine man began chanting softly to drive out the *chendi,* or evil spirits that invaded his body, Redhawk felt the warm trickle of sand over his head, shoulders, arms, and then his legs. The sun was hot overhead, beating down with an intensity that made the sand feel almost cool to the touch in contrast. As the sand fell away from his body, Redhawk felt an odd relief, as if a weight had been lifted from him.

It was good. He began to feel a healing of his bruised spirit, of the months of terror and of forcing his emotions to remain hidden. The words of the medicine man curled around him in a protective shell, taking away the bad and giving back good, until he could remember how it was before he had joined the Marines.

When the ceremony was over, when Redhawk and Johns once more rode ponies across the hard-baked land of Arizona, he could recall the friends he'd made and lost without sadness. Bell Wood, the Navajo code talker they'd met in boot camp, had been killed in the Gorge in those last days on Iwo Jima, but most of the code talkers had returned home.

General Vandegrift had said that the Navajos had contributed an invaluable service to their country, and he was partially right. All the men of the Marine Corps had done the same, from the lowest private to the highest-ranking general. Most Americans did not know about the Navajo code talkers, who had given and received over eight hundred messages on Iwo Jima alone, all without a single mistake and without the enemy being able to decipher them. But there were many marines who knew and remembered, and many marines this code talker knew and remembered. Maybe it was a fair trade.